THE DESTINY STONE
The War of Powers: Book Three

The Princess Moriana has done a dumb thing. Not only has she sliced up her lover, Fost Longstrider, in a battle for a magical amulet—but she has stolen the *wrong* amulet. She now has the dangerous Destiny Stone, while Fost's corpse clutches the real Amulet of Living Flame.

Fortunately for Fost, the magic brings him back to life. Unfortunately for Fost, it leaves him to fend for himself with only a foul-minded genie for company. And this whole affair may have scrambled Fost's brains: He still loves Moriana and wants to save her from the effects of the Destiny Stone.

Meanwhile, the evil Queen Synalon and her repulsive cousin, Prince Rann, are also interested in Moriana's whereabouts. Only they don't want to save her, they want to torture her, cut her up into little bits, and feed her to the talking ravens. For fun and profit—since Moriana could displace Synalon from the throne.

But Moriana's relatives think she wears the powerful Amulet of Living Flame; they don't know she has another amulet instead. And none of them realizes the stone will disturb the balance of powers that chains a sleeping demon. The Destiny Stone will cause a new

WAR OF POWERS

"A lively and humorous tale. The further adventures of Fost and Erimenes should be fun."
—Stephen R. Donaldson, author of
The Chronicles of Thomas Covenant the Unbeliever

THE WAR OF POWERS SERIES

THE DESTINY STONE

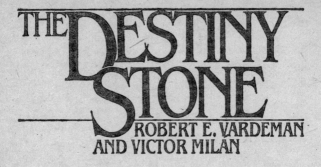

ROBERT E. VARDEMAN
AND VICTOR MILÁN

PLAYBOY
PAPERBACKS

THE DESTINY STONE

Copyright © 1980 by Robert E. Vardeman and Victor W. Milán

Cover illustration copyright © 1980 by PEI Books, Inc.

Published simultaneously in the United States and Canada by Playboy Paperbacks, New York, New York. Printed in the United States of America. Library of Congress Catalog Card Number: 80-82223. First edition.

Books are available at quantity discounts for promotional and industrial use. For further information, write to Premium Sales, Playboy Paperbacks, 747 Third Avenue, New York, New York 10017.

ISBN: 0-872-16763-1

First printing December 1980.

For good friends
Steve,
Fred,
and Roger,
with appreciation

— vwm & rev —

A Chronology
of the Sundered Realm

—20,000   The reptilian *Zr'gsz* settle the Southern Continent and begin construction of the City in the Sky.

—3,100   Istu sent by the Dark Ones to serve the *Zr'gsz* as a reward for their devotion.

—2,300   Human migration begins.

—2,100   Athalau founded by migrants from the Islands of the Sun.

—1,700   Explorers from the Northern Continent found High Medurim.

—1,000   Tension increases between the *Zr'gsz* and the human settlers.

—31   *Zr'gsz* begin active campaign to exterminate all humans.

—3   Martyrdom of the Five Holy Ones.

0   *The War of Powers:* Unable to wipe out the human invaders, the *Zr'gsz* begin to use the powers of Istu. Most of the Southern Continent is desolated. In Athalau, Felarod raises his Hundred and summons up the World-Spirit. Forces unleashed by the struggle sink continents, tip the world on its axis (bringing Athalau into the polar region), cause a star to fall from the heavens to create the Great Crater. The *Zr'gsz* and Istu are

defeated: Istu is cast into a magical sleep and imprisoned in the Sky City's foundations. Conflict costs the life of Felarod and ninety of his Hundred. Survivors exile themselves from Athalau in horror at the destruction they've brought about.

Human Era begins.

100 Trade between humans and *Zr-gsz* grows; increasing population of humans in the Sky City. Medurim begins its conquests.

979 Ensdak Aritku proclaimed first Emperor of High Medurim.

1171 Humans seize power in the Sky City. The *Zr'gsz* are expelled. Riomar shai-Gallri crowns herself queen.

2317 Series of wars between the Empire of Medurim and the City in the Sky.

2912–17 War between the Sky City and Athalau; Athalau victorious. Wars between the City and Athalau continue on and off over the next several centuries.

5143 Julanna Etuul wrests the Beryl Throne from Malva Kryn. She abolishes worship of the Dark Ones within the Sky City, concludes peace with the Empire.

5331 Invaders from the Northern Continent seize Medurim and the Sapphire Throne; barbarian accession signals fresh outbreak of civil wars.

5332 Newly-proclaimed Emperor Churdag declares war on the City in the Sky.

5340 Chafing under the oppression of the Barbarian Empire, the southern half of the

Empire revolts. Athalau and the Sky City form an alliance.

5358   Tolviroth Acerte, the City of Bankers, is founded by merchants who fled the disorder in High Medurim.

5676   Collapse of the Barbarian Dynasty. The Sky City officiates over continent-wide peace.

5700   The Golden Age of the City in the Sky begins.

6900   General decline overtakes Southern Continent. The Sky City magic and influence wane. Agriculture breaks down in south and west. Glacier nears Athalau. Tolviroth Acerte rises through trade with Jorea.

7513   Battle of River Merchant, between Quincunx Federation and High Medurim, ends Imperial domination everywhere but in the northwest corner of the continent. The Southern Continent becomes the Sundered Realm.

8614   Erimenes the Ethical born. Population of Athalau in decline.

8722   Erimenes dies at 108.

8736   Birth of Ziore.

8823   Death of Ziore.

9940   Final abandonment of Athalau to encroaching glacier.

10,091   Prince Rann Etuul born to Ekrimsin the Ill-Favored, sister to Queen Derora V.

10,093   Synalon and Moriana born to Derora. As younger twin, Moriana becomes heir apparent.

10,095   Fost Longstrider born in The Teeming, slum district of High Medurim.

10,103   Teom the Decadent ascends the Sapphire Throne. Fost's parents killed in rioting over reduction in dole to cover Imperial festivities.

10,120   Jar containing the spirit of Erimenes the Ethical discovered in brothel in The Sjedd.

Mount Omizantrim, "Throat of the Dark Ones," from whose lava the *Zr'gsz* mined the skystone for the Sky City foundations, has its worst eruption in millenia.

10,121   Fost Longstrider, now a courier of Tolviroth Acerte, is commissioned to deliver a parcel to the mage *Kest-i-Mond*.

CHAPTER ONE

Princess Moriana Etuul stared from the bloody knife in her hand to the corpse of her lover. The only sounds in the vast chamber were the frenzied beating of her heart and the slow, *drip-drip-drip* of Fost Longstrider's blood as it fell from knife point to the cold stone floor.

The princess fell weeping to her knees, covering her face with trembling hands. The courier's blood had drenched them. They turned her finely boned features into a ghoulish crimson mask.

"Oh, Fost. Oh, my only love."

"Hypocritical bitch," Erimenes said from his earthen jar.

"Be silent!" she shouted at the genie, beating gory hands on Fost's satchel, which contained the jug.

"Why? Haven't I ample reason for complaint? I have lost my only chance to live again. Oh, ashes, ashes!"

Moriana sat back, wiping tears from her eyes. The siren's lure of immortality had forced her into killing the courier. She swallowed hard, remembering Fost as he had been, a big man, self-assured and clever, a man grasping life with both sword-callused hands.

Now Fost lay sprawled in the gracelessness of death before the altar of the Palace of Esoteric Wisdom in glacier-locked Athalau. A rude stone amulet tied to a leather thong lay on his chest like an offering. His eyes gaped at the ceiling, framing the last of all questions.

"I have lost my love," Moriana cried. "Don't talk to me of your need for the Amulet of Living Flame, Erimenes. Each of us needed it more than you."

"Each? Fost wanted eternal life only for an eternity

11

of carousing, of brawling and wenching and gorging."

"No!" denied Moriana. "He wanted it for more. He wanted to savor the knowledge locked in all the world's libraries. That use would surely be better than yours. All you wanted was to enjoy firsthand the earthly pleasures your miserable philosophy had denied you when first you lived."

Erimenes sniffed and said nothing.

Moriana felt the heavy weight of silence in the room. The polar chill had begun to congeal the blood around her boots. She moved away, leaving behind a sticky trail of red.

"I . . . I need the amulet, Erimenes. I will never be able to depose my sister Synalon without it. Her oppression of the Sky City grows daily. My need for the amulet is the greater. *I need it!*"

"Pure rationalization, nothing more," said Erimenes, still sulking. "You cared nothing for Fost. Otherwise, you could never have driven that knife so firmly into his back."

"I loved him, damn you, spirit!"

"Love," Erimenes snorted. "A deadly way you have of showing it. More like a spider than a woman. What happens now? Do you devour the body?"

"I'll have no more of you, spirit." She went to the altar and paused a moment. The great stone amulet shone like a black sun from its silver starburst setting. Even in her numbness she marveled at it. First it appeared all white, then half light, half dark. The amulet now radiated the color of midnight. She shuddered, realizing the high price she had paid to obtain this trinket and the gift it bestowed.

Moriana picked up the amulet and looped the chain around her neck. An electric tingle passed through her. She sighed and let the gem drop between her breasts. Its touch chilled her.

She turned and knelt by Fost's body, fingertips pressed into his throat to seek even the faintest thread of pulse. There was none. She closed the eyelids, crossed his hands on his chest over the gray stone that rested there. It was a poor thing, but it must have possessed some mystic importance to have hung on the altar next to the Amulet of Living Flame. Moriana hoped it would buy his soul an easy passage now that he had answered the Hell Call.

Tears spattered the lifeless face as she bent to kiss him. "Farewell, beloved," she said. "I promise you shall not have died in vain. When I have freed my city and sent my sister shrieking to Hell to join her lackey Rann, I will return and erect a shrine to your memory."

"I'm sure that will bring his solace," said Erimenes caustically.

"And I hope you will enjoy his company here until the sun itself receives Hell Call." Fighting to hold in the sobs that threatened to wrack her body again, she turned her back on the satchel and walked away. The golden glow of Athalau beckoned to her through the opened doors of the Palace of Esoteric Wisdom.

"Wait," called Erimenes. "Don't go! You can't leave me here!"

"Fost deserves better company than yours, faithless one," Moriana said. "Still, here you will stay to guard over his body until my return. And ever after as well, accursed spirit. I shall see to that!"

"Don't be hasty," Erimenes called, his voice turning to honey. "I know something yet, something that could be of advantage to you and . . ."

Moriana paused, then fled, tears pouring down her cheeks, the amulet beating like a second heart between her breasts. Erimenes called after her, voice rising in desperation.

His pleas pursued her.

She paused on the steps just outside the massive copper doors. The city's glow enveloped her. She breathed deeply, tasting chill and the mustiness of age, letting the polychromatic pulse of Athalau soothe her.

Her breathing slowed. The princess let her head sink down, almost forgetting for an instant her grief, her remorse, her self-hatred. . . .

An ominous crack from overhead brought her head up. Not twenty minutes before, she and Fost had fought side-by-side against the bird riders from the City in the Sky. The bird riders' numbers and her cousin Rann's lethal sword had seemed certain to overwhelm the pair. But Erimenes was in his home and at the center of his power. With his psychic abilities magnified in this glacier-surrounded city, he had dislodged an immense block of ice from above. It had smashed down, crushing the end of the marble portico fronting the palace—and Prince Rann and his men. The ceiling of the bubble that arched over Athalau was now veined with cracks, the ice rotten with age. The falling block had loosened others and the ponderous groaning from above warned of more icefalls. With a last heart-wrenching glance into the darkness of the palace, now the tomb of her love, Moriana dropped from the broken steps and lightly ran up the street.

The deserted edifices gazed down upon her, calm and empty, serene with the wisdom of millennia. The peculiar street paving gave slightly beneath her boot soles, adding energy to her stride. She found it almost impossible to remain depressed when she was surrounded by the glory and beauty of Athalau.

Almost impossible.

Impulse turned her from the street to climb a few steps and enter a tall, narrow building. Its face shimmered in the constantly shifting light. As she neared the door, she saw the façade was of some pale yellow metal scored with a billion shallow scratches cunningly placed to cast back light in all directions. Even in her dark gloom, Moriana marveled at the blend of diversity and harmony the Athalar had achieved in the building of their city.

Still unsure why she did so, she explored the inside of the building. The princess came to a foyer flanked by closed doors. She tried one. Locked. Humming a half-forgotten song of her childhood, she proceeded into the hallway, checking the doors as she went.

It occurred to her that she might find something of use in one of these long-untenanted rooms. Erimenes had spoken of great wealth stored within the city. Mere gauds and gold meant nothing to her. She was a princess of the City in the Sky, born to riches. Besides, she could not carry much on the difficult and dangerous journey out of the glacier—provided that a way *out* of the glacier existed.

She remembered the ever-filled water flask and gruel bowl Fost had found in the castle of Kest-i-Mond the mage, where he had first learned of the Amulet of Living Flame and the gift of immortality it bestowed. She had no provisions; she couldn't bear to ransack the body of her lover for the flask and bowl. Perhaps some similar objects were hidden away in this building. Or magical artifacts that could prove useful in other ways. She shook her head, blonde hair cascading around her pale face and masking her sea-green eyes. She had no real purpose to her search. She just had to keep moving until the great, raw, throbbing pain inside her eased and she felt ready to try escaping from the glacier's guts.

A door opened. Instinctively, her hand touched the wire-wound hilt of her scimitar. She dropped her hand and laughed nervously. In a city buried within a glacier for a thousand years, it was unlikely any menace awaited her behind a closed door.

The room proved bare. No furniture on the floor, no decoration on the walls. Perhaps an ascetic's cell, she thought, recalling Erimenes' philosophy of self-denial, long ago shed with his corporeal being. The princess reconsidered. Perhaps the room had been left unused or had been stripped of its furnishings when the Athalar escaped the ponderous advance of the glacier. She shut the door and tried another.

This one revealed a desk and four-legged stool. An irregular lump of dark green crystal lay on the desk. Lights flickered randomly within it, chasing one another like berserk fireflies, then winking out of existence. She closed the door on still another mystery in Athalau. It would take as many lifetimes as the amulet could give her to begin to comprehend the city and the people who had constructed it. She thought of Fost's childlike lust for knowledge, nurtured since his childhood in the slums of High Medurim, and strained again against tears.

Two more doors failed to open. As Moriana reached for the latch of the third, a wave of panic swept over her. She froze. Her throat constricted with the impact of the almost palpable dread. There was no smell, no sound, no sight of anything dangerous. But black dread pounded inside her skull and a frantic voice cried *no!*

Her fingers slipped toward the latch. Fear grew to almost intolerable intensity, but her determination to find what lay behind the blank wooden door also mounted. Her fingers found the latch and twisted it convulsively. She yanked open the door.

Death rushed her with a clacking of black jaws.

Reflexes honed in battle saved her. She threw herself aside as the ice worm hurtled past. With a splintering sound, it struck the door on the far side of the corridor. Giving a sinuous wiggle, it doubled back on itself, hissing in rage. Its putrid breath turned her stomach as the sword in her hand swept forth and struck.

The hideous head recoiled. A great gash opened in the translucent, corpse-white flesh. Foul yellow gore defiled the floor. In wounding the ice worm, Moriana had gained the initiative. She didn't waste that advantage.

Another sword slash parted rubbery flesh. The worm screamed. The head darted forward as Moriana swung her sword again. The ceramic-hard jaws had not yet opened. They slammed like a battering ram below her ribs.

She sat down heavily, gasping for breath. The room spun around her, knocked loose from its moorings by her dizziness and nausea. She tried to raise the sword and strike but she failed. It was a struggle even to keep the hilt in her numbed fingers.

The monster reared above her. The four jaws parted, the toothed sphincters within the maw pulsing in expectant spasms. Moriana looked into that mouth and saw more than her own death. If she died, the hope she held out for defeating Synalon died also. Her beloved Sky City would perish.

She waited for the head to descend, the black jaws to slice through her flesh. Oddly, the worm did not move. The sickness slowly ebbed. Moriana edged away, watching the beast warily, certain that her movement would bring it out of its inexplicable lethargy. The thick annular segments that comprised its body rippled in exertion, but the monster remained still, as if held by some compulsion.

Moriana rose. A sudden uncoiling of well-trained muscles sent her sword whistling through the air to land with a blubbery *thunk*. The blunt head of the ice worm slumped forward, half-severed by the face of her blow. Rage exploded inside the princess. She swung the sword again and again, taking out the fear of death and failure on the unresisting worm, purging herself of the unbearable emotions that had wracked her since she'd murdered Fost. When only a goulash of severed flesh and stinking blood and fractured jaws remained, she fell back against the wall. The poison emotions she harbored within her had been worked out.

Then Moriana remembered the amulet around her

neck. It granted her immortality. She'd really had little to fear from the ice worm—except that the beast could devour and digest her before the amulet effected her return to the living. Immortality would then have resided in the ice worm's belly along with the Amulet of Living Flame. The nearness of her escape made her shudder—she realized that even the possession of a magical device giving immortality did not make her invulnerable.

When she'd regained her breath and controlled the quivering of her limbs, she started off again. Purpose moved her now. She was still dazed by the closeness of death and her unexplained salvation. All she could do was wonder wanly as her feet led her through a maze of twisting corridors.

She came to a door no different from any of the others, but she knew this was *the door*. It opened readily. Her sword still in hand and her normal instinct for self-preservation returned, she stepped inside.

Well met, my child, a voice echoed in her head.

Moriana tensed. Her eyes swept the room. The walls were lined with shelves that at one time had been lined with clay pots. Some past disturbance had shaken those pots down, and they had shattered on the dark onyx floor.

For a moment, the princess was mystified. Only slowly did she comprehend what she saw. The fractured pots were simple enough, round-bodied vessels of wheel-worked clay. But they weren't common jugs.

Each was identical to the one that held the soul of Erimenes the Ethical.

I cannot clearly read your thoughts, child. The words flowed into her mind like soothing balm. *Yet I perceive that you walk near the truth.*

Some unseen force drawing her, Moriana turned to a corner of the small chamber. An unbroken pot leaned against the juncture of walls.

"Is someone there?" Moriana said hesitantly.

"I am," the voice said aloud. There could be no question the words issued forth from the jug. "I guided you here. Aye, and tried to save your life. I sorrow that I couldn't stop you from opening that door."

Moriana stared. Realization dawned on her. Erimenes had thought himself the sole survivor of old Athalau. More likely, he had only been the first; others had followed his path, finding immortality bounded by clay walls.

This spirit, unlike Erimenes, had shown her kindness in trying to warn of the ice worm. Erimenes would have done everything in his power to make Moriana fight to the death—and then would have cheered both sides impartially.

Weakness surged inside the princess. The floor seemed to bow and buckle under her. She'd thought herself alone in the city, except for ice worms, corpses loved and corpses hated, and the treacherous spirit of Erimenes. Now she'd found another presence. It flowed into her now, as beautiful and serene as Athalau itself.

Moriana sank to the floor, covered her face with her hands, and wept.

"Aye, child, weep. Let your feelings flow freely. If you dam them up inside, they soon will swamp your soul." Moriana did as she was told. She cried until the blood-soaked and grimy sleeves of her tunic were sodden with tears. When Moriana raised her hand, the crying stopped, she felt calm. The momentary catharsis of butchering the ice worm had been replaced by a more stable emotion. While not a feeling of well-being, it was less jagged and wracking than what had filled her before.

Her sword had fallen from her hand and lay beside her. Ignoring it, she leaned forward to pick up the single intact jug. It felt precisely like Erimenes'. She examined the lid. Like the one capping the philosopher's jar, it was a disk of dark basalt forced into the mouth of the jug. It resisted her attempt to pull it free, then abruptly came loose.

"Ahhh!" came the satisfied cry. A red vapor curled from the jar in a long unsweeping plume. Motes of energy danced through the pinkish cloud as it swirled, formed, and congealed into an astonishingly solid figure.

The rose-colored figure of a woman stood before the princess. What Moriana had sensed from her communication with the spirit was confirmed by its appearance: this survivor of Athalau was the opposite of Erimenes in every detail. Where Erimenes was stooped and scrawny, the woman was tall and robust. Her face was lined by the passage of many years of mortal life, but it retained a calm and dignified beauty. Erimenes' face was hatchet-lean and shrewd, dominated by the blade of his nose and etched by years of repression of every worldly desire, though his newly professed hedonism kept his lips curled into a perpetual half-leer. The female ghost's hair hung unbound down her back like a pale misty waterfall. Erimenes' smooth dome of a skull was decorated by a fringe of scraggled hair. The shade reached out to touch Moriana's cheek. Feeling a spiderweb tenuous contact, the princess yelped and jerked away. The woman smiled at her.

"Do not be afraid. In the middle of Athalau, I can almost regain the solidity I knew in life. Outside the city, far across the mountains, it would be different, I think." She frowned and added, "But my years of solitude have left me sadly lacking in courtesy. My thanks, many and eternal, for releasing me from a durance lasting thirteen hundred years."

"It . . . it was little enough to do for someone who'd saved my life. You made the ice worm pause before striking, didn't you?"

"The beast's emotions were simple and blunt, and it took me a moment to find one to manipulate that would keep it from slaying you. They are feral creatures, those worms. Their lives consist solely of seeking and slaying." Her face creased with concern. "My lack of swiftness nearly cost your life. Accept my apologies."

"Apologies?" Moriana said in confusion. "But you tried to keep me from entering the worm's chamber and then kept it from killing me when it had the better of me. I owe *you* my life."

"It was my mental touch that guided you into this building. You were far away, and I failed to mesh my thoughts with yours at such a distance. But closer, I found it easy to deal with your emotions. I manipulated you, I fear. But your will is strong, child. When you wished to enter the room into which the worm had laired, I couldn't dissuade you." She watched Moriana intently. When the princess smiled, the spirit also smiled. With a start, Moriana realized the wraith was practicing facial expressions, unsure of herself after thirteen centuries.

"But come," the ghost said, "I am less than courteous. I am Ziore. What name are you known by, child?"

"Moriana Etuul."

"Etuul? I remember such a name, though we knew little of the outside world in my convent. Are you related to the ruling house in the City in the Sky?"

"I am of that blood," came the proud reply.

"A princess!" the spirit cried. Moriana blinked, a headache blurring her vision. "Forgive me, child. I pried into your thoughts again. But a princess!" The spirit smiled more broadly. "High company for one who was a lowly nun in life."

"A nun? I didn't know the Athalar practiced that form of devotion."

"We didn't." The spirit sighed gustily. "It was my misfortune to fall under the influence of a philosophy propounded by one who died fourteen years before my birth."

Moriana stared at her, a premonition dawning. "And who was this philosopher?"

"A foolish man," Ziore said with a frown, an expression out of place on her serene countenance. "And a bad one, I think. Erimenes the Ethical. I am sure you've never heard of him."

"But I have, Ziore! And your assessment of him is perfect. I came to Athalau with him. It was because we accompanied him that the Guardian—the glacier—let us in."

"But how is this?" cried Ziore, dumbfounded. "He died!"

"Just as you did. He survived, in spirit, much the same way."

"Tell me of it."

Moriana looked around. The remnants of shattered jugs about her feet gritted like dried bones under her boot soles. Her every impulse was to flee this forlorn graveyard of ghosts, to escape Athalau, to put distance between her and the city in which she had slain her lover.

Ziore's eyes went round.

"I know little of these matters," she said quietly. "We Sisters of Denial kept ourselves apart from the world and its ways. But I know this, child. The pain within you will fester and grow if you hold it in. It will destroy you as surely as the cancer that took my life."

Moriana sighed. The spirit's presence soothed her, though she realized she was responding to a deliberate effort on Ziore's part. She sensed truth in what Ziore said. She sat on a low bench and told her story.

It took an hour.

The words began in a trickle. Then the dam burst, and they flowed forth in a torrent that Moriana later thought she would have been unable to stem, even if she'd wanted to do so.

She told of her life in the City in the Sky. She was one of Queen Derora's twin daughters; as the younger, she was heir to the Beryl Throne. But her sister, the lovely, black-haired Synalon, had been a strange and sullen child. Moriana had been bright, compassionate, effervescent. Synalon had been the antithesis. Resentment sprouted within the elder twin and flourished with the years. In time, dark Synalon had recognized the seedling and actively nurtured it.

Moriana matured into an intelligent, responsible woman. She studied history, statecraft, trade, and arts magical and military. She was an apt pupil. Her mother the queen doted on Moriana.

During this time, Synalon drew ever more into herself. Her interest in external matters manifested itself in a growing entanglement in palace intrigue. She studied the darker branches of sorcery, which were of particular horror to the people of the City, who lived with the knowledge that a demon slept beneath their feet. Derora had looked on in distress but had done nothing to curb Synalon's dangerous magical leanings.

Two factions had gradually emerged in the Palace of the Skyborn: one favoring Moriana and the other Synalon. Moriana at first refused to take part in the unpleasant vagaries of palace intrigue. A series of near-fatal accidents in which her sister's complicity could never quite be proven had changed her attitude.

Life in the City had slipped further and further from the happy simplicity Moriana knew as a child. It was further complicated by the tragedy that befell their cousin when he was eighteen. Two years older than the royal twins, and barred by gender from ever ruling the matrilineal City, Prince Rann Etuul had shown every sign of growing into a strong and capable leader who would be an invaluable adjunct to Moriana's rule. He was a remote boy given to strange moods and fits of emotion; like his cousin Synalon, he dabbled in the black arts. His mother, Derora's sister Ekrimsin the Ill-Favored, had been similarly involved. Palace rumor had it that her death a few years after the prince's birth had been caused by her summoning an entity she couldn't control.

But Rann, to his humiliation, discovered that he lacked any trace of magical ability. He threw himself completely and wholeheartedly into military matters, a pursuit for which he soon showed surprising aptitude.

As a young cadet in the elite bird riders, he was forced down as he escorted a trade caravan through the Thail Mountains. He had been captured and tortured by the mountain savages. They disfigured his face with an obsidian knife, leaving behind a network of razor-thin scars. Not content with this simple torture, they robbed him of his manhood with repeated applications of flambeaux.

Rann returned to the City. After recovering, he threw himself into military affairs more vigorously than ever before. And he emerged on Synalon's side in the growing struggle for power.

The situation between the sisters had deteriorated almost to the point of civil war. When Rann's spies on the surface learned of a jar containing the spirit of Erimenes the Ethical of glacier-swallowed Athalau, even further rivalry was touched off. If the rumors were true, he would know not only the location of the lost city but might well find out where within it rested the Amulet of Living Flame.

"The Amulet of Living Flame," mused Ziore. "I've heard of it. There were a number of magical items in the Palace of Esoteric Wisdom, but by my time their use had been forgotten. Athalau grew senescent in its final years, even as people do."

Moriana bit her lip. She sensed trouble ahead. Yet her story impelled her onward of its own momentum.

She had left the City and her ailing mother in search of Erimenes. Synalon was much stronger than she in magical application, and the dark princess made a specialty of the sorceries of destruction and devastation. A magical struggle between them would be no contest at all—unless Moriana possessed the Amulet of Living Flame. With its life-restoring property, it could revive her even if Synalon's death spells struck her down. Her own magic required lengthy preparation, time Synalon would never give her in a real contest of wills. With the Amulet of Living Flame providing the needed time to weave spells not even her sister could counter, she would emerge victorious. Perhaps she might even be able to use the energies stored within the amulet to fuel her own magic. If she seized the amulet and returned to the Sky City, she had a fighting chance of overcoming her sister.

The jar containing Erimenes had turned up in the possession of a Realm courier named Fost Longstrider. She had tried to steal it from him in the middle of the night, but she was caught. She fought with him sword to sword. He had grappled her, and their wrestling bout had turned from struggle to ardor. Without quite understanding how it came about, the pair had made love.

For all her confused and confusing feelings toward Fost, she still had her mission. As he slept, she had again taken the jug and slipped away. Then, driven by concern over her mother's welfare, she returned to the City in the Sky.

It had been a mistake. She learned that her beloved mother had just died. Before she had time to properly mourn, she was arrested by Rann and charged with Derora's murder. Convicted of regicide and matricide, she found Synalon usurping the Beryl Throne.

Moriana was sentenced to die—and the manner of her execution still caused her to shake uncontrollably at the thought of it. Death by torture was mild in comparison. She was to be given as bride to the Vicar of Istu in the Rite of Dark Assumption. During the early millennia of human rule in the City, that Rite had cemented the loyalty of the sleeping Demon of the Dark Ones to the humans. It involved summoning a part of the sleeping demon's subconscious and using it to animate a hideous statue at the City's center. The effigy accepted only those of the Royal Blood as victims.

Suitably bribed by the ravishment, it would lend its power to the City's ruler. Even bound and eternally asleep due to the magic of Felarod and the Earth-Spirit after their triumph in the War of Powers, Istu remained a potent force.

Fost had rescued Moriana. He had followed her into the Sky City by hijacking a military balloon and made contact with an underground force opposing Synalon. Though the members of the underground ineptly failed to aid Fost, he had succeeded in freeing the princess.

Fost had learned of the amulet from Erimenes himself and claimed he had rescued the princess only to reclaim what was rightfully his. But there had been a more complex reason for the rescue. When Fost left the City with Erimenes back in his possession, he had taken Moriana with him. Moriana's skills in flying and aerial combat had assured his escape.

Together, they had trudged southward across miles of peril from cold, hostile nomads and Rann's Sky Guardsmen. They had finally passed through the Rampart Mountains and to the very glacier enveloping Athalau. The glacier possessed a rudimentary intelligence granted it by energies released during the War of Powers ten thousand years before. They had a final confrontation with Rann that ended with the eunuch prince's death and a last desperate struggle in which Erimenes tried to seize the amulet to restore himself to physical being. The bottled spirit had developed a taste for the carnal pleasures he'd eschewed in life. His desire to remedy the lacks of his prior existence had almost cost Moriana the amulet.

During their journey, Moriana had come to love Fost. He returned her love even though a barrier lay between them. Fost had a lust for knowledge that bordered on obsession; he had a lust for life, also, which delighted Erimenes when they first came together. The lecherous spirit couldn't have found a better companion through whom to pursue vicarious sensation. Fost intended to use the Amulet of Living Flame in learning all he could, drinking all there was to be drunk, and sleeping with all the women there were to be slept with. Moriana wanted—needed—the amulet to save the Sky City from Synalon and her insane ambitions to conquer all the Sundered Realm and reunite it under her iron rule. Neither Fost nor Moriana budged from desire for the amulet.

The dispute was settled once and for all in the Palace of Esoteric Wisdom when Moriana thrust her knife through Fost's back.

Finishing her tale, Moriana surrendered immediately to tears. She saw the truth in Ziore's warning of a festering emotional tumor inside her. The telling had sliced out much of the cancer.

Ziore let her weep, then calmed her with a gentle mind-touch.

"I do not know that I can approve of your actions," the spirit said, "but it was a terrible decision confronting you. Perhaps you chose wisely. I am no judge of such things. In spite of killing Fost, you are good. You have been touched by the powers of the Elder Dark, but it has left no taint upon your soul."

Moriana raised her eyebrow skeptically.

"Do not mistake scars for taints, child," the spirit said.

Moriana nodded, understanding. She leaned back against the wall, cool and firm against her body. The chill of the glacier seemed to seep into her bones. She felt adrift as if all the cause for her urgency had vanished. She suspected this was Ziore's doing, too. But Moriana felt her strength returning and did not resist.

"What happened here?" she asked, gesturing around the room littered with broken pottery. It felt good to change the subject from her own sorrows.

"Some centuries ago—I've lost count now—ice fell from the roof of the glacier. Only a small chunk, but it struck this building a powerful blow. The spirit jars

were knocked from their shelves. From within our jugs
we cannot influence material objects, though from what
you tell me of Erimenes, once released our powers appear to be considerable." Ziore looked in sorrow at the
broken jugs, emotion rippling through her form. "But
when this happened, we were helpless.

"I felt them die. They were kin to me. I felt their
agony, their fear—and for a few, their exaltation. Life
within the jugs had become wearisome, and it seemed
a blessing to be released. But still, the shock of their
final passing unsettled me for centuries." Sadness radiated from her face, a desolation and loneliness that
made Moriana's troubles dwindle into insignificance.
"But pain remembered pales quicker than other, more
pleasant memories. I recovered. But, ah, so long have
I endured loneliness!"

"You're not alone now," said Moriana. "I'll take
you with me."

"You will?" Ziore exulted. She clapped vaporous
hands together in silent glee. "I hardly dared hope!"

"That is . . . if you can guide us out of here."

"I can sense the ice-worm tunnels, even from here.
For all their unthinking voracity, I find beauty in their
works. Many paths lead to the outer world. And once
there it's a short journey to the Gate of the Mountains
and lands beyond!"

"It can be an impossible journey without food."

"Don't worry, child. Traveler's fare has been stored
in the buildings nearby."

The thought of eating centuries-old food appealed to
the princess as much as eating the reeking, rubbery
flesh of the ice worms.

"It's been so long," she protested. "You need no
food in your state. I need something more than hand-
fuls of ancient powder."

Ziore laughed.

"We knew how to use our magic to keep food from
spoiling. An especially potent spell was used on food

intended for travelers. I think you'll find it as palatable after a millennium as the day it was laid down." Ziore chuckled, looking like a small girl caught in a prank as she added, "Not that it was very palatable when fresh. From what I remember, the stuff tastes like plaster. But it will nourish."

"I've eaten worse than plaster," said Moriana, thinking of Fost's gruel bowl and its tasteless contents.

"In fact," continued Ziore, hand under her chin in thought, "there are numerous items not far from here that might be of considerable worth in the outer world. I see no harm in helping yourself to them. The original owners can lodge no protest."

She drew up her arms and laughed, more like a happy, innocent child than the ghost of an elderly woman.

"Oh, to be free, to know companionship!"

Moriana smiled wryly. She wondered if the spirit would feel otherwise after she had renewed her acquaintances with humanity. Or perhaps her knowledge had never been that great, stultified as it was by Erimenes' arid doctrines. Still, the spirit's joy diminished Moriana's own pain for the moment.

"But what of Erimenes? He was your spiritual master, I suppose. Do you want to bring him out, too?"

"No." The expression on the pale, rose-colored face surprised Moriana. In her brief acquaintance with Ziore, she had come to think of her as a creature of gentleness and loving strength, not of the bitter anger appearing now at the mention of Erimenes' name. "His teachings led many to waste their lives as I did in contemplation of empty wisdom, empty because it denied experience and served no human end. And from what you tell me, he has caused hardship enough in the years since his death. How many of history's evil men weave such an enduring net of duplicity? I waste no sympathy on him. Leave him."

Moriana shrugged as she picked up the jar. She made

her way out of the room of smashed jugs, wondering what became of the ghosts of ghosts.

They paused to rest near the wrinkled, shiny inner skin of the glacier. This had once been the highway to the Gate of the Mountains. The road had long since been blocked by millions of tons of ice, but up to the glacier itself the road was still the most convenient path to travel. Moriana sat down on a bench of unfamiliar substance. It yielded beneath her form, molding itself to her body's contours. It was marvelously restful, and she wondered at the skill of those whose magic remained potent after so many years.

It was here the question she dreaded most was asked.

Ziore floated free of her jar in a fashion familiar to Moriana after her travels with Erimenes. The spirit now looked diffident as she asked, "The amulet—might I look at it?"

Color rushed to Moriana's cheeks. Her impulse was to shout *no!* and pull back. Yet she didn't do it. She didn't wish to hurt the spirit's feelings. She owed her life to Ziore.

Moriana hooked her finger into the silver chain from which the amulet hung. Slowly, she drew forth the jewel. Ziore stared. The stone glowed white with only a thin crescent of black around the edge.

"It's beautiful," exclaimed Ziore, "but . . ."

"But what?" Moriana asked sharply.

"Nothing. Only . . . I thought it would look different."

Moriana shrugged. Looking like a child marveling at an intricate toy, Ziore stretched insubstantial fingers out to touch the amulet. Moriana tensed. Her heart almost stopped beating. Erimenes had believed he could make the Amulet of Living Flame restore him to life by "touching" it, even though he lacked physical substance. Would it return Ziore to her mortal shape if she brushed fingers over it? And would that exhaust its stored power and render all her torment for naught?

Ziore sensed the tension in Moriana and looked deeply into the princess's eyes. Moriana recalled the great hunger for life Ziore had displayed in the chamber of broken spirit jars. Was it less fierce than Erimenes'? Yet slowly, grudgingly, she felt the mistrust leave her.

Ziore nodded, withdrawing her vaporous hand.

"You need not fear me, child," she said gently. "I would give much to live again, but not at your expense. I will not redeem the folly of my life at the expense of your dreams."

Moriana dropped the amulet. It still burned like a white beacon. She smiled gratitude, eyes misting with tears. She envied Ziore her strength of character.

Thunder made her look back at the city. The lofty buildings enthralled the eye, subtle and magnificent, as ethereal as spun sunlight. But the slimmest spires seemed to waver slightly. Disturbed by the fall of the block of ice that had killed Rann, the ice overhead shifted, settling back into its ancient equilibrium.

Moriana stood silently for a moment, staring toward the distant Palace of Esoteric Wisdom. Then, with Ziore's jar under her arm, she started climbing for the black cavern of the nearest ice-worm tunnel.

CHAPTER TWO

Fost lay on the floor of the Palace of Esoteric Wisdom, a small eddy of silence in the oceanic silence that was the again-deserted city of Athalau. Hours made the soft transition from future to past. A sound rippled the silence, dimly at first, then growing. It began as a rustling, became a crackling, and ended as a rushing roar. Blue glow oozed between Fost's dead fingers. It seeped out, enveloped him, and leaped upward in a sudden wild dance.

He opened his eyes to flame. The fire wrapped him in pain. A shuddering inhalation filled his lungs with agony. An incandescent point seared the flesh of his chest and ate into his palm. He snatched away the hand and sat up, beating at the flames.

They were gone. He looked down at his chest. The mail had been burned away in a perfect circle yet the flesh beneath was not charred. An angry red mark glowed there, but the skin was intact. To the side, the rent in the mail left by the ice worm's jaws exposed unmarked skin.

He blinked and shook his head to clear it. Gradually, memory seeped into his skull. His eyes widened with astonishment.

"I . . . I live," he mumbled. Then, louder, "I live!"

"A brilliant observation," a voice said at his elbow. "I didn't think you had it in you."

"Erimenes?"

"Who else? Certainly not that backstabbing slut of yours. She took the other amulet and left you for dead."

"Other amulet?" echoed Fost numbly.

"The Destiny Stone, which hung beside the Amulet of Living Flame."

"Which hung beside . . ." His words trailed off. He stared stupidly at the satchel containing Erimenes' jug.

"Need you repeat everything, fool? Yes, your beloved princess stabbed you in the back. You died and in dying seized the amulet. Moriana took what you both stupidly assumed to be the Amulet of Living Flame."

Fost examined his back gingerly. A tear in his mail revealed where her dagger had made its way through his heart. He felt a twinge of admiration for anyone strong and sure enough to drive a knife through linked rings of steel.

He stood, his knees feeling like springs. Steadying himself against the altar, he brushed fine gray powder from his chest.

"Where is the amulet if she didn't take it?"

"You're brushing it off your chest, dunce."

The round burn on his chest ached with the throb of permanence. On the black marble flagstone by his foot lay a leather thong charred in two.

"As I said before, the amulet had only a finite amount of energy stored in it. I feared it was near exhaustion and I was right. You misused the last of it in being restored." The spirit sniffed as though on the verge of tears. "It could have given *me* life! And you took it, you stupid, selfish lout!"

"It was hardly my doing," said Fost defensively. Erimenes began to weep violently. The sound was so forlorn Fost almost wished he had the amulet back to give to the shade.

Almost.

"Cheer up, old ghost. This stone of yours has healed my minor cuts as well as the largest malady of all— death. I'm ready to leave this wormy lair of a city. Will you come along?"

"Whatever would I wish to stay for?"

"This is your home. And your powers are greatest here."

Erimenes made a rude noise.

"Much good they did me. They failed to free me from this miserable jug. No, I'll come with you." His voice cheered noticeably. "I look forward to adventuring with you, Fost. What do you intend now? To fare north through the Gate of the Mountains and sample the fleshpots of Kara-Est?"

"I fare north but not to Kara-Est. Unless Moriana's trail leads there."

"You follow the bitch to kill her?" Eagerness caused the spirit's voice to pulse with vitality.

"Not at all." Fost laughed, amazed at his feelings. "I should hate her for what she did to me, and yet I can't. She murdered me but she thought she did the right thing." He laughed again, more loudly. "Maybe I don't feel animosity because the death wasn't permanent."

"Maybe she'll do a better job next time," grumbled Erimenes.

"None of that," Fost said. "I want to warn her, Erimenes. She thinks she's got the Amulet of Living Flame and if she goes against Synalon . . ." He paused, considering the implications. "What does this Destiny Stone do, anyway?"

"A mere bagatelle," said Erimenes. "Now, let me tell you of the rich treasure troves all around you."

"Think, Erimenes," said Fost, "how marvelous it will be, all the centuries of peace and solitude alone in this glacier, nothing disturbing your meditations . . ."

"Sadist!" Erimenes declared with ill-grace. "Very well. It alters the luck of whoever wears it. Sometimes for the better, sometimes not."

"It alternates, then?"

"No. There's no predicting the sequence, although

many have tried. The Destiny Stone, while in ways immeasurably more powerful than the Amulet of Living
Flame, was reckoned less valuable."

Fost weighed the information. The Destiny Stone
could enable Moriana to best Synalon at a stroke—or
betray her instantly. There was no way to guess.

"I've got to warn her!" said the courier. "She's in
danger."

"Let her die," said Erimenes. "Or join with Synalon.
Let vengeance fire that pallid soul of yours. Why not
betray her as she betrayed you?"

"Because I love her," Fost said.

"The more fool you."

"Yes, the more fool I." He hitched the strap of
Erimenes' satchel over his shoulder. "Now, my nebu-
lous friend, what's this you say about plunder? I'll do
better chasing our wayward princess if I've gold in my
purse to go along with my determination."

Blood seeped into the ancient streets of Athalau.
Blood congealed, blood froze, blood streamed from
fingertips scraped raw on the pavement.

Inch by tortured inch, Prince Rann Etuul dragged
himself from beneath the block of ice partially pinning
him. In falling, the ice had struck the marble steps of
the Palace of Esoteric Wisdom, saving him from instant
death.

Though he delighted in the pain of others, he was not
immune from feeling his own. Many of his bones were
broken; he didn't know if even the surgical arts of the
Sky City would mend him. The vicious pain shooting up
his legs every time he moved at least assured him his
spine was intact.

A rumble from above hastened his strugglings. The
ice dome overhead had been fractured by slow shiftings
and pressures within the glacier. With one ice block
fallen, the others would soon follow. A fist-sized piece

ricocheted off the larger block in a spray of glass-sharp shards and went whistling off down the street. He fought harder to escape.

With a last convulsive heave, Rann pulled his legs free. He was hardly the picture of a Sky City prince. The black and purple of his uniform had been stained the color of dried blood. The clothing had dried stiff. He felt as if the pressure of the ice had squeezed the blood from his very pores.

He coughed, spat, then eyed his injuries critically. He saw no blood; internal bleeding could finish him before any possible rescue. He knew better than most physicians of the Sundered Realm how much abuse a human body could take. He had pushed others screaming past those limits often enough.

Exhaustion darkened his vision. The smell of age and blood and death clotted in his nostrils. He wondered if he wanted to live. The savage Thail tribesmen had already robbed him of that pleasure most men reckoned indispensable. The tortures were a surrogate, as was driving his small, hard body through ceaseless exercise with sword and bow. If his injuries could not be healed, still more of his feeble pleasures would be torn from him. Would life be worth much then?

The thought formed calmly in his mind: *Yes.* Those of Etuul blood did not yield easily, even to death.

He must report to Synalon and assure her he had not failed her once again. He and his men had been about to best Moriana and her consort when the world had fallen on top of them. He assumed the princess and courier had been mashed as thoroughly as his own men. He knew that the Amulet of Living Flame lay somewhere within the Palace of Esoteric Wisdom, even if he was in no shape to recover it personally. At the moment, his main concern was getting out of the path of more falling ice cubes.

Haven awaited him in a doorway on the left side of the street, flanked by decorative glass bricks running to

THE DESTINY STONE 37
THE DESTINY STONE 37

street level. Like a broken-backed snake, Rann painfully hunched over to it. The world dipped and whirled about him when a groping finger touched smooth hardness. It was impossible to tell the difference between his own pulse and the creaking of overstressed ice. He forced his eyes open, blinked away the sweat that filled them, and forced his mind to focus on a face.

Magical power as well as political passed through the female side of the Etuul clan. But Rann was not without some basic sorcerous lore. He struggled to contact the one who was trying to contact him.

"My lord." For a moment, Rann looked without comprehension at the face appearing in the milky glass before him. "My lord prince, is it you?"

He sighed with mingled relief and disgust. He recognized the nasal, whining tone of the apprentice magician, Maguerr. The youth kept watch from outside the glacier by means of a magic seeing stone, looking in every hour to note the progress of the prince and his party. The rest of the time he was to maintain a loose rapport with the stone. By concentrating on Maguerr's thin and pimply face, Rann had drawn his attention.

The boy tugged his sandy beard in dismay.

"Milord, it's been the *longest* time since I've heard from you. Why, it's almost daylight!"

"Enough!" Somehow Rann found the strength to bark out the word. "I'm hurt. Send for help." Each syllable produced a spear thrust through his broken chest.

"I already did, milord," Maguerr said, his head bobbing. "When I no longer found you with my geode, I called the Sky City for aid. They are sending bird riders. They should be here soon after dawn."

"Bird riders!" Rann spat in disgust. "What can they do to get me out? Chisel a way through the glacier with their eagles' beaks?"

"They bring powerful elementals with them, lord."

"My cousin's idea, I take it?"

"Yes, lord. The queen herself commanded that the sprites be sent." A shadow crossed the pimply visage. "She desired that you report immediately on making contact with me, most noble one."

"I . . . can't talk now," Rann said, exaggerating the difficulty of speech. "Damn block of ice fell on me. Later."

Maguerr blanched.

"But, lord, I . . . but . . ." He was caught between conflicting commands. Rann savored the consternation radiating from the sorcerer's face. At last Maguerr came to the prudent conclusion that Rann, being closer, commanded temporary priority. He swallowed his gibbered protests and said, "Very well, O lord, to hear is to obey. But I must communicate with Her Majesty. What shall I tell her?" Maguerr's expression made it clear that he wanted to report success.

Rann smiled mirthlessly at the young sorcerer's understanding of the situation. Synalon was indiscriminate with her wrath. If Rann failed, Maguerr, not being high-born, would suffer no less—and possibly more.

"We overtook Moriana and her accomplice. We fought; they died."

Maguerr's throat worked like a frog's. His eyes bulged. If an insect had flown by, Rann would have expected to see a long forked tongue dart out of the boy's mouth and snare it.

"And the amulet, lord?" Maguerr stammered. "Do you have it?"

A vast, flat boom cracked across the city as Rann started to reply. The prince looked up. An irregular piece of ice detached itself from the arched vault of Athalau. The ponderous ice spear moved as if it were dipped in clear molasses, then gained speed, smashing into the ground barely a hundred feet distant. The shock wave stunned Rann momentarily.

"My lord," called Maguerr. "Are you there? Do you have the amulet?"

With a sardonic smile, Rann regarded the huge block of ice that had landed next to its icy brother. The front half of the Palace of Esoteric Wisdom lay crushed now. Getting inside would require exhausting work; he dare not damage the amulet by allowing a fire elemental to approach too closely.

"Not exactly," he said.

The long drum roll of the ice falling brought Fost's head up abruptly, a spoonful of tasteless gruel halfway to his mouth. The sound rolled like thunder splashing off the frigid walls. The taller buildings swayed to the beat of the massive impact.

"Glad I wasn't under that," commented Fost, swallowing the gruel. He plunged his spoon into the ebony bowl again and scooped up more, which was dutifully replenished by the spell that animated the bowl. The courier almost savored the slop. He'd never felt this ravenous in his life. Being raised from the dead did wonders for a man's appetite.

"You almost were," was Erimenes' dour comment. He peered into the city, blue brow furrowed. "That landed smack atop the Palace of Esoteric Wisdom, I see."

Something seemed to stick in Fost's throat.

"Desecration," Erimenes sighed. His thin shoulders moved with such exaggerated despair that Fost laughed aloud. Erimenes looked daggers in his direction. "Laugh if you will, barbarian. But this was once my city—the greatest on earth!"

"No offense meant, spirit," Fost said, waving his spoon placatingly. "But don't look so at me. If it weren't for you yanking that chunk of ice off the ceiling, I doubt the new block would've fallen."

"And if I hadn't, you wouldn't be here to carry on so witlessly."

"Well taken." Fost forced down another mouthful of gruel. "At any rate, I wasn't laughing at the damage done to your precious city; I was laughing at you. The thought of such beauty laid to waste depresses me, too."

Erimenes did not look appeased. He folded thin arms, elevated his nose, and in a lordly fashion gazed out over Athalau. Ignoring him, Fost turned back to his gruel. But food would cure only part of the hollow ache he felt inside.

"Man Fost."

The words rolled forth in a thunderous bass. Fost jumped off the bench spilling Erimenes in one direction and his gruel in another. The spirit turned into an agitated blue tornado as he tried to resume his form. Fost looked about him, hands on sword and dagger.

"You humans are an excitable lot," the voice rumbled. It came from all around at the same pitch and volume as the falling ice. "I had forgotten that, along with your poor eyesight."

"It wasn't poor eyesight, dammit!" Fost shouted. "And I'm not excitable. It was—is—I'm not used to being addressed by glaciers."

The pause fell as heavy as the glacier's voice. It took Fost a few moments to realize he'd hurt the glacier's feelings.

He sighed. It wasn't enough to be saddled with a treacherous, lecherous, hypercritical spirit and a beautiful but idealistic princess; he had to cope with a tempermental glacier as well.

His bowl lay tilted against the end of the bench, disgorging a steady stream of fluid that ran down the ice-sheathed road in a stream the color of dirty wool. He wondered whether it would keep issuing gruel until the whole bubble enveloping Athalau was filled with the stuff. He was appalled with the idea of the timeless beauty of the city being drowned in murky, colorless, salty glop. He capped the bowl, still needing it.

"I'm sorry, Guardian," he said. He looked around for a way to clean the bowl. He finally broke up some ice and rinsed off the bowl with it. Erimenes re-formed and stood by, watching with his usual expression of disdain.

"I didn't mean to insult you, Guardian," Fost went on. Several minutes had elapsed between the first part of his apology and the second. He was beginning to adopt the glacier's speech habits. "I was taken by surprise when you spoke."

"I see."

An ominous crack echoed above as the words rolled around the bubble over Athalau. Fost looked up uneasily. At its highest point several hundred feet up, the hollow containing the city must come within a few score feet of the glacier's exterior. It wouldn't take much to bring the entire roof hurtling down.

"I thought you might be glad to know that the other two members of your party passed this way not long ago."

Fost's heart soared. Moriana took the road out of the city leading northeast to the Gate of the Mountains! With luck, he might catch up with the princess in a few days. How surprised Moriana would be, that lovely, golden-haired bitch . . .

Slowly, the courier realized that Erimenes looked at him strangely. At the same instant, his subconscious reran the glacier's words.

"Wait a minute! You said, 'the other *two*.' *What* other two?"

"Why, the yellow-haired one who claimed Athalar descent . . ."

"Go on," Fost demanded, his boot tapping impatiently on the ice.

"And the other was, why excuse me, Ureminus, I'd thought it to be you who accompanied the princess."

Erimenes' jaw dropped. The news was scarcely less surprising to Fost.

"Impossible!" raged the spirit. "There's only one of me! I and only I, Erimenes the Ethical, last survivor of Athalau! Accept no substitutes!"

"But there was another such as you," the glacier said. Erimenes turned the color of squid's ink. He beat impotent fists against the air. If he'd been alive, Fost would have thought he was seized by a demon.

"An impostor!" Erimenes roared, his form shifting with passion. "O gods, O Five Holy Ones and the Three and Twenty of Agift, witness now how I am wronged!"

"You said you didn't believe in any of those," pointed out Fost. Erimenes ignored him.

"Hmmm, yes, ah, I was wrong. My apologies, Irreminas."

Erimenes pulled together rapidly, so mollified by the glacier's retraction that he forgot to take exception to the mangling of his name.

"I remember now that this shade was pink and feminine in gender." The Guardian sighed, rattling Athalau's foundations. "I have *such* a hard time differentiating between you humans. You're so minute."

Erimenes puffed up like a lizard in rut, preparing to flirt with the netherworld's approximation of apoplexy again. Fost hastily jammed the lid back into the spirit jar. The outraged philosopher faded from view. A wail emerged from the jug.

"Let me out! This instant, Fost, let me out! I must tell that oversized icicle a thing or two!"

Fost heartily thumped the jar with his fist. Erimenes gulped and quieted. Inside the jug, he was susceptible to motion sickness.

Stuffing Erimenes' jar back into its satchel, Fost set off at a rapid pace into a tunnel the spirit had adjudged to be the way out. A mere twenty paces shut off the light of Athalau. Blackness as thick and heavy as velvet engulfed him. He tried a few experimental steps, bumped his nose into a wall, cursed, and stopped. Even with Erimenes guiding him through this maze of iceworm tunnels, he might encounter one of the builders. Memory of hard black jaws stayed him.

"Erimenes? If I let you out, will you promise not to squabble with the Guardians?"

"Why should I promise you anything?"

Fost sighed. A century of life and fourteen of death and Erimenes still acted like a spoiled child.

"Because I can't see where I'm going."

"Ahh," said Erimenes cagily. "You need my glow to illuminate your way. And Moriana has your torches. *You* need *me*. Not the other way around."

"Tell me," said Fost, "how many centuries would it take before an ice worm decided to see if a discarded clay pot was tasty?"

"A pot like mine? Oh, very well. But I won't forget this, Fost. You're brutal. *Brutal.*"

Fost opened the satchel and allowed Erimenes to waver into being beside him. Fost smiled broadly and got a scornful sniff in return. The light cast wasn't bright, but it did prevent him from colliding with tunnel walls.

Fost walked rapidly, avoiding the cold walls until a slab of ice slammed sideways into the courier and knocked him off his feet.

Erimenes shrieked in terror as his jug flew into the air. The satchel cushioned it enough to prevent it from shattering. Another tremor rocked the passageway. Erimenes swirled like a tornado, jittery blue lightning crackling through his being. He squealed like an orphaned shoat.

"Guardian," Fost bellowed. "What's going on?"

"In-intruders, O man." Agony etched the great voice. "They come from above like the ones who came after you professing to be your friends." The words came as quickly as any human's. Something caused the Guardian incredible anguish.

A lull in the quaking gave Fost opportunity to recover Erimenes' satchel and lash it securely to his hip. The philosopher still vibrated.

"Negligence! Criminal negligence! You, a Realm courier, allow your valuable cargo to be endangered by carelessness. I shall complain to your employer, sir!"

To think of his employer Gabric—fat, black-moustached and oily—made Fost grin. Gabric had enough grievances with his star courier already. Making off with the property of a sorcerer and failing to report back in were definite violations of the rules.

"Pain," moaned the glacier, shuddering. "Such agony!"

Fost felt tons of ice poised over his head. Guardian was shaking himself apart. The courier crawled along as fast as he could.

"What's hurting you, Guardian? Tell me!"

"The bird folk. They brought with them some demon of northern witchery. Ohhh! It burns. It burns into my bowels!"

"A fire elemental," said Erimenes, voice jittering to the tempo of the quakes rocking the tunnel. "The Sky City men are burning inward."

"Yes!" The glacier's voice was the sound of tortured, yielding metal. "Their leader, the lying manling, still lives. They rescue him with the fire fiend. O Felarod, O Athalau, I have failed you!"

Ice shards erupted from ahead as the tunnel collapsed.

Face cut and bleeding from the icy knives, Fost dropped to his knees and crawled. Over the roaring of new ice falling, he heard Erimenes shouting, ". . . other way . . . back up . . . yards . . . tunnel to north!"

The din deafening him, Fost raced for the cross-tunnel, death nipping at his heels as he went.

Steam geysered from the hole in the ice. The bird riders huddled around, filling their lungs with the astringent steam and feeling the war between the heat that bathed their fronts and the chill wind that lashed against their backs. The glacier shifted under them like a beast gone mad.

Shapeless in his heavy cloak, Maguerr hunched over his geode.

"The elemental is almost through, noble prince," he said. "Do you see it yet?"

Rann rolled onto his back. The city moved around and beneath him in constant randomness. The view above was obscured by debris, flecks and chunks of ice falling to shatter in the streets. All around him, soaring buildings had been hammered to rubble by plummeting blocks.

"Yes!" he shouted. His hand clawed at the glass brick as though actually clutching the young mage's sleeve. "A yellow glow—red now—I see it! Water's beginning to drip down this side."

Maguerr fought to keep the fire elemental in check. They were fickle, tricky beings, as were the nobles of the Sky City in their own way. A single wavering of purpose, of concentration, and they would all be screaming torches. The salamanders loved to dine on human flesh.

The bird riders kept well away from the sorcerer. They knew the risks of distracting him at a crucial moment since ice was not a normal diet for fire sprites. Only the strongest spells of obedience known to the Sky City mages forced the fire elementals into contact with water.

To bore a rescue tunnel down to the injured Prince Rann, the salamander needed fuel, vast amounts of it, to maintain its existence. And it needed to be bribed, as well.

The bird riders around the steaming hole in the Guardian's back cast glances at their tethered birds, shrilling and thumping wings nervously at the nearness of such potent savagery. Not one of the men could make himself forget that there were now three more birds than riders. No extra mounts had been brought.

Service to their City in the Sky could be costly.

Under their boots, the salamander bored ever deeper into living ice.

Fost barely noticed the cessation of the tremors. The impossible crashing, like all the world's forges in one, dinned on within his brain. His bruised, weary limbs still felt the glacier's shaking. Had the whole mass of the Guardian's bulk fallen on him he couldn't have ached more.

He lurched along, sometimes erect, sometimes swaying, sometimes dragging himself on hands that had become senseless clubs of meat. He was conscious of Erimenes hovering at his side like a nervous guardian angel. The philosopher's lips moved ceaselessly, but Fost heard nothing.

Blinding glare caused him to recoil. Fear clutched at him. Wondering if he had become turned around, he confronted the elemental impaling the helpless Guardian. He blinked, forcing his eyes to confront the hellishly intense light.

It was the sun. The pale, distant, antarctic sun.

He was out, safe, free. The journey through the bowels of a nightmare had ended. He'd lost precious hours in his pursuit of the woman he loved and was far away from the Gate of the Mountains, but the noise and pain battering his head had ceased. And the fear, too, the soul-rotting fear that filled the mouth with bile and the mind with white howling had subsided. He couldn't be trapped in a closed-in space now.

He pulled himself along the stony, snowy ground. A slope fell away before him. He rolled down, listless, limbs flailing helplessly. At last he hit bottom. The sun dripped warmth into his chilled soul. His eyes closed. He slept and dreamed of . . . *nothing* . . .

He awoke. The sun had fallen low and was about to douse its fires in the distant Gulf of Veluz. Dying light stained the world orange.

Fost was conscious of separation. *Shadow.* He was somehow shaded and exempted from the dying umber sunset. He raised his head in pain.

A great, misshapen figure loomed over him, blotting out the sun.

CHAPTER THREE

A round swell of petulance drifted up through the Sleeper's mind. Black in blackness, the creature stirred. Its mind and body were bound in eternal darkness. Yet the dreaming mind, the mind beneath, refused to be still.

Tenuous dream memory fragments of color, feeling, smell, floated through a mind that had not known these alien intruders for ten thousand years. Yet it had known these sensations recently.

Hadn't it?

Colors, pale, pinkish blurs—faces. Thousands of faces, faces of the soft folk, the folk of the ancient foe, turned toward it in fear and awe and—expectation. One face in particular contorted in a fear so intense that the Sleeper's mind experienced a thrill like freedom, like the destruction of suns, like a boiling in stone loins. The soft one was bound and helpless; its nude form awakened desires buried deep in the mind of the demon. Nostrils newly returned (how? why?) had drunk in the sweet smell of fear and excitement and the harsh musk of anticipation, not from the shape upon the altar but from the thronging multitudes. They awaited the captive's degradation like the blessing of a god. In its dream the Sleeper felt soft flesh yielding to it, enfolding it, causing hot pleasure to blast in pulses up its spine.

And then pain. *PAIN!*

The dream dissolved in a crimson wash of rage. Betrayed! The Sleeper had been betrayed again! Drawn forth from senselessness with the promise of pleasure, it met only the reality of pain.

Betrayed!

The word burst forth and shrieked through the stony corridors of its mind. It was ever this way. From the freedom of the gaps between suns it had been drawn to this insignificant ball of offal. It had been promised consummation of all desires left unsated in the void by those who granted it life. It had reveled for a time in the nearness of benchmarks, by which it measured the immensity of its power. But that had begun to pall. It had come to see it was being used, bound by the strength of its makers to serve beings inferior to itself.

And then the great struggle with the ancient foes, the time of triumph and ultimate loss. Its lords assured it that it could not be defeated by the pale ones. They had lied. It was brought low, cast down, immurred in stone. The black soul that had known the freedom of galaxies now knew only the inescapable confines of a tiny womb of rock and magic. Worse than this, its intelligence had been forced inward and down into this endless slumber. Awareness came in fleeting fragments, yet it knew it had been more.

It suffered.

Betrayed! Always betrayed. It had served its makers well, and they had abandoned it to this prison. In blackness a black shape twisted in wrath and impotence. Black limbs thrashed at invisible binding walls. The ancient stone remained impervious even to fists capable of smashing mountains. Black waves of hate flowed from the sleeping mind like flaming gas from the explosion of a star.

In the City above, thousands of other sleepers stirred uneasily. Unlike the Sleeper below, they slumbered only from the labors of the day. Most slept on and soon forgot the formless dread that had for a brief instant invaded their dreams. Others, more sensitive, lay wakeful. Some rose and looked out at the gelid winter stars above with a new uneasy familiarity. After a time they, too, shuddered and returned to bed. Perhaps some sensed the nature of that which roused them, but if they did, they kept their minds carefully averted. Some things are too hideous to confront directly.

Like a great stone cloud, the City in the Sky floated northeastward. Below, the jagged Thail Mountains began to ease and flow into foothills that would become the central plain. A thousand feet below, Thail tribesman in reeking furs shook fetish sticks at the City.

The City would continue on its path whether or not the Thailint mystics danced and gibbered. No one, not even the powerful mages who inhabited it, could swerve the Sky City from its slow but unpredictable course around the Great Quincunx of cities. It had followed the Quincunx since the War of Powers had stripped its original owners, the lizardlike folk now called the Fallen Ones, of their dark sorceries and confined them to the City. Humans had seized the Sky City by treachery and cast out the Fallen Ones, who had then shut themselves in a castle in the heights of the Mystic Mountains. They had played no further role in the affairs of the Sundered Realm except as occasional villains in tales told to frighten small children into obedience. The City in the Sky now followed its own whim switching course at the cities forming the sides of the Quincunx—Wirix, Kara-Est, Brev, and Thailot, and Bilsinx at the center. Following no known or knowable scheme, it proceeded a mile every hour of every day.

Vast wings reached into the sky. Eagles rose from the battlements bearing small, wiry men on their backs. A score, two score, then fifty of the warbirds took wing, orbited the City once and flew off to the south. Thailint watchers cowering in the rocks far below marked the grim manner of the troop. Not even the wild cry of an eagle floated down the wind as the Sky Guardsmen beat their way into the teeth of an icy wind.

A hundred miles to the south, just beyond the lower reaches of the Thails, they encountered another smaller party flying out of the snow-sheathed Southern Steppes. Now the eagles throated strident cries to greet their kin. The men saluted one another with weapons but did not speak. The party coming from the south brought a slight, still form strapped amid heavy furs on an improvised pallet. The newcomers swung about and took up stations surrounding the three eagles that bore the burden. Though every man was ceaselessly alert, eyes roving the horizon for sign of danger, none expected trouble. The City ruled the skies over the Sundered Realm. But it was not for protection that the men had flown to meet the stretcher bearers.

Gravely wounded, Prince Rann Etuul, commander of the elite Sky Guard, was being borne home to the City. His men had come unbidden as a guard of honor.

The Sky Guardsmen did not love their prince. They feared him. But despite his personal taste for inflicting pain, his discipline was severe but fair; enemies of the Sky City and its capricious, lovely ruler provided partners enough for the only sort of lovemaking the eunuch prince was able to partake of. A slacker could expect no mercy at his hands, but those who did their duty well had nothing to fear. Prince Rann did not have his men's love but he had from them respect bordering on worship.

High-piled clouds paced the City as it floated toward Wirix. With the wind at their backs, the returning bird riders made good time. They returned home just as dusk began to tint the sky scarlet. The unconscious Rann was removed from the stretcher and taken to his chambers in the royal palace. Nervous mages, their shaven skulls painted with cabalistic symbols, hovered like a cloud of gnats. Synalon had convinced them that Rann's life was more precious than their own.

For three days Rann hovered in the gray no-man's-land between life and death. His injuries should have killed him outright. Yet Rann had retained consciousness until the rescue party had finished strapping him to the makeshift sling. He only vaguely remembered the eagles lifting from the street up through the steaming hole far above. After that, all was black.

His own natural resilience joined forces with the sorcery of the City. By the third morning after his return, the crisis had passed. At midday his eyes opened, and he asked for refreshment. The mages on duty exchanged looks of almost unbearable relief and went flapping into the hall to spread the good news.

He was sipping boiled poultry broth when his cousin swept in. Synalon Etuul was a woman in her early twenties, soft-voiced and self-assured to the point of arrogance. Her sorcery and skill in intrigue had accomplished the death of her mother and the seizure of the throne that was, by tradition and law, her sister's. She was the greatest enchantress of her age, and she was determined to restore the City in the Sky to its former glory.

"Your Majesty," said Rann, looking sardonically over the rim of his pewter mug. "I'd abase myself, but my physicians forbid me to leave my sickbed."

Synalon bowed her head in reply. Her jet-black hair was unbound and fell in gleaming coils past the shoulders of a gown the same color. Her creamy skin glowed in vivid contrast.

"It is we who should abase ourselves to you, Prince Rann," she said, clasping her hands on her breast. "You are the hero of the hour."

Rann raised a skeptical eyebrow.

"You have brought the traitor Moriana to justice. The hearts of our people are lifted to you in gratitude. Moreover, you have secured for us the Amulet of Living Flame, a guarantee that we will be able to spread the benefits of our reign over this noble City for all time to come."

"I haven't exactly secured the amulet for Your Majesty." It took a conscious effort to keep from saying "Your Majesties." He found Synalon's affectations amusing—amusing and lethal. "The amulet lies buried under tons of ice. I must, in all honesty, point out that the ice fall might have smashed it to powder. Magical artifacts of such antiquity are notoriously fragile."

"No matter," said Synalon, dismissing the possibility with a wave of her hand. "My prime concern was that Moriana be denied the use of the amulet. I desired it for my own immortality, of course, but no matter. When the Sundered Realm lies conquered at my feet, then will be the time to experiment and increase my sorcerous lore. Perhaps I can make peace with Istu. With the resources of a continent at my disposal, I can find some way to break damned Felarod's restraints and free the Soul of the City. Then nothing would be beyond my power! Nay, cousin, this is but a setback. It is not to diminish the glory of your achievement."

Rann shut his eyes and lay back. He stifled a moan. A few weeks before, Synalon had been frantic to get the Amulet of Living Flame. Now she dismissed it as a mere trinket. For all her power and wiles, the self-proclaimed ruler was little more than a spoiled child. She could focus her interest on one thing only so long; then her desire skipped gaily to some new toy.

He opened his eyes. Hers burned like blue suns. He was slow to recognize that there might be shrewd calculation behind her apparent fickleness. With Moriana out of the way, the major threat to Synalon's power had been removed. Now the usurper could put her grand schemes into motion.

For that she would need her cousin.

Recuperation was a slow process for the prince. Not even the magic of the Sky City could heal wounds such as his overnight. And his iron will could demand only so much of broken limbs and battered muscles.

Still, the next weeks were a time of activity for the prince. He observed, considered, and planned. Within four days of his return to the floating city, he had himself carried to a great-windowed chamber where he looked out on the Sky Guardsmen drilling on their mounts. Shortly after that, he supervised the drill personally. He could not sit on an eagle, but a sedan slung between slow cargo eagles allowed him to fly among his troops to watch, criticize, refine.

Militarily, the Sky City possessed both advantages and disadvantages. The troops of the City had a base that was virtually proof against assault or even against attempts at assault. Several times in her wars with Athalau and the Empire, the City had been assailed by balloon attacks, but such clumsy transports proved bloody jokes when confronting the superbly trained and equipped bird riders.

But as far as the City was concerned, targets for bombings with rocks had to be directly below—and the Sky Citizens had no more control over the movement of their floating home than did their enemies. The only cities vulnerable to attack from above were the five cities of the Great Quincunx. And the attacks brought courted reprisals of the most devastating form.

The Sky City's existence depended on trade. No raw materials were produced within the City. All food had to be purchased or produced on plantations owned and run by the City's agents and then lifted thousands of feet upward to feed the small but well-fed populace. Over half of the water had to be raised by balloon; rigorous water discipline, collection of rainwater, and use of the Fallen Ones' "magic fountains"—the aero-aquifers—alleviated the problem but did not solve it. Military materiel especially strained the supply system. Even rocks to be dropped on enemies far below had to be lifted laboriously by the great dirigibles.

If the Sky City wished conquest—and Synalon did— it had to begin by conquering the Quincunx. Fortunately, there was no difficulty in reaching the targets. Sooner or later the City passed over all its earthbound trading partners. And the land dominated by the Quincunx lay in the middle of the Sundered Realm, giving the territory definite strategic value in terms of further expansion. But the City's war with the Quincunx had to be fast and it had to be successful. A cessation of trade would starve the aerial city quickly.

Further complicating Rann's task as commander in chief was the lack of knowledge as to which target the city would attack first. They'd just departed Thailot on the savannah west of the Thail Mountains and were bound for Wirix, fifty miles southwest of mighty Mount Omizantrim. Wirix, surrounded by twenty-mile-long Lake Wir, was dependent on water trade. If the Sky City captured Wirix, that city could be easily cut off. On the other hand, since the City had never been known to double back on its course, from Wirix there were only two possible destinations: Kara-Est at the head of the Gulf of Veluz, and Bilsinx, central city of the Quincunx. Of the two, Rann thought Bilsinx the easier target. The Estil had domesticated huge jellyfishlike creatures from the swamps west of the city which produced lighter-than-air gas within their bodies sufficient to raise themselves and considerable loads. Though still inferior to the eagles of the City, the *ludintip* of Kara-Est gave the Estil the best aerial defense of any of the cities.

The wind blew sharp and evil a fortnight after Rann's return. The night before, it had brought clouds from the south to plaster a blinding white stucco of snow across the land. For all its brilliance, the sun above lacked warmth. And the very air sucked heat from unsuspecting bodies until Rann felt as if he'd been slashed with a hundred knives.

His body was still one throb of pain. The cold was torture this morning as it magnified every ache. Later he would welcome numbness as a blessing, but now he forced himself to continue with his task in spite of the discomfort.

A cup of medicinal tea gave the illusion of warmth.

Rann sipped it as he shifted his bandaged body on the divan, trying to find the best view out of the balloon's wicker gondola. Beside him, looking like a small freak of a bear in his furry coat and hood, stood the balloon operator. And huddled against the curving wall of the basket like a fur-bearing crane was Maguerr, hugging his geode and breathing mist on his blue fingers to keep them warm. He was Rann's communications officer. In the past few days, the prince had grown almost resigned to the journeyman mage's presence. Rann had come to view Maguerr's presence as punishment for the muddle he'd made of the quest for Moriana and the amulet.

It had been a pity to lose Moriana, he thought. Sighing inwardly, he peered over the gondola's rim to watch the workers laying out strips of dark cloth several hundred feet below. Soon those dark patches would be real enemy troops and not practice targets. Still, better to have his mind on war then on the loving touches he could have given Moriana.

He sipped at his tea, so lost in thought that he hardly noticed its bitterness. Maguerr muttered his grievances endlessly to himself. Rann idly turned his attention to the mage. He hadn't yet caught the words of the youth's aggrieved litany, but from its rhythms he guessed Maguerr repeated himself too much to leave room for inventiveness in cursing.

It had been a pity to lose Fost as well. With the collapse of the Empire centuries before, the Realm had lost all central authority. Its roads and byways were constantly alive with brigands ranging from skulking cutpurses to young armies of cutthroats that occasionally grew bold enough to ransack unwary towns. Those brigands were the reason for the City's large numbers of highly trained troops. The trade arterials had to be kept free. Sky City bird and dog riders guarded caravans, its spearmen held innumerable outposts along the major routes into and through the Quincunx, and its patrols attacked known bands of highwaymen from the air.

Because of the prevailing anarchy of the Realm, the men serving as couriers had to be very special, tough, smart, and resourceful. Fost Longstrider had been no exception. Rann could recall no single outlander who'd given the Skyborn such difficulty. Even before teaming with Moriana, he'd bested several patrols of dog riders sent to take Erimenes from him. To add further insult to his crimes, he'd infiltrated the Sky City and stolen away Moriana. That and the pursuit leading up to his injury inside Athalau made Rann view the courier with a mixture of admiration and hatred.

He could use men like Fost. Mulling over the prospect, an idea came to the prince. Why not recruit as many Realm couriers as possible to use as rangers and raiders? Because of the Sky City's lack of population, tactical doctrine depended on small, well-trained units. For serious conquest once the Quincunx cities had been subdued, Synalon would hire mercenaries to flesh out her ground forces. Even here, the couriers could be of use. They would know the best places to recruit such men.

Spun downstream by the wind like flotsam, the notes of a trumpet reached Rann. He craned his neck. A company of eagles rose from the City, formed an echelon, and winged toward his tethered balloon. Another company followed and then another.

Overhead, just out of the reach of missile fire from the ground, the bird riders formed a wide circle. These weren't Sky Guardsmen. Their eagles didn't maintain the awful, foreboding silence until the moment of attack. Their voices rang down fierce and wild, full of challenge.

From a fold in the land appeared a body of dog-riding cavalry. The bird riders broke formation and streamed in a raucous, squalling line to take up a new orbit above the heads of the ground troops. The wind whipped the dark cloth laid out to represent the enemy army. The cloth cracked with a splitting sound, crisp and harsh in the morning chill.

The first company of bird riders dove on the "enemy." They held until their front ranks were twenty yards from the flapping cloth. Then a hailstorm of arrows broke from the flyers. The projectiles fell like deadly rain onto the cloth, pinning it to the ground in half a hundred places. The second company followed with the third close behind. When they finished the attack, they circled again, pouring down missiles. The ground-borne skirmishers came whirling forward, casting their own darts and arrows. The cloth strip lay still like a great beast freshly slain.

Rann nodded. This was his drill for attacking formed troops: soften the front ranks with an arrow storm from the air, further disorganize the foe with the skirmishers while the eagles continued to harry from above, and finally drive in with lancers for the killing stroke. Variations would be used as the battle required. His troops had performed well, but his keen eyes saw flaws.

"Get me Captain Sunda," he growled at Maguerr. "That first volley was as ragged as a molting eagle's tail. Maguerr bobbed his head and waved spidery fingers over his geode. Rann sat back, at ease in spite of the cold and agony enveloping him.

The Sky City's great conquest was soon to begin.

"You are sad, child," came the gentle, clear voice through the moaning of the wind. "Tell me of it. A burden is lighter when shared."

Moriana sighed and let the amulet drop from her fingers. She had been contemplating it for some time, oblivious to the chill rush of the wind and the acrid stink of the small campfire. The amulet's color divided now between light and dark, but it was never still. The balance shifted from one moment to the next so that she was barely able to perceive the subtle flux. Neither shade predominated. Whatever the interplay of black and white meant, it was in equilibrium for the present.

The wind brushed fluffy snow in soft sibilance across the top of the makeshift shelter. Drawn back to her surroundings by Ziore's words, Moriana tried and failed to keep down a shiver. The lean-to provided poor shielding against the relentless storm sweeping down from the northwest. But it was better than no shield at all.

It had been sheer luck to stumble upon the herd of grazers. It had been greater luck still to find an aged cow, her white winter pelt yellow and dingy with age, resting amid tall, dead grass at the perimeter of the herd. With the wind blowing out of the Ramparts at her back, Moriana had stalked within striking distance of the beast without alerting any in the herd. A bellow of fear turned to pain is she slashed her scimitar across hamstrings and then against the softness of throat skin. The hailstone of hooves as the herd took flight had faded into silence.

She stripped the skin from the dead animal, cut off as much meat as she could carry, and continued on her way. The Sky City beckoned. She had unsettled business with her twin sister.

The single-horned ruminant's flesh was stringy but a welcome relief from the monotony of the Athalar rations. But the important item was the hide. The wind marched ceaselessly across the steppe this time of year, as frigid and merciless as a horde of army ants. The hide offered some protection. This southeastern corner of the Southern Steppes was crisscrossed by streambeds running down out of the Ramparts toward the Gulf of Veluz. In spring they'd froth with the runoff of melting snow, but now they were dead and dry. The long roots of the steppes grass held the topsoil firm, forming almost perpendicular banks. An hour's labor with her knife gave a snug cubbyhole that could be roofed with the grazer hide. With dried grazer dung for fuel, Moriana indulged herself with a campfire, though only a tiny one so she wouldn't smoke herself out.

She sighed again. Rolling idle reminiscences through her mind was merely a way to put off answering Ziore. On the endless loneliness of the steppe, any human companionship was welcome, even a ghost's. And Ziore provided more than mere companionship. Her affection and concern sometimes seemed to cover Moriana like a warm, soft blanket. Yet even such snug comfort grew cloying at times.

"I'm afraid," she said flatly. "My sister knows more sorcery than I. With the amulet, I stand more chance against her. If I can find some place secure against her minions, I can engage her in a battle of magics. When her deathspells strike me down, I'll rise again to challenge her anew. Sooner or later, I will exhaust her." Moriana fingered the glassy facets of the stone as she added, "I hope."

"And for this you must be physically within the City?" asked Ziore. Moriana nodded. "What if you cannot gain entry into the Sky City?"

"I will gain entry," the princess said, letting go of the amulet to draw figures in the yellow dirt. "If stealth doesn't serve, I'll raise an army and force my way in." She laughed abruptly, bitterly. "I'm being grandiose today, aren't I? To speak of forcing entry to the City in the Sky when I sit huddled over a reeking manure fire in the middle of a blizzard with nothing but sore feet to carry me across hundreds of miles of barrenness. The way I talk, you'd think I was a princess and not a wretched refugee."

They sat in silence. The fire burned low. Moriana dug into her pouch for a dried dung chip and threw it into the embers.

A feathery touch caressed her cheek. She started, her eyes darting. Ziore hung beside her. The aged and beautiful face showed concern.

"I believe," the spirit said at length, "though I cannot know, for foretelling what will come to pass is a talent never granted me, that you will find some way to reach this reckoning with your sister." Ziore's eyes were sad. "I also know that's far from all that troubles you."

Moriana nodded, acknowledging the pain, grateful there was no need to put a name to it.

"Did I do right?" she asked.

"Don't be foolish, girl," said Ziore, her tone brisk. "You know quite well that only you can answer that."

"I have to feel I did right." She felt warm tears fill her eyes. "I feel the anguish of my people as Synalon's tyranny grinds them down. And I feel there's more at stake than even the welfare of my City. Synalon is quite insane. She's in tune with the power of the Dark Ones, more so than any of the City since the ancient time of Queen Malva Kryn. I dread her ambition, not so much for what she might achieve herself but for what she might unleash in her mad striving after power."

A wave of sickness, starting in the depth of her loins and washing outward, passed through her. She hugged herself and clenched her teeth against a mindless scream. Tears rolled down her cheeks, and blackness yammered at the fringes of her mind. She had been close, so close to that black maelstrom. The Vicar of Istu, animated by the sleeping demon's life, had held her in its stone embrace. The formless dark that swirled behind the statue's yellow eyes as they burned into hers had left its imprint on her soul.

More than anyone else alive, she understood the nature of the forces with which her sister so blithely toyed.

Another feathery caress touched her arm. To feel purposeful contact out in this friendless, icy waste sent a ripple of eeriness down her spine. The feeling passed quickly, and in its place came a strange serenity.

Moriana turned her head. Ziore paused, slim fingers on the princess's arm. The heavy maroon fabric of

Moriana's cloak dimpled as though to the touch of solid fingertips. Moriana looked at the spirit in surprise.

"An illusion," said Ziore, her voice a whisper in the strong wind. "Another trick I learned as a nun in Erimenes' cult. Not all the master's gifts proved worthless."

Bitterness tinged the words. After the ghost woman's initial vehemence at the mention of the sage's name, Moriana had been little inclined to press for an explanation. But those few words on Ziore's part said it all.

The princess reached out, taking one of Ziore's hands. The not-flesh seemed warm and dry in her fingers. She drew a ragged breath.

"Oh, daughter, daughter," the spirit said. She stroked Moriana's cheek. "You have need. Great need."

Her fingers slid down Moriana's face, over the rounded jawline and down her slender throat. Moriana felt a stirring in the depths of her belly. She shied away from it, from the strangeness of it. Again she felt the touch of Ziore's mind on hers, gentle and sweet as the illusory touch of her fingers.

"Don't hold yourself apart from what you know you need. You must have surcease from your worries, or they will consume you."

Moriana knew the truth of what the long dead woman said. Fear of the future, dread of the present, remorse of the past, these were cancers eating at her from within. She let down her barriers and felt her soul fill with Ziore's warmth.

The makeshift shelter filled with a rich red glow banishing cold and reeking smoke. Moriana felt fingers slip over her clavicle and down the sloped plain of her breastbone. Despite herself she tensed in disbelief. She wore a tunic and thick cloak yet felt the touch with her bare flesh.

"Fear not," soothed Ziore. "Do not disbelieve. Erimenes' vile, life-spurning doctrines robbed me of much while I lived. Yet when my life was over I learned many things before the glacier drove the living from Athalau and before the ice fall robbed me of my un-living kin." Her fingers cupped a breast. Moriana gasped with unexpected pleasure.

She reached out her arms. What they enfolded seemed no less real than Fost the last time they had embraced.

But no, she thought, I must not think of him. Now of all times . . .

She let herself slip into the sweet vortex of ecstasy. Outside, the wind keened, unheeded.

CHAPTER FOUR

Breath rattled in Fost's chest. He felt as if he inhaled sharp-edged pebbles. He tried to rise, but it felt as if the glacier had rolled forward and lay crushing his battered back.

He knew he had to rise. The shape outlined against the setting sun couldn't be human.

He groped for his sword. The motion sent pain lancing up his arm and stabbing through his chest. He gasped. His hand found the pommel and tried vainly to close. His fingers were stone clubs, unbending.

A moan answered his. A guttural, unearthly sound, it rasped like a potsherd along his spine. Trying to blink down the dazzle of the sun, he looked up desperately at the looming bulk.

The image swam in the dying glare. It finally resolved into two figures, still vague, still inhuman.

"I don't know why I came," a voice said.

Fost blinked harder. Sweat burned his eyes. He shook his head savagely in defiance of the pain it caused. His eyes finally focused.

Tall in the saddle of her great brown bear, Jennas, hetwoman of the Ust-alayakits, somberly regarded Fost. Resting on his haunches beside her mount was a riderless bear, his red fur touched with gold by the setting sun.

"I should have left you," the hetwoman said. She looked at a point somewhere over and beyond the courier. "You made your choice and chose to follow your northern woman on her quest. Why should I care what befalls you? Answer me that."

Fost tried to speak and couldn't, his throat filled with gravel.

"Ust came to me in a dream last night and said that I would find you as he rolled the sun-ball down behind the world." She sighed, her sad brown eyes sinking to Fost's. Moisture glittered at the corners of her eyes. "Your destiny is still tied to that of the People of Ust, it seems." She added, in a hoarse whisper, "And to mine."

Fost sat up. With his limbs numb from chill and the beating he'd taken, he felt like he was pulling several hundredweight of sandbags along with him. Bright lights orbiting inside his skull were his reward for the effort.

The red bear lumbered forward. It tongue lolled over deadly teeth. Confronted with those ivory pikes, Fost recoiled. The jaws widened. As it licked, the tongue hit him in the face like a heavy, wet towel.

He fell backward, squawking. The bear was all over him in a flash, as nimble as a racing hound, plying the courner's face with vast swipes of rough tongue.

"Grutz is glad to see you," said Jennas, "though you abandoned him."

Fost struggled under the bear's loving attack and stifled the impulse to hit the immense, shaggy head. No matter how glad Grutz was to be reunited with his former master, the bear might lose his temper if batted around the ears by accident. Finger-length fangs inches from Fast's face kept the courier quiet. He managed to bury his fists in the fur on either side of Grutz's muzzle and pushed the bear's face to one side. He gulped a frigid breath. Air recycled through a bear's lungs wasn't the sweetest in the world.

He stood, using Grutz's fur for handholds. The polar waste wheeled crazily. He leaned against the bear's flank and finally fell forward, draping himself across the creature's back. He managed to straddle the beast, then lay like a limp rag. Without a word, Jennas turned her own mount and started off at a rolling gait for the mountains. Grutz followed. Fost hung on precariously, never having been much of a rider. And riding one of the Ust-alayakits's bears was like trying to keep astride an avalanche.

"I take it you know this rustic person, friend Fost," a voice complained peevishly. "I can't say much for her choice of pets, but wherever they are taking us must be a substantial improvement over this miserable wasteland."

Grutz snapped upright, snarling in alarm. Arms and legs feebly wheeling, Fost arced through the air and landed hard on frozen earth. Grutz swayed back and forth, growling low, hunched to spring on the unseen intruder.

"Declare yourself, apparition," demanded Jennas, whipping her longsword from its sling across her back. "Are you demon or magic of the Sky City?"

"Neither one," a voice from behind said. "Merely the shade of a great but unfortunately demised philosopher. Since my loutish companion has neglected to do so, I shall introduce myself. I am Erimenes the Ethical, madam, late—if I may allow myself the clever turn of phrase—of the glorious city of Athalau." The ghost chuckled at his own wit.

With great effort, Fost turned his head. His satchel had fallen a few feet from him, dislodging the lid of Erimenes' jar. A thin umbilicus of blue vapor wisped from under the satchel's flap. Fost was pulling himself to his feet when an ominous rumbling echoed down the mountain. Erimenes turned the color of winter sky.

Seeing a strange blue being appear from nowhere confused Grutz. He was bright—for a bear—but in his mind he held many of the insular attitudes of the Bear Tribe. It didn't take much for him to form the basic equation: unknown = danger. He attacked with a deep-throated roar.

Erimenes barely had time to bug his eyes and utter a

strangled squawk before Grutz lashed out with a fore-paw. The huge scythe-clawed paw swept through the philosopher's midsection.

Fost yelled in surprise. The ghost poised above the satchel, a gap the width of the bear's arm separating his top from his bottom. Then he collapsed into himself in a swirl of blue vapors.

Fost regained his feet. Concern for the philosopher filled him with urgent energy. Erimenes had been a trial for him, but they were comrades. It would be bitter irony for the sage to have survived his own body's death, the fall of his city, and the many strange perils of the quest to Athalau only to be destroyed by a startled bear.

Grutz loomed over the satchel, his wet nose sniffing. An outraged cry caused him to jerk back.

"Awk!" cried Erimenes. "Outrage! Indignity! To be manhandled so by such a noisome brute—arrgh!"

Fost watched the blue vapor boil out of the satchel, shot through with blue-white sparks of anger. Relief gave way to amusement. Fost had never seen Erimenes reduced to such sputtering, wordless rage.

The philosopher wasn't mollified with Grutz scooped up the satchel with his paw and hoisted it off the ground. When Grutz swatted a foe, it stayed swatted. He shook the bag until finally curiosity won out over fear of the unknown. The bear stuck his nose into Erimenes' jar.

Erimenes howled. He winked into being above the bear and drummed the flat, shaggy head with immaterial fists.

"Oaf! Monster! *Get your snout out of my jug!*"

Jennas's sword drooped in her hands. She gaped as she tried to assimilate the spectacle of a war beast beset by an infuriated ghost. As Grutz took the jug in both paws and shook it, Erimenes' complaints soared an octave. Fost did the only thing he could. He fell down, laughing.

Strain, danger, and exhaustion took their toll. Fost's laughter quickly turned to shrill hysteria. Alarmed by the sound of his friend's voice, Grutz tossed the jar away, provoking a fresh outcry from Erimenes, and came to stand over Fost. He licked the courier's livid face.

The danger of being drowned by the bear's sloppy goodwill brought Fost a measure of sobriety. He only giggled now as he pushed the bear away. From off in the rocks, Erimenes vented language unlike any Fost had heard since his days on the docks in High Medurim. Fost wiped bear slobber from his face.

Jennas stared at him. The only sounds now were the wind whispering through the Ramparts, Grutz's stertorous breathing, and Erimenes' chanson of profanity. The nomad woman shook her head in wonder.

"It is truly said," she sighed, "that those touched by the gods are touched with madness." Reslinging her sword, Jennas turned her bear around and again set off for the mountains.

It took three days to cross the mountains and a fourth to reach the winter camp of the Ust-alayakits. During most of the journey, Erimenes kept still, sulking over his ill treatment by the bear. Fost enjoyed the respite.

Explaining the spirit had been hard enough. The People of Ust, ingrained by long years of war with their neighbors, the Badger Clan, had an instinctive dread of magic. The semi-nomadic Hurinzyn had been under the sway of their shaman Kleta-atelk, whose obscene magical experiments transformed animals and humans into monsters. His depredations of the Ust-alayakits had proven too much even for the valor and skill of the Bear Tribe. They had just embarked on a final, all-out suicidal raid on Kleta-atelk when they happened upon Fost. Rescuing him from the bird riders, they had extracted the promise of his aid against the Badger Clan sorcerer. The Ust-alayakits custom of killing all strangers in their realm helped wrest this promise from him.

All had worked out for the best. Fost had led an attack and had come upon the Badger clansmen from above. Kleta-atelk had been directing his horrors in the destruction of the Ust-alayakits when Fost dropped a twenty-pound stone on him. Her people released from the threat of further sorcery, Jennas had agreed to guide Fost through the treacherous Ramparts Mountains, though she had pleaded with him to remain and become a member of the Bear Tribe.

The fear of sorcery remained even after Kleta-atelk's death. Jennas suggested dropping Erimenes into the next abyss.

Erimenes talked her out of it. His continued survival, he explained, was due to his tremendous intellect and strength of character which had allowed him to live on incorporeally after his body died. Athalar magic was a misnomer; the Athalar used their mental powers, not spells and captive spirits to work their wonders. Jennas hadn't been fully convinced, but like Fost, she came to the conclusion that a being so utterly garrulous posed no threat, unless it was death by boredom. But that night Fost found himself agreeable to Jennas's suggestion of tossing the philosopher down a crevasse.

They had pitched a tent in the lee of a snow-burdened tree and had eaten supper by the smoky yellow light of a brazier fueled by resin pellets. Chewing the tough, jerked meat, Fost told the story of his foray into Athalau with Moriana and Erimenes. Jennas nodded knowingly at the account of the princess's backstabbing and expressed satisfaction at the thought that Moriana had the wrong amulet.

"If it is capable of wreaking great misfortune on its bearer," she said, "perhaps it will bring fitting retribution for her crime. To stab a comrade in the back . . . honor knows no fouler breach."

"She did what she thought best," said Fost, staring into the tiny flames. "I want to catch up with her and warn her of her mistake."

Jennas only shook her head.

They soon crawled into their bedrolls. Fost wasn't surprised when a warm and naked Jennas wriggled into his bag with him. Her mouth covered his, tongue probing deep, hand searching for the sudden hardness between his legs. Lust burst like a bomb inside him. Later he would reflect that he had needed the reaffirmation of life provided by lovemaking, that his need sprang from soul as well as loins. He had no such thoughts now. His mind filled with his need for her as his hand fumbled with the thatch between her smoothly muscled thighs. She rolled atop him.

"If you'd remove yourselves from that ridiculous gunny sack," Erimenes said with marked asperity, "you'd not only be more comfortable, you'd also be affording me a better view of the proceedings."

Jennas jerked herself off Fost as though his manhood had blazed white-hot inside her. They thrashed like drowning kittens in a bag, then she stood over Fost, shivering, bare skin sheened with the sweat of desire and goosefleshed with chill.

"You make sport of me?" she raged, dividing her rage impartially between Fost and Erimenes. "You think me nothing but a plaything for your dirty games?" She burrowed back into the depths of her own bedroll.

In the library at High Medurim while he was under the tutelage of the pedagogue Ceratith, Fost had read a text on ethnology prepared by the Imperial University. The treatise had said that nomads tended toward sexual conservatism and even prudishness. The teenaged gutter urchin had stuffed this morsel of knowledge into his voracious mind and read on, digesting it as thoughtlessly as he did the food given him by Ceratith.

He had thought his earlier experiences with Jennas had given the lie to that Imperial text; she had led Fost through a series of erotic combinations that would have been the envy of a Kara-Est courtesan. Now he learned a new truth about the bear-riding people of the Southern Steppes: what they did in privacy was one thing, public exhibitionism was another. Erimenes being dead, it hadn't occurred to Jennas that he might prove an avid voyeur. The spirit's suggestions filled her with a righteous indignation that included Fost. In her outrage, the chieftainess assumed Fost wanted his vaporous companion to witness their passion.

Fost had been too exhausted in mind and too aroused in body to give any thought to Erimenes. Jennas's powerful body writhing against his, her musk heady in his nostrils, had driven all else from his awareness. His attempts to tell her this elicited only stony silence from the woman. Fost finally gave up and rolled onto his back. He stirred himself to reach over and give Erimenes' jug a hearty thwack when the sage complained at the sudden cessation of his evening's entertainment. The courier eventually went to sleep, feeling robbed and angry.

Fost assumed sourly that his physical liaison with Jennas was done. The woman felt her honor besmirched. She wouldn't forgive him. Or so he thought until the small hours of the morning when Jennas emerged from her bedroll, heaved a protesting Erimenes out the front flap of the tent, and rejoined Fost in his sleeping bag. She uttered no word but her mouth spoke eloquently.

In the morning, Erimenes brooded upon the injustice of his summary eviction as well as the mistreatment at the paws of Grutz. Crushed by the weight of indignities heaped upon him, Erimenes fell into a sullen silence all the way to the bear-rider's camp in the foothills north of the Ramparts.

Somehow, Fost didn't miss the philosopher's repartee, especially in the dead of night when he and Jennas fought the cold in their own very special way.

* * *

"You're determined to go on, then?" the fat woman asked. Fost nodded, distracted by his effort to keep his gorge from rising due to the aroma wafting up from his earthen cup.

"Good!" the woman cried, a hearty backslap knocking the breath from his body. He slopped the hot, stinging brew into his lap. "Small is the soul craving no adventure. Jennas may sit there looking baleful, but mind you, boy, she'd have it no other way."

Vancha Broad-Ax took a healthy swig of her own steaming tea and beamed at Fost as though she'd just finished sculpting him from clay. Fost, feeling the tea corroding his crotch, managed a grin in response. The subchief of the Ust-alayakits was a vast, coarse woman, outstandingly ugly with a squashed nose spread across a visage reddened by wind and drink. Her hair was a faded reddish-orange tangle. Her eyes gleamed like emeralds inset in the fatty rolls of her face. She wore a leather harness studded with bronze, and bronzen torques as thick as two of Fost's fingers encircled arms as big as the courier's thighs. Vancha was loud, exuberant, mercurial, and apparently seldom sober.

Fost liked her immensely.

He felt the pressure of Jennas's hip against his. A warm tingle stirred his crotch, only partially dampened by the now-cooling tea. He took a sip from his cup and shuddered. The four of them in Jennas's tent were drinking *amasinj,* the favored drink of the Ust-alayakits. He didn't mind the astringent herb tea; it was the distilled *ofilos*-tree sap liquor the bear people added to it in liberal quantities to give it strength that watered his eyes and crisped his nose hairs.

Vancha poured the stuff down her throat in torrents until Fost expected smoke to pour from her bangled ears. Jennas downed it with a will, too, though not with the relish of her second chief.

As always, Fost felt time pressing him onward. Yet now he had stayed with the People of Ust for a week.

His hurts needed healing, but the luxury of relaxing among friends uncovered deeper wounds. Sometimes in the night he clung to Jennas and whimpered like a whipped puppy. She held him, comforted him, and thought no less of him. The Ust-alayakits did not believe in hiding their emotions. And any who could answer the Hell Call and return sane need no further proof of strength and courage.

But the time had come for leaving. Tomorrow Fost would go north in pursuit of Moriana. Tonight he, Jennas, Vancha and Vancha's young consort Rinzi— and Erimenes—had gathered for a quiet celebration.

"Care well for my people when I am gone, Vancha," said Jennas smiling. But her expression wasn't reflected in her eyes. Vancha laughed uproariously.

"I shall be a mother to them all," she declared. "But it hurts me to be left behind. Put Lurnum or Vixo in charge and let me accompany you. Little Sister is vexed at having missed the bloodletting at the caves of the Hurinzyn." Little Sister lay on a pillow on the other side of Vancha's bulk from the slender Rinzi. Vancha patted her affectionately. Little Sister shifted, sending shafts of reflected firelight dancing from her blue steel blade.

The ax was of the same monumental proportions as its owner. A three-foot shaft of black hardwood from the Tanzul Forest, as rare as valuable silver on the treeless steppe, was affixed to a broad, spike-backed head weighing fully five pounds. The weapon filled Fost with awe. Despite the exploits of the brawny heroes of Medurimite romance, five pounds total weight was usually the maximum. Vancha could wield Little Sister with one meaty hand while he held a beaten-brass buckler in the other.

He had always assumed the barbarians of the Southern Steppe chose their leaders by combat. Vancha was easily the strongest of all the several hundred Ust-alayakits. She outweighed Fost and Jennas combined and could break either like a reed in the wind. Yet Jennas seemed to feel no compunction about naming her subchief guardian of her daughter Duri and going off with Fost, leaving Vancha to rule in her absence.

"I fear your Little Sister will drink her fill all too soon," said Jennas, staring moodily into the flames.

"What's that, girl?" Vancha demanded. "Have you had a vision?"

Jennas nodded.

"What are you talking about?" asked Erimenes. "Is there a nice, bloody war in the offing? If so, I may stay here and let Fost wend his dreary way north without me. I shouldn't like my jar to get cracked by some ignorant ruffian."

"Ust should so favor me," Fost said dourly.

Jennas's glance was sharp.

"You, of all people, shouldn't use Ust's name so lightly." Fost dropped his eyes from hers, feeling warmth touch his cheeks. The hetwoman gripped his arm in an iron band. "I go north with you because you have done the Ust-alayakits greater service than we can ever hope to repay—and because I want to be with you, though your heart is with that northerner wench. But these things aren't enough to make me leave my people, even in Vancha's capable hands."

Fost looked up at her, the question in his eyes.

"No," she said with a bitter laugh. "I'm no young girl to go mooning off after you like a pet goat. You're a man like no other I've known, Fost Longstrider, but not even you can take me from my people, not even if you gave me all your love and forswore this princess." She shook her head. "Not unless the welfare of my people lay in my going with you."

Fost stared at her. Her proud, high-cheekboned face was set into grim lines. He looked at the others. Erimenes looked bored, Rinzi diffident. A hard glint showed in Vancha's eyes.

"What do you mean?" he asked.

"Danger is building in the world like a storm gathering thunderheads," Vancha said. "Our hetwoman fares north to assess the danger. She fears the wind may soon blow foul for the People of Ust."

"I don't know what you're talking about. There's peril, to be sure, but that lies on the path before *me*. It doesn't have anything to do with your folk."

"But it does," said Jennas. "I feel it. Ust sends me dreams. There is a power—and malice—in the north. They grow. They shall soon break free, and their fury will not spare the people of the steppes."

"Do you mean the Sky City? They plan for war, true enough. They might conquer the Quincunx Cities, but they can't harm you here. Their city won't leave its travel pattern, and the bird riders have too much trouble with the winged foxes in the Ramparts to carry on a campaign against you."

"It's not their soldiers we fear," Vancha said, "but their sorcery."

A chill wind blew along Fost's spine. He recalled the ape-thing that had pursued him through the keep of Kest-i-Mond the mage. And unbidden came the memory of the yellow hellfire glowing in the Vicar of Istu's eyes as it lustfully raped Moriana.

"But they're hundreds of miles to the north. And Synalon can't come here to work her magic against you. She's tied to the City itself. She derives her power from it. . . ."

"From the Child of the Dark Ones," whispered Jennas. "From That Which Sleeps in the foundations of their accursed city. Whom Felarod bound in the War of Powers . . ."

". . . for all time," Fost finished.

Vancha leaned forward. Joviality slipped from her as if it were a cowl. Her face glinted like brass in the flamelight.

"We live here beneath sky and wind, outlander. From them we've learned *nothing lasts forever*."

"But Felarod had the aid of the Three and Twenty Wise Ones. The World-Spirit itself helped him bind Istu. That's a power not easily overcome."

"Not *easily*," Vancha agreed. "But the Dark Ones have had ten millennia in which to work. In that time, a tiny rivulet can wear a deep cleft through the hardest stone. *They* are no tiny dribbling. Their evil is a rushing torrent."

He looked from one to the other. He accepted the existence of beings beyond his plane of existence. Fire elementals, the occasional demon, even Erimenes, were more or less part of everyday existence. The gods, though, whether the Wise or the Dark, were distant beings aloof from the affairs of men. Fost didn't entirely believe in them for all that Jennas claimed he was a sending from Ust. And if they did exist, it seemed to him they ought to keep a decent distance from the mortal world. That they might again take more of a hand in earthly events . . .

"I think you go too far. You're talking about a Second War of Powers." He shook himself as a wet dog sheds water.

"I am," Jennas said flatly.

Uneasy quiet filled the tent. Fost gulped his *amasinj*, welcoming now the acrid taste. It distracted him from the foreboding that grew in his guts. A War of Powers! But that was ancient history so far in the past that it had slipped into legend. Something so distant, so immense could not belong to the present day. The cosmic disruption, the deadly struggle of powers that tipped the very world on its axis couldn't intrude on the life of Fost Longstrider.

Could it?

Vancha sighed, belched, and drained her cup.

"Ahhh," she said, smacking her lips in satisfaction. "We're in deadly danger of becoming serious. Let us drink, my friends. Drink to Fost and Jennas and their epic journey to the wild and unknown lands of the north!" She caught up the *amasinj* pot from the brazier and filled their cups to the brim. A robust infusion of the beverage brought gaiety back. But it was strained, fragile, as if the revelers sensed an intruding monstrous presence lurking in the shadows of the tent.

When the evening was done, when the two moons had come down from heaven and Vancha had gone reeling off to her own tent with one arm wrapped around Rinzi, Fost and Jennas turned blindly to each other. They strove furiously, savagely, bodies guided by the dying light. When their passion and energy had been spent, they fell into a troubled sleep.

Fost would always try to convince himself that he did not dream that night. But in later days he often wondered if that were true.

Moriana scarcely believed her good fortune. The blizzard that had blown for two days out of the Thail Mountains to the northwest had left most of its snow on the prairies of the Quincunx, with only flurries and biting winds to lash at the steppe. She need fear no further snowbanks, but still she was almost out of her mind with worry thinking of what her sister planned—accomplished—while she plodded endlessly beneath the lifeless gray sky. Neither Ziore's soothing touch on her mind nor the nimble erotic tricks that left Moriana gasping with passion could ease the princess's fear.

But now chance gave her a gift so great she scarcely believed the testimony of her eyes.

She huddled in an arroyo beneath the husk of a ground-hugging bush, peering over the lip of the cutbank. Not fifteen yards away sat a man. He was small, and the tunic sleeve on the arm appearing from within the folds of his cloak was purple edged in black. Near him stood an eagle, almost twelve feet tall at the crest of his skull, wings spread over a tiny fire for warmth.

The bird was a lean, wide-winged scout and not a deep-chested warbird like Moriana's lost Ayoka. But it was a riding bird of the City. The storm winds from the north and west had brought snow, but they had brought this hapless bird and its rider, blowing them miles from Sky City–patrolled terrain.

The princess rolled her amulet between her fingers as she pondered. The many-faceted gem showed only a thin fingernail of black along one edge. Otherwise, it was as white as the snow left behind by the blizzard. Ziore had given her warning that they approached another human. Moriana had ducked into the gully until the spirit told her they were near the presence she sensed. By good fortune, the stranded bird rider had his back to the gully.

The eagle shook its wings and gave a racking cough. This wet, frigid weather didn't agree with him. The cold didn't agree with the bird rider either. His form trembled beneath his cloak. Now and then he shook his head, muttering curses to himself. The wind died to sporadic blustering. It wouldn't be long before he took to the sky again and began the long flight to the blessed warmth of barracks and aerie.

Moriana consulted with Ziore. She had no wish to kill this unfortunate soldier because of her need to remain anonymous. Synalon thought her dead, and she must remain that way until she confronted her sister.

Fortunately, she didn't have to kill him. She had only to walk up to the soldier and ask him for his mount. He would be only too happy to oblige, never caring that it would put him afoot in the middle of the Southern Steppe. Such was Ziore's power to mold emotions. Moriana would leave him enough of her Athalar rations to keep him alive for several weeks. He could walk out on his own, or maybe if—*when,* she amended mentally—she overcame Synalon and recovered the Beryl Throne she could send out search parties to bring him in.

She drew the edges of her capacious hood forward to hide her face and distinctive hair and boosted herself up over the bank.

The sighing wind covered the sounds of her approach until she was within a few feet of the bird rider. The eagle raised its head, saw her, and shrilled alarm. The man rose smoothly, sword poised before him. His jaw dropped at the sight of the tall, cowled figure who had stolen upon him out of nowhere.

"I require the use of your mount, my good man," she said from the shadows of the cowl. "I will leave you rations. You will come to no harm."

The trooper opened his mouth to scorn this impertinent offer.

"Yes, my lady," he said, confused that he mouthed those words. And yet . . . yet he couldn't refuse. He had been offered rations. It was a fair exchange. He was only too happy to oblige the wishes of this mysterious apparition with the glowing black-and-white pendant.

Or was it a black pendant?

A gust of wind struck Moriana in the face. Before she could react, it peeled the hood from her head. Golden hair spilled forth.

"Princess!" the soldier cried, his eyes widening in recognition. "But they said you were dead!"

Moriana cried in despair as her fingers found the hilt of her sword. Steel glinted dully in the leaden light. The eagle drummed its wings and screamed at the copper smell of blood.

Moriana's secret remained intact—at the cost of a human life.

CHAPTER FIVE

Prince Rann stood at the window watching the ground slowly slide by.

The Sky City was an immense stone raft two thousand feet long and eleven hundred at its broadest point. At the fore and aft ends of the great ellipse, stone piers jutted like the mandibles of some giant insect. Between these piers and the ground moved the hot-air balloons supplying the City with foodstuffs and other necessary supplies.

A broad avenue ran the length of the City from pier to pier. In the center of the City it was bisected by another artery running from port to starboard. At their juncture, the Circle of the Skywell ringed the great Well of Winds, through which malefactors were "exiled" to the ground five thousand feet below. The avenue running to port from the well had a peculiar, bumpy, off-white appearance due to the materials used in the paving stones: the skulls of past rulers of the City in the Sky. At the end of the Skullway rose the Palace of the Winds, sharply arched, fluted, attenuated, looming high above even the tall buildings.

The far side of the Palace lay flush with the guard wall ringing the City. Standing now at the narrow arch of a window partly opened to admit a chill blast of air, Rann had an incomparable view of the Sundered Realm.

At the moment, port meant northwest. Looking straight out from the City, Rann saw the Thail Mountains reaching their northernmost extent and dwindling into the high hills of Kubil and the Black March, duchies that gave nominal allegiance to the much-shrunken Empire of High Medurim. To the left, the Thails rose to become a wall blocking all sight of Thailot, westernmost of the Quincunx cities. To the right, if Rann put his head out into the rush of the wind, he could see the sheen of Lake Wir glinting like a sheet of beaten silver in the early morning sun. Beyond that a pall of thick black smoke gripped the horizon like an iron band. Omizantrim breathed today.

Throat of the Dark Ones, the name meant in the harsh speech of the Fallen Ones who had built the City millennia before human feet trod the soil of the Realm. The alien, humanoid, reptilian folk had hewn the foundations of the City whole from the lava flows of the twenty-five-thousand-foot volcano. They had made smaller rafts from the skystone the Throat belched up from the bowels of the earth, but by what arts no man living could say. Rann doubted if even the degenerate remnants of the Fallen Ones still possessed the knowledge to fly the skyrafts. The City itself was the sole surviving artifact of that era.

He sighed and drew his head back inside. It was unhealthy to brood oven the Fallen People. They'd been gone from the City for thousands of years, but still, deep down, every inhabitant of the floating citadel had the unvoiced conviction that some day they would attempt to reclaim their creation.

He looked down again. The land below teemed with movement. Miniscule toy wagons pulled by insects crept across the snowy plains. Around them milled ants, dark against the snow. They were really vast freight wagons drawn by dray dogs and horn bulls broken to harness dwarfed by distance. Northeast, in the path of the City, bloated gray finger-shapes lifted from the ground, the block-long balloons raised on air heated by captive salamanders. The wind brought him the cries of birds and men as one of the gigantic sausages was steered to its mooring on the forward pier by harnessed eagles.

Day and night now the cargo balloons moved between City and earth. The enormous legless, sightless ruby spiders in the catacombs of the City were being forced to turn out ever more of the silk from which the skycraft were made. And still there were too few balloons. Even the mightiest could only hoist a few tons to the skydocks. The City armed for war. Its appetite had become voracious.

The prince shook his head. He was responsible for the success of that initial stroke in the coming war.

The Quincunx Cities had become nervous due to the City's recent feverish trading activity. It was widely known that rule in the City had changed hands. Expansion of the City's trade was given as a reason for the sudden influx of materiel, with the concomitant increase of military reserve to keep surface trade routes secure. In the past, such a move had always pleased the Quincunx Cities, who otherwise bore the expense themselves. Unofficially, the rumor also went forth that internal unrest had followed Synalon's succession to the throne. While nothing serious, the new ruler felt it necessary to import large quantities of arms from the foundaries of Port Zorn and North Keep.

Rann had authored both stories, official and otherwise. Each contained a germ of truth. Civil disturbance had followed Derora's death, and the City was definitely planning to increase the scope of its dealings with the surface.

How long the Quincunx would accept the stories remained an unanswerable question. Spies reported uneasiness in Wirix. In three days, the Sky City would be above the island city. When the City passed by and committed no aggression against Wirix, the fears of the other Quincunx Cities would ease.

And after the transit of Wirix . . .

The City would change direction over Wirix and head for one of two destinations, Bilsinx or the great seaport of Kara-Est at the head of the Gulf of Veluz. Whichever city the floating fortress crossed, there the first blow would fall. With surprise, the Sky City bird riders had a chance of subduing either. To be certain of success—and Rann could afford no less—required allies on the ground.

Small garrisons of Sky City dog riders bivouacked in both Bilsinx and Kara-Est to escort caravans across the brigand-plagued prairie. Neither was large enough for Rann's purposes, and he dared not augment them without exciting suspicion. He needed a dependable, discreet, competent ally whose presence wouldn't be connected with the Sky City's approach.

The unwieldy balloon now rising to meet the City carried a man Rann hoped would be that ally.

The breeze blowing in the window began to make his wounds ache. While no longer bandaged like a corpse in its shroud, the prince was still far from fully recovered. He shut the window and went to a table on which a large map of the Quincunx had been spread. He began to study and plan.

Moriana's mount failed her as the Sky City came into view.

It had been a tense flight. It should have taken less than two days to arrive at her destination. She'd been in the air for three. When her stolen mount touched ground the day before, the princess hadn't known whether or not she'd ever get the bird airborne again.

She had spent half the night awake, caring for the bird. When the wind stilled, Moriana had gathered dried dung, built a roaring fire, and moved the stricken eagle as close to the flames as possible without singeing feathers. He coughed incessantly, a racking, convulsive sound. A hint of bloody froth touched the hingles of his beak. Moriana had massaged him, trying to soothe tortured muscles. Her fingers were expert. She had known the secrets of an eagle's anatomy before she learned the mysteries of her own.

She found no proper herbs for healing. Moriana had strained herself to call up the strongest healing magics she knew—in this branch of magic she was far superior to her sister. Perversely, the healing spells took the same soul-wrenching exertion as spells of harm. The princess had reached down inside herself and had drawn out the essence of her soul, even daring contact with the black blight left there by the Vicar of Istu. She wove the spell to restore the eagle's strength. The royalty of the Sky City had an ages-old obligation to their eagles, an obligation not even Synalon would think of denying.

So she worked, struggled, wept. Despite the midwinter cold, sweat rolled off her in rivers. Exhaustion permeated her body and poisoned her muscles, bones, mind. A cloud of stink rose to assault her: the acrid reek of the dung-fed fire, her own body long unwashed and overworked, the stench of terminal sickness gushing from the eagle with every heave of his chest. It had required all her determination to keep working until she'd done what she could. Only Ziore's masterful calming and soothing and encouragement enabled her to finish her task. And when the princess had at last collapsed into a deathlike sleep, she knew all she'd gained was a pitiful few hours flying time.

The new day dawned cold and bleak. The wind blasted in from the west, quartering her line of flight. It was as if fate had decreed that she would not gain entry to her City for the final confrontation with Synalon. Her amulet, her secret weapon, shone mostly black like a sun partially eclipsed, and she played with it as she flew. A croak from the eagle drew her from the fog of tension. She looked up, alarmed. Did the bird sense danger? Or was it calling above to its comrades on patrol?

The eagle cried again. This time she heard the glad note in its voice. A low, humped darkness appeared on the horizon, an anomalous isolated storm cloud. But it was no ordinary cloud. The City in the Sky floated heedless of the wind. The tempo of the wing-beats picked up. Her mount strained to the utmost, striving to reach home to die.

But this last exertion proved too much. The City grew in Moriana's vision until she made out details, picked out the steep roofs of homes and businesses, the tracery of the palace on the far side. She even saw movement on the walls. Monitors patroling. The bustle of activity on the ground and the cargo balloons sprouting from the strange, prairielike fungi didn't surprise her. Using a scrying spell, she had scanned the City. The palace was denied to her vision because of routine magical precautions, but she saw that the City girded itself for war.

For conquest.

She had just noted the exceptional number of bird riders in the air when her mount coughed and shuddered mightily.

Her attention instantly focused on the bird's dying cough. A sigh from Ziore touched her mind. The spirit sensed it, too. The bird had made it all this way only to fall short by less than a mile, almost near enough to touch the skystone of the City itself.

The wings fluttered, losing strength perceptibly. The City canted and veered away as the bird banked into a descending spiral. War eagles were trained to land when they felt their strength failing them. Moriana felt the bitterness in the creature; it longed with all its fading being to die, if it must, in a last desperate effort to get its claws on the rock of home. But duty lay in protecting its rider. The ancient compact between rider and eagle bound both equally.

The bird straightened its wings. Gliding down, it conserved strength for landing. The irregular ground hurtled upward at a dizzying rate. An incautious landing would kill Moriana as surely as if the bird's heart had burst a mile up.

Moriana tensed. Thoughts chased one another through her mind with terrifying speed. Her plan had been to fly openly into the City. Citizens didn't question bird riders, and if she rode in purposefully enough, no Guardsman would question her, either. But that scheme lay shattered now because of her bird's fading life-force.

"Say-y-y! Ho there, a rescue!" came the cry from above. Five birds had detached themselves from the unusual number that flocked around the City. Five powerful pairs of wings propelled bodies and riders through the air toward her with purposeful speed.

She had time to appreciate the irony of this rescue. The Sky Guardsmen did not for an instant suspect they were on the verge of apprehending the fugitive Princess Moriana, presumed dead. They saw only a bird rider in distress, and the only bird riders in the Sundered Realm were soldiers of the Sky City. They thought they flew to the rescue of a comrade in trouble.

Moriana knew they'd realize their mistake soon enough. Then the ground came spinning up to meet her.

"I take it for granted, my lord count," said Rann, toying with the skull he had been using to hold down a corner of the map, "that you appreciate the need for utmost discretion in this matter."

"Certainly, Your Highness," said the count, his manner courteous but clipped, verging on impatience. The edge in his voice would have thrown Synalon into a homicidal fury at his impertinence. It only reassured the prince. The man refused to waste time. Rann needed such a man.

He gingerly put down the skull. He had stripped the flesh from it while its still-living owner thrashed and howled in exquisite agony. The whole experience had been so rewarding that Rann had desired a memento.

He studied his guest carefully. A small man, scarcely three inches taller than his diminutive host, but as stockily built as Rann was spare. He stood in his severely cut, blue tunic and loose trousers with black riding boots rolled down to his calves. He wore a sword hung from a black baldric, a rare privilege for an outsider permitted into the presence of Sky City royalty.

It was deliberate. Rann let the man know how utterly he trusted him. The look in the visitor's watery blue eyes showed his understanding of the situation.

Rann picked up a goblet of hot spiced wine and sipped. The drink spread soothing warmth through his body, erasing the effect of the chill wind, and soothing him while he bided his time. His visitor stood waiting, but not patiently. Though not a muscle of body or face moved, he gave the impression of vibrating with ill-suppressed energy. Even the tips of his prematurely white, waxed moustache stood quivering at attention.

The goblet clanked to the tabletop with sudden decision.

"You will need to arrive in the target city well before we do, with, of course, some ostensible business not at all associated with the Sky City." The count's only reply was a curt nod. "That's why it is necessary to meet now before our transit of Wirix. Preparations must begin immediately."

"It shall be done as you command, Highness." The visitor smoothed an imaginary wrinkle from the front of his tunic.

"Our friends below are nervous. But they are also

complacent. Years of peace have turned them soft. They doubt anyone would dare attack them. The Sky City has made no overtly hostile move toward them since the humans conquered it. As a result, for all their apprehension at our recent activity, they cannot bring themselves to believe that we will attack. *But . . .*" He drained his drink and set the goblet down with a thump of finality. "But should they receive intelligence —reliable intelligence—of our designs, even the most lethargic bourgeois would be goaded to action. Properly forewarned, they might even successfully fend us off. It is a matter of concern to Her Majesty and myself."

His tawny eyes moved sidelong to study his visitor's reaction. The man's face betrayed no emotion, but his manner clearly said he was irritated. He grasped the obvious as readily as any other man.

"Well, then," said Rann, smiling, nodding his head as if to change the subject. "If my lord will excuse me, I've an appointment in the palace dungeons. My monitors caught a spy trying to sneak in. The slut rode up in a cargo balloon. I anticipate a most diverting afternoon." He turned a bland countenance on his guest. "Unless my lord wishes to come and watch . . .?"

"Thank you, Highness," the man said with a courtly half-bow, "but I fear I must return to the surface at your earliest convenience. There is much to set in motion." His toneless, staccato voice did not waver. But his florid face had gone pale at the suggestion that he share in Rann's "diversion." Rann felt a delicious tingle of amusement. Inflicting emotional upset was, in its own way, as gratifying as dealing out physical pain.

The stone's color shifted to black. Moriana kept it tucked into her tunic while flying, but the eagle's whirling descent steepened as the bird lost control and pitched it free. It seemed uncongruous to the princess that the stone's color mirrored her own fortune. Then the tip of the bird's lower wing caught on a tree limb and the eagle spun in.

At the northern edge of the central plains, the occasional trees sometimes banded together into woods. As her mount had started his final descent, Moriana had steered him for the nearest large cluster of trees. It was dangerous landing among trees. But to land in the open was fatal.

A limb laden with snow hit Moriana in the face as her mount cartwheeled down through the trees. A blow to her ribs knocked the breath from her. She saw clear, snowy ground below and threw herself from the saddle.

She hit and rolled expertly, coming to rest against the bole of a tree. The eagle floundered on, smashing through the bare limbs in a flurry of white powder. The snow muted the sound of its passage so that it sounded distant, unreal. The noise of wings cracking branches ceased abruptly. A heartbeat later, Moriana heard a sickening thump. A cloud of snow marked her mount's final resting place.

She raised her head, shaking it to clear snow from her eyes. A lump hung tenaciously to her forehead like a cold, wet hand.

She silently saluted her fallen eagle, then began moving. The ache in her ribs jabbed into pain with every step. Possibly she'd broken a rib, but this wasn't the time to check. She had to find cover before the bird riders descended.

She knew what to expect from those above. Seeking cover, the princess found a spot where interlocked branches had formed a framework roofed over with snow, bent low, and scurried beneath it. For all her care, she brushed the limb. It dumped snow down the back of her cloak.

Ignoring the snow turning to water on her back, she examined herself. Her ribs hurt, but after a few experimental breaths she decided she hadn't cracked any. An ankle throbbed painfully; she'd twisted it and hadn't noticed till now. Her face was scratched, her lips swollen from the limb that had swept across her face. But she was relatively healthy.

She remembered Ziore's jug. Guiltily, she reached around and felt her backpack. The jug seemed intact.

I'm here, she heard the nun's voice say inside her head. *Don't fear for me, child. I'm not harmed.*

Moriana sighed in relief. Overhead, the bird riders swept by.

Instinctively, she hunched down. The eagles flapped by, their wings making the sound of sails flapping in a stiff breeze.

"Look," came a man's voice. "That's where he went down."

Through gaps in the trees Moriana saw the five birds circling over her fallen mount. She held perfectly still. The slightest motion would betray her. She tried to ignore the discomfort of her cramped position as her mind raced.

Moriana knew she was finished if they landed. She considered shooting at the Sky Guardsmen with the bow she'd taken from the lost scout. She dismissed the idea at once. She could bring one down, but with the trees in the way that would end her life then and there. The only way she could escape was to bring down all five at once.

Ziore? she thought. *Can you help me?*

She felt the spirit's negative response. She thought fleetingly of her own sorceries, but these were Sky Guardsmen, warded against anything she could do on such short notice. Her hand slipped to the reassuring firmness of her sword hilt. Her heart hammered in her ears. She waited. It was all she could do.

"I don't see the rider," called one of the orbiting Guardsmen. "He may have been thrown free."

"Ho!" another shouted. "Ho, down there! Can you hear me? If you can't answer, make some sign. We can't see you!"

The minutes moved as ponderously as the glacier guarding Athalau.

"He's in no shape to respond," a third voice declared. "Let's go down and look for him."

"No!" a fourth voice rapped.

"But flight corporal," the second said. "We can't just leave him."

"We're under orders not to land." A bird shrilled irritably. The mounts disliked the wing-cramping circle they flew.

"Corporal, he's one of ours!" the second complained.

Hardness pressed into the palm of Moriana's left hand. She realized she clutched furiously at the Amulet of Living Flame. She stared at it.

Its surface glowed mostly white.

Irrationally, her heart beat faster. She had no reason to think this meant her luck had changed, but . . .

"I'm sure Prince Rann will be impressed with your spirit of comradeship," the corporal said ironically, "when we're strapped to the torture frames in his playroom. He commanded that no one land under any circumstances. Rescues are to be left to the dog humpers. Our place is aloft, flyer, and aloft is where we're going to stay."

No grumbling greeted the corporal's words. The prince's name acted like a potent spell. One of the Sky Guardsmen shouted down, "Sorry, but we can't land. We'll have the dog boys out with stretchers as soon as we can."

Then the sound of wingbeats diminished.

"Ziore, did you have anything to do with that?" Moriana trembled with the nervous release of tension.

"No," the spirit said aloud, sounding puzzled. "As soon as the corporal spoke, I probed his mind to harden him to the idea of flying off if he started to weaken. But he didn't. In fact, I don't think I could have *made* him land."

Moriana emerged from the shelter, stood up, and stretched. Hours in the saddle coaxing her eagle along had left her muscles wound into knots.

"These bird riders are afraid of this Rann," said Ziore. "I thought you said he was dead."

"I thought he was." Moriana shook her head. This was a bad turn.

She looked to the northwest. A ballon grew like a tumor from the forward edge of the City, distended, broke away, and then began to descend as the flyers vented air from the bag. A feeling of despair washed up like bile from her belly. The City was near—and infinitely far away.

"Why, child?" Moriana started. She constantly forgot that Ziore read her thoughts. The nun was better at it than Erimenes ever had been. "You've gotten this far on a stolen bird. Can't you steal another, or ride up in one of those unsafe looking contrivances?"

"No. If Rann died under the ice as I'd thought, it would be worth trying. But if Rann lives, no. He's suspicious of his own shadow. The City's sewn up like a balloon; trust in it."

"What will you do now?"

The words played over and over in her mind, clanking like lumps of rusted iron. *What will you do now?*

Her choices were few. But she wouldn't give up. There had to be a way someone as resourceful and daring as she could sneak into the City.

Somewhere, a snow clump dropped to the forest floor. Moriana shook herself. When the groundling rescue party failed to turn up a downed flyer, they would report back to the Sky City. Suspicion would be roused. A full-scale hunt would be fielded.

The disappointment of her failure to reach the City

was swept away by a swell of emotion. Rage, hatred, determination flared.

"What will I do now?" she asked harshly. "I'm going to show my sister that two can play the game of conquest.

"I'm going to invade the City in the Sky."

CHAPTER SIX

Shadows writhed and capered among the vaults of the ceiling. Shadows pursued each other along the walls, ducking into alcoves, flashing up the piers of the pointed arches that supported the roof. Shadows held court in the throne room of the City in the Sky.

Shadows wrapped Synalon like silk. Clad only in their dark substance, the Queen of the City knelt in a chalk circle scribed carefully on the dark stone of the floor.

Within the seven-foot circle was a triangle, its apexes touching the circle. At its three points burned fires— one yellow, one blue, and the last red. A different scent rose from each: sandalwood, cinnamon, gall.

Thus protected by her magics, Synalon addressed herself to the spirits held captive before her.

She rose and shook back midnight hair. Shadows caressed her thighs, her belly, the palely glowing moons of her breasts, the shadows moving like lover's hands. She inhaled sharply as though she felt the touch.

"As Stone worked with Fire becomes Metal," she intoned, her hair rising of its own accord like a deadly black halo, "as Stone mixed with Water becomes Mortar, as both are shaped by the hand of Man, I shape you as I have bound you. You must serve my ends, or Wood shall be your pain!"

The creature she addressed stood splay-footed within its crystal prison, its arms crossed over the round jut of its belly. Bat ears flanked a domed, wrinkled skull. Its skin was rough, knobbed, and pitted like

94

pumice. Its obsidian eyes gleamed forth with white-hot fire.

"You have drawn me into being, mistress," it rasped with ill grace. "Say what you would have of me and be done with it." It spoke slowly, with obvious effort, its tone hovering near inaudibility at the lower end of the scale.

"Hear me. This is my pleasure. Convey my submission to the Lords of Darkness. They have but to render me their bidding, and I shall do it. The greatness of the City shall be as it was, and the glory of the City was ever the glory of the Dark Ones."

"No." A stony head lowered to a stony breast.

Synalon's head snapped up. Her hair crackled with furious energy.

"The stone I called on you to animate was gathered from the flows of Omizantrim, manikin. Speak thus, with the Throat of the Dark Ones. Bear me their bidding." The last words rushed out in a sensuous whisper. She bent forward at the waist, body sheened with sweat. Her nipples stood erect, casting shadows on her breasts.

"Stone is Stone, from wherever drawn," the stone spirit said. "I am touched with Darkness, perhaps. But not with madness. I will have naught to do with the Lords of Infinite Night."

"Then you must suffer." Synalon hissed the words, face contorted with rage.

"Better your punishment than to draw the notice of the Dark Ones," the spirit replied.

She pressed palms together before her belly. Slowly, she raised her hands. A green shoot sprouted from the floor of the chamber within the domed cylinder that imprisoned the spirit. It grew, touched one ankle of the lavalike homunculus and began to twine up the leg. The spirit stood immobile.

The queen raised her hands higher. The shoot

climbed with them, swelling and hardening, green turning to brown along its length. The leafed tendril at the tip of the shoot touched the juncture of the stone man's thighs. It pressed upward with the inexorable pressure of growing plants.

The bat-winged visage lifted. Its lips stretched in a grin of growing agony, but still the spirit uttered no sound. Synalon's arms pressed before her breasts, her throat, her face. The stone head arched up and back, as though drawn by an invisible cord. Muscles stood out on its arms in stark relief.

Synalon began to spread her fingers. A ripple passed through the spirit's body. A shoot burst through stony skin at the juncture of neck and shoulder, curled coyly, green, and seemingly tender. Other sprouts broke from the creature's chest, its sides and belly, thickening into the branches of the tree that grew within the spirit, impaling it as it stood.

Remorselessly, Synalon's hands rose. The growing green and brown cancer rose up in the stone figure. Synalon raised hands above her head and pulled them apart. Stony fragments fell to the floor as fresh branches broke from the cheeks and ears of the spirit. One obsidian eye was pushed from its socket. It rolled down the face like a black teardrop and shattered on the floor. At last the spirit opened its mouth to scream. Instead of sound, a shoot emerged, thick and leafy, reaching for the ceiling of the crystal cylinder. A shudder wracked the body. The fire died in its remaining eye.

Synalon dropped her hands to her sides. The ineluctable, unnatural growing ceased. It was now a stunted tree and nothing more.

The sorceress stood panting, a sense of frustration suffusing her. She had been so near the consummation she sought. And she had been denied. Her body trembled with rage and thwarted yearning.

Stone had been the likeliest choice as intermediary with the Dark Ones. Darkness was the great Sixth Principle. The other five acted upon each other, Fire consuming Wood, Water stilling Fire, Air dispersing Water, Stone negating Air, and finally Wood sundering Stone. Darkness was aloof, inviolate, the First Principle from which the rest derived. Light, that waste product of Fire, produced the illusion of dispelling Dark; but Dark remained, ever-present, hiding just beyond sight, biding in shadow until the Light vanished.

Dark alone was eternal.

She turned to the captive sylph. The water sprite oozed within its crystal pen.

"You," Synalon said, her hair waving as if it were caught in a breeze, "you shall serve me. Great will be your reward, O child of the oceans. Bear my message to the Dark Ones. This I ask and no more."

The sylph's voice was pleasing, fluid, and as elusive as quicksilver. But it, too, refused the sorceress's command. Quivering with fury, Synalon waved her hands before her in a whirlwind gesture. The sylph's body became agitated and was drawn up in a whirlpool around the insides of its prison. The spirit squealed, an aching, candescent sound. Synalon gestured. Vents at the bottom of the cylinder opened. The dying sylph puffed outward, mist. It filled the chamber for a moment and then was gone.

Synalon rounded the third cylinder. It contained the dryad, a lovely naked maiden whose toes were root and whose fingers were supple branches, her hair a green rustling of leaves. She sang with a voice like wind in spring-sweet branches, but her answer was the same. She dared not contact the Dark Ones.

She screamed lingeringly in her very human voice as a fire sprite consumed her loveliness. It left behind only ashes.

Sparks flickered in Synalon's hair, popping and snapping electrically. Ozone was rank in her nostrils. And fear began to seep in around the edges of her determination. Her voice was edged as she addressed the shimmer that was the spirit of the upper air.

It defied her in the tones of chimes.

Dark crystals appeared on the inside of the vessel. They rapidly obscured Synalon's view of the sprite as they grew together and inward. The spirit taunted Synalon with its tinkling laughter even as the hardness crushed out its life.

Blue radiance bathed her body. Lightning traveled her limbs in a violet corona discharge. Her hair floated in a glowing spark-shot nimbus around her head. There remained only one captive elemental: Fire.

Fire, the elemental best understood and controlled by the mages of the City; Fire, the elemental most inimical to Darkness. It had been the humans who brought salamander lore to the City. The builders had venerated Dark alone.

Fire was the best choice and the worst. And if Fire defied her, too? The thought threatened to melt her resolve. She needed the power granted by the Dark Ones, she *needed* it, if her world-girdling ambitions were ever to be realized. And after Fire there remained no elementals to try to bend to her will. There were no lesser spirits of Darkness. The closest thing to a Darkness elemental was Istu, sleeping in chains of power in the depths of the City. Synalon knew too well what would befall her if she dared stir the Sleeper. The last time she had roused a fragment of his sleeping mind and animated the Vicar of Istu for the Rite of Dark Assumption, the demon had been given pain such as he'd never known before. He would not forget the sorceress who summoned him to anguish.

"Salamander," she said, fighting to keep the quaver from her words. "Strength of my City, ally of my folk. I command you and beseech you to bear my message to the Dark Ones." She stood straight, flames spilling from her outstretched, supplicant hands.

The salamander's vessel exploded.

Flying shards of glass scored Synalon's stomach, thighs, and breasts. One glittering fragment laid open her right cheek. She flinched but held her ground. The salamander was loose. The fire sprites were fickle, vicious beasts and never predictable—and never entirely controlled. Something had gone horribly wrong. The enchanted vessel should have held any power less strong than Istu himself.

The flame creature danced in the middle of the throne room. The stone floor ran and puddled like water beneath it. Synalon threw up her hands to shield her eyes from the yellow incandescence.

In a few trip-hammer beats of her heart, she sensed that the binding radiance had dimmed. Carefully, she lowered her hands. And gasped.

The thing was no normal salamander. They were usually shifting, indistinct beasts. Their only form appeared vaguely reptilian and sinuous. The horror confronting her was like a goat, an ape, a grossly misshapen human. It had a bulky body with ever-changing outlines, and yet its lineaments didn't change with the quicksilver speed and smoothness of an elemental. The thing had hooves on its four feet—two? more?—clawed hands, and bizarre paired horns sprouting from both sides of its head. With a start, Synalon recognized what she had conjured.

"Aye, little one, you guess the truth," the apparition said. The words came not in a salamander's familiar sibilance but in a dry sound that made her think of dead leaves and blighted lands. "The Lords of Darkness have taken note of your petition. They have sent me to bear their tidings to you."

Joy exploded in Synalon's heart, a joy magnified by the frantic fear clutching her. Would they favor her or cast her to shrieking damnation?

She dropped to her knees, throwing her arms wide. "O harbinger of Darkness, accept my subservience. Take me, Lords! Make me the instrument of your revenge for the wrong done you by accursed Felarod!"

"The Dark Lords hear your voice, little one. They bid me tell you this: their time is almost come. But . . ." A wave of a tentaclelike member cut off her glad cry. "But they are as yet undecided as to whether you are the proper tool by which they shall accomplish their vengeance—and their return."

"Tell me," she cried, wringing her hands. "I beseech thee, tell me how I may prove myself!"

The creature's smile was unmistakable in spite of its slowly changing features.

"Your chance arrives soon." And it vanished. But not entirely. The torches in their brackets on the walls blazed to life. Blinking back the spots swimming in her eyes, she saw only darkness beyond.

Dazed, she rose and walked from the circle and triangle. She noted that the three ward fires had been extinguished. She didn't doubt that the emissary of the Dark Ones had put them out to show how ineffective her spells were against their minions. She slumped into the Beryl Throne.

The stone chilled her buttocks and thighs, reviving her. She brushed sweat-lank hair from her eyes and tried to think.

Synalon tried to tell herself she had nothing to fear. The Dark Ones had been banished for millennia, and few outside the City dared even think of them. They needed an ally on this plane, a powerful one with the skills and ruthlessness to carry out their designs. She was unquestioned ruler of the City in the Sky, the City of Sorcerers. Her winged legions would soon spread out to cover the Sundered Realm. Who would they find better suited to their ends?

Yet she couldn't shake the feeling that the Dark Ones only toyed with her, that she'd been found want-

ing and they had chosen their earthly instrument—
and she was not their choice.

Synalon reached for the golden bell by the throne
and rang. She needed wine and restoratives and, after
that, the attentions of one of her many lovers. Or perhaps more than one. Perhaps even the trained horn
bull.

She did not want to sleep and dream this night.

Tolviroth Acerte had no army. Contrary to popular
belief, war is *not* good business. And the Tolviroth
were consummate businessmen.

The City of Bankers was not without its defenses.
Twenty-five miles of sea separated it from the nearest
mainland. The seamen and marines of the Tolviroth
Maritime Guaranty Corporation, largest insurance firm
on the island, were famed well beyond the Realm for
their fighting and naval skills. But that was merely
good business. Pirates, with or without letters of
marque, interrupted trade. *That* was intolerable. The
merchants of Tolviroth paid and paid well to see that
their vessels were safeguarded. And the Maritime Guaranty, with a half-dozen competitors only too ready to
claim its market share, made certain its customers got
their money's worth. Not even the Imperial Navy in its
heyday centuries before would have undertaken to protect the wallowing bottoms of an invasion fleet against
the lethal black ships of the TMG.

Moriana had spent eight hours in the forest near
the City in the Sky as patrols of dog cavalry scoured
the woods for the missing bird rider. Her senses, turned
animal-sharp, had gotten her through the cordon. One
of the searchers had strayed too far from his comrades,
and Moriana was soon bound southeast for Kara-Est,
a stolen black-and-white war dog bunching and straining between her legs.

Weeks passed as she made her way to Kara-Est and
from there by sea to Tolviroth Acerte, paying for her

passage with the klenors gained by selling her stolen dog. And after reaching Tolviroth Acerte, she headed directly for the House of Omsgib-Bir, the bank that held the accounts for the Sky City.

They'd given her no satisfaction. She'd established her identity without difficulty. She'd been to Tolviroth Acerte twice before and knew the passwords and countersigns that proved she had legitimate access to the accounts. Or at least the records of the accounts. Tulmen Omsgib, chancellor of the bank, had politely but relentlessly refused her request to release the money to her.

"Your bona fides are not questioned, Highness," the syndic had said unctuously, stroking his beard. "Yet we can only disburse funds to the government of the City in the Sky, or its rightful representative."

"But I'm the rightful heir to the throne!"

"I can appreciate that," he said with spurious compassion in his sad, round eyes. "By the laws of ultimogeniture followed in your City, you are the rightful successor to Derora, may the Great Ultimate bring her soul repose." He sat back and pressed his palms together as if in prayer. "But you are not in the City. You are here before me in my office, an honored guest, to be sure, but a guest without official standing."

He held off her protest with upraised hand.

"No, I am most sorry, Highness. But it is not the custom in Tolviroth Acerte, or in the House of Omsgib-Bir, to deal with what might be, or even what ought to be." He reached down and took a jellied sweet from a salver at his elbow and popped it right down his throat. "Your title is clear by right, but it is your sister who rules the City. It is she, therefore, whom we must recognize and deal with as the lawful government."

He tilted his head back and regarded her down his crooked nose. The look in his eye was unmistakable. Moriana's garb was rough and functional and not precisely what one expected of the rightful queen of the City of Sorcerers. It did nothing to hide the curves of her body. Omsgib's oily tongue slipped from the cavern of his mouth and slowly circled his lips.

"Has your highness made arrangements for accommodation? If you are in difficulty, please allow me to offer the hospitality of my own humble villa."

She got up and walked out in the middle of his offer.

She didn't even bother to ask him for a loan. He would be as smooth and slippery as a slug's track, saying nothing to offend, but he would not give it to her. It didn't matter that she was an "honored guest," or that she'd dealt with him personally before. She was the bitter, deadly enemy of the person who controlled one of his bank's largest accounts. She'd get nothing from him financially, and she wanted no part of what he was obviously only too willing to give her.

She left Omsgib and went to the second largest bank in Tolviroth Acerte. And then the third, the fourth, and on down until she ended up in the boardroom of Iola Trust, the eighth bank she'd visited that day.

The seven members of the Board of Directors regarded her from behind veils of professional politeness. She looked away from the ascetic face of the man who'd just refused her request. She saw no sympathy anywhere. Of the four male directors, at least two would obviously be willing to offer the same "accommodation" Omsgib had hinted at. But not even they showed the slightest inclination to advance her the money to raise a mercenary army.

"Look," she said, eyes flicking from face to face. "I'm not asking you to involve yourselves in the affairs of the Sky City. I am applying for a loan. Isn't my credit good?"

A look of pain passed over the face of a female director named Bovre Coudis. A person's credit rating was all but sacred to a Tolvirot, and Synalon had good credit. Refusing a loan to someone with good credit moved perilously close to blasphemy. But obviously that did not extend to Synalon's renegade sister.

"I know the Sky City as well as any person living. Do any among you doubt that? I know the military doctrines of the City, I know the caliber and training of its troops, I know its commanders. If I'm given the proper backing—*if*—I can conquer the City. And then you, gentlefolk of this board, will see a handsome return on your investment."

"War's bad business," grumbled one. Another twitched an impatient finger to silence the speaker.

"So you say," said the man introduced as Kolwyl, dabbing languidly at his lips with a scented handkerchief. Moriana pegged him as totally disinterested in "accommodations" of any sort with her. "But no one has ever invaded the City before. For any loan, we must have a reasonable assurance the money will not be frittered away. Success must loom large or it is a poor loan. What makes you think you can succeed in this mad venture?"

She met his gaze levelly, unspeaking. After a moment, he turned his eyes away and coughed delicately into his handkerchief.

"The City *has* been invaded successfully before," she said. "My ancestors wrested it from the Fallen Ones."

"They used treachery," replied Kolwyl sharply.

"They succeeded. Your objection to my proposal seems to be that it can't succeed. What does it matter to you how it comes about as long as you realize your profit?"

Kolwyl looked about him for support. Anathas, a small mousy man wearing a thick fur collar despite the heat within the chamber, shifted in his seat with a rustle of expensive cloth.

"You know," he said nasally, "it is not impossible that we are being unfair to Princess Moriana. She is, after all, rightful Queen of the Sky City. Surely, she has some popular support among the, uh, the masses."

"That may be," said Bovre Coudis, leaning forward so far that her jowls swung like a bulldog's. "But her sister controls the secret police. And from our intelligence in this matter, the masses would be well advised to keep their place."

Moriana scarcely heard her. She stared at Anathas, who huddled down inside his fur-lined robe, uncomfortable beneath her gaze. She tried to fathom his sudden reversal. He had seemed against her at first.

Sunlight filtered through the windows, casting a yellow-brown light on the vast oaken table. Servants passed through the room, ignoring the conversation and being ignored, refilling wineglasses and replenishing the trays of dainties. Moriana had the impression that if she touched one of them, she'd find it as insubstantial as Ziore.

"We have a great deal of venture capital at our discretion," said Anathas, looking everywhere but at the princess. "Surely, there's no doubting her Highness's resourcefulness. Recall, gentles, how many years we've tried to wrest the City's account from that lascivious hound, Omsgib."

The decorous tone of the meeting lapsed for the first time. Everyone spoke at once, clamoring for attention. With sinking spirit, Moriana realized the others were unanimous in their opposition to Anathas.

The gaunt man uttered the first refusal and restored order by rapping bony knuckles on the table.

"Gentles, gentles, please! Is this any way to conduct *business?*"

That quieted them.

"Now," he said, nodding. "Now, Anathas, it pains me to say this but you seem to be suffering from a lapse of good judgment. This young lady comes to us with a harebrained scheme to conquer the City in the Sky, a City never taken by conquest. It has been taken, as our lovely guest so thoughtfully pointed out, but not by battle. The gradual infiltration of human traders into the City originally made it possible to expel the Fallen People. No outside intervention was used. While military matters are somewhat beyond my province, I must say that the Sky City seems to be impregnable. Even if I am wrong, it is not the place of this bank to become involved in such a risky undertaking as a war. And not just any war, but a *civil* war, as it were."

He turned to Moriana.

"I might also point out that we've no way of knowing if this woman is who she claims to be." Moriana stiffened. Her hand dropped to her side, clutching empty air. She'd left her sword in the anteroom according to standard banking practice. Her fingers brushed the rough cloth of her knapsack.

She blinked twice rapidly. She hadn't been asked to surrender the knapsack before being ushered into the august corporate presence of the board as she had at every other institution she'd visited that day. A sudden intuition into Anathas's change of mind made her smile. Her spirits rose in spite of the firm hold she kept on her expectations.

". . . further enjoy the services of Prince Rann Etuul, cousin to the queen, and widely acknowledged to be one of the most astute military minds of our day," the gaunt man was saying. He turned to Moriana and attempted to smile benignly. It made him look as if he'd just bitten into a spoiled sweetmeat and was trying to pretend he hadn't.

"I trust Your Highness will forgive my bluntness," he said. "It isn't that I personally doubt your assurances that you are who you claim to be. Nor do I doubt your competence as a leader and planner in a venture such as you've outlined. But you must understand that my decision is based on more than my own preference. The investors in this bank had given their trust—and their money—to the Board of Directors to safeguard. Before we venture any of *their* hard-won capital, we must entertain no doubts whatsoever about the feasibility of the project under consideration. I— and I think I speak for my colleagues as well—would like nothing so much as to grant to your request." He shook his head sadly. "But we do not believe, to speak frankly, that aligning ourselves against the Sky City's current regime is in the best interests of our bank or its investors."

Kolwyl turned and said to Anathas, "Really, old man, I'm surprised at you. Falling for a piece of fluff like this. She's pretty enough, I suppose, if you like the type, but is she worth the risk of impecuniation?"

Anathas turned white. Moriana's spirit came crashing back to earth. "Impecuniation" was the Tolvirot euphemism for the severest of civil penalties, the confiscation of all properties and assets. A true merchant of the City of Bankers would rather be flayed alive in public than suffer impecuniousness.

The other directors glared reproachfully at Kolwyl for his rudeness—and in front of Moriana. But the damage was done. Anathas shrank so far into his cloak that only the tip of his nose showed. Whatever the reason for his support, it had evaporated like mist under the morning sun.

"Thank you for your time, gentlefolk," said Moriana, rising. Her voice was clear and firm, though inside she felt as if she were melting. "I apologize for any inconvenience I may have caused you. In return for your indulgence, I'd like to offer some advice." She looked from director to director, her gaze sharp and fierce. Even pugnacious Coudis cringed away from it.

"If you think to gain advantage by dealing with Synalon, or by doing nothing which might offend her, you are doing your investors small service. My sister's ambitions encompass much more than the City and the Quincunx. There's little room for the likes of you in her grand design, no matter how much you try to ingratiate or appease. You prattle on about her power; do you think she will sit by and *not* use it?"

She took a deep breath. Silence held sway. Even the servants stared at her.

"And if my sister fails," she said, "give thought, gentles, who will rule the City in her place."

She left, panicked mutterings following her out the door.

CHAPTER SEVEN

"I am sorry, Moriana," said Ziore mournfully. "I failed you."

"You tried," the princess said, patting the knapsack.

"It is with me as you said it was for that pious fraud Erimenes. The farther I go from Athalau, the more my powers wane. I was lucky to influence that mousy Anathas for as long as I did. Strong conviction or passion negates my talent for controlling emotions. My best couldn't override Anathas's fear of—what did they call it?—impecuniousness."

Moriana crossed her arms under her breasts. A landau rolled past, drawn by four black dogs, each with an identical white patch over its left eye. The carriage body was white painted wood with gold trim in severe lines. The vehicle couldn't be described as ornate, yet neither was it strictly functional. The gilt added a touch of garishness. It epitomized all Moriana had seen in Tolviroth Acerte. The citizens wished to appear reserved but at the same time they hinted at extravagance.

"Why don't you go to the Quincunx Cities and warn them of your sister's intentions?" suggested Ziore.

"The burghers of the Quincunx could give the Tolvirot lessons in smug complacency. They'll not believe themselves threatened until the Sky Guardsmen drop from their skies. And then it will be too late." She smiled humorlessly. "And once the first Quincunx city falls to my sister, it wil be my life if I set foot in any of the others. They'll not trust *any* of the City's royal family."

Approaching darkness sent its tentacles creeping up the block. Across the hewn stone street the most distinguished of Tolviroth Acerte's banking houses stood as stately as spinsters and, for Moriana, as impenetrable. At her back a fountain played, complete with water-spewing fish and naked little boys with urns and gilded bottoms.

"If you can't hire a mercenary army," Ziore said, "why not try to raise a popular one? Surely, not all the folk of the Sundered Realm are as phlegmatic as the Quincunxers? In my day, folk feared the City's might, and that was long past the fall of its builders. Can't you awaken the countryside to the dangers of your sister's ambition?"

Moriana gave the unseen spirit a pitying smile. Ziore was wise in some ways, but life in the cloister hadn't prepared her for the harsh reality of the world.

"You're right," she said, "about the folk of the Realm dreading the Sky City. Long ago we treated them with contempt—even we Etuul. "Groundlings" we call them. We sneer at them for never rising above the dirt into the freedom of the sky. They fear us, even hate us. The common people will believe Synalon threatens them, but they will also suspect that I wish to entangle them in a war for my own ends."

"But what of justice? The throne belongs to you!"

"I think it's safe to wager that not a single citizen of the Realm loses so much as a minute's sleep worrying about the fortunes of the City."

"You are cynical, child. It is your hurt that makes you speak thus."

"It's reality, Ziore, reality."

They sat in silence. Darkness deepened and with it the gloom enfolding Moriana. Perhaps, she thought, I should return to the City. Could Rann's perverted amusements be so much worse than the agony of helplessness?

"Don't!" cried Ziore. "Never think that, child, never! Such thinking is always a trap, a pit without bottom. Once you fall into it, you can never . . ."

The sound of a footfall nearby cut her off. Moriana looked around. She expected to see one of the constabulary come to collect the tariff for sitting on the bench and enjoying the view of the rich statuary. Her hand went instinctively to her sword hilt.

A man stood there, a tall silhouette against the fading sun.

"*Fost!*" she gasped.

"I fear not my lady," came the warm but unfamiliar voice. "Just a plain passerby whose heart is torn to see one so lovely in distress. Can I be of service? A kind word? A sword to fight beside you?"

Moriana blinked. The words, coming soft in the accents of the City States, should have repelled her as mere puffery. Yet sincerity flowed through them like a warm, rich current. Something made her want to believe the offer was real.

"I am grateful, sir," she said, gesturing for him to sit. "But my troubles are larger than the two of us."

"That may be so, and may be not," he said, smiling. She studied him as he took a place—not too close, but not far either. She saw why, with the sun at his back, he had made her think of her lost lover. He had the same big-boned build, and he was well muscled and lithe. He moved with the assurance of the competent.

But up close he was quite different. His hair, she now saw, was brown touched with gray instead of Fost's night-black. The stranger had known far more than the courier had—or ever would. The stranger's eyes were brown and set in a network of fine laugh lines. His clothing was patched and travel-worn, but it was plainly of high quality. As was his manner, as well. He was no guttersnipe but a man of birth and breeding.

"If you'll pardon the impertinence of self-introduction, lady, I am Darl Rhadaman, Count-Duke of Harmis."

"Lord Rhadaman," she gasped. Darl Rhadaman, swordsman, strategist, orator, crusader ever in search of some new cause to champion, was no less than a legend. He'd fared around the world in his way, yet his finest hour had come in freeing his hereditary fiefdom of a wizard bent on subjugation.

A kiss on her hand brought her from her daze.

"And you, my lady? To whom have I the honor of offering my service?"

"Moriana Etuul, Heir to the City in the Sky."

"So," he said. "Your pardon, Highness, for my unseeming familiarity."

"Don't be ridiculous," she said, pulling at his sleeve to prevent him from dropping to a knee in obeisance. "How do you know I'm not lying, anyway? I could tell you anything."

"I have seen you, Highness, and heard of your sister's . . . assumption of the Beryl Throne."

"Seen me? Where?" she asked, surprised.

"In this very city, Highness, not three years ago. The Festival of Debentures was underway and you were pointed out to me. I am appalled I could see you now and not remember your stunning beauty."

"I remember!" Moriana cried, clapping her hands. "I had come to discuss the City's accounts with . . ." She couldn't give name to the banker who'd so recently denied her the means of conquering the City. "Yes," she said shortly, "I was here. If I'd only known a man such as yourself was nearby!"

"I have a confession, Highness. I'm no longer Count-Duke of Harmis."

"I didn't mean . . ."

"No offense taken, milady. I suppose I am still count-duke, when all is said and done. But I've renounced claim to my homeland."

"Why?" Such a question would normally have been discourteous, but something in the man's manner told Moriana he wouldn't regard it as such.

"Peace," Darl said, "is a wonderful thing, a blessing for the people. The borders of Harmis are secured against foes within and without, and since I helped the people of my country find their pride again, few will issue a real challenge."

He looked at her and said in a lower voice, "Peace is a marvelous thing. And it's also boring as hell."

Moriana's laugh started her. It sounded strange, alien. It had been long since she'd laughed.

"So now my life story is yours. What of you, bright princess? I know some of the affairs of your City; the Realm lost a great leader in your mother. Tell me why Synalon sits on the Beryl Throne while you are desolate and alone on a bench in Tolviroth Acerte."

Moriana started to speak, then halted herself. Could she trust this man? He had come to her precipitously, out of the night, a coincidence. Was he a spy for Rann? She cast that notion from her fatigued mind; Rann still did not know she lived. And she would have been wisked away to a dungeon by now. Rann's perverted sense of torture didn't extend to assignations like this.

Ziore, she spoke with her mind. *Ziore, can I trust this man?*

The pause drew her muscles taut. Darl looked at her expectantly with his kind brown eyes. In a moment expectation would turn to impatience. She couldn't afford to irritate him if he could help her. Had Ziore caught her thought?

I have scanned his soul with care, child, Ziore's thought poured smoothly into her mind. *His heart is good. Trust him.*

Moriana tried to speak, but her words were drowned in tears.

* * *

The day had been warm for winter, but as dusk deepened into night the bench became uncomfortable. They drifted to a restaurant specializing in Port Zorn cuisine. Island cooking proved dull, but Tolviroth Acerte had an excellent assortment of foreign eating establishments. Moriana told the balance of her story over a meal of sea-grass salad with spiced, boiled crab, a main course of fillet of yellowharp boiled in butter and sweet wine.

Afterward, they walked along the palisades overlooking the harbor to the north. The wind blew off the Jorea, but the highlands of the island absorbed much of its fury. Still, a winter chill gave a steel edge to the wind. In the penetrating cold, it seemed only natural for Darl's strong arm to slip around her shoulders.

"You have done many fantastic things," he told her, "But Erimenes is perhaps the rarest treat of all. To have lived in Athalau of old! How I envy you that meeting."

"Perhaps I should introduce myself," Ziore said shyly from the depths of her jug. Darl stepped back a half pace, then slowly smiled, accepting. Then he laughed at his own reaction.

"I have indeed led a sheltered life," he said. Never before have I met a jug of spirits quite like you!" He paused, shivered, and drew Moriana closer, saying, "I could do with other spirits. Milady?"

It seemed only natural for Moriana to accompany the nobleman back to the small but snug room he had engaged at a nearby inn.

Darl poured her wine.

"I am in awe of you, princess," he said, seating himself on the bed. "You've braved incredible hardships and survived unearthly peril. Take no offense, but without the amulet and an Athalar to confirm your tale, I'd find it impossible to credit you. But one thing I'm unclear on." He sipped his wine. Light danced in his eyes and reflected the image of a single tallow candle. "What actually happened to this comrade of yours, this Fost? I'd be honored to meet him."

"I'm . . . that's impossible," Moriana said, her eyes dropping to her lap where her hands intertwined helplessly. Her throat knotted up with tension as she realized she must tell Darl the truth.

"Fost is dead," she said in a small, cracked voice. "I killed him myself."

Darl said nothing. She looked up and into Darl's eyes, seeking some sign of reproach or repulsion. She read nothing. Only . . . a waiting for explanation.

"Fost wanted the amulet for his own," she said, the words beginning to tumble out in a cathartic rush. "But I needed it to help overthrow my sister. It's not just for me but for my City! It's for the entire Sundered Realm that I must destroy Synalon. He couldn't see that."

She covered her face with her hands. Uncontrollable weeping seized her. She knew she'd done right. She also knew she'd never be done reproaching herself.

Then Darl was beside her, holding her, soothing her. She turned her face to his chest and soaked his shirt with hot, bitter tears.

Though neither seemed to will it, they rose and went to the bed. Her face lifted, seeking his. Their clothes fell without conscious effort as their hands explored each other's body. Moriana's loss and pain crystallized into sudden flaring passion. She needed to open her soul and let her grief pour out.

She lay back. He smiled down at her, gentle, compassionate. And suddenly she remembered Ziore.

What did the spirit think? They'd shared love through many a bleak night in secret ways Ziore knew. Now, how would the shade of a long-dead nun react to sharing her lover with another?

Do not be foolish, child. Your pleasure is mine, however you may come by it.

Darl hovered above her. He had sensed her tension

and held back. Her arms went around his neck and drew him down.

Then he was inside her. She moved passionately against him, almost fighting, and lost herself in a frenzy of release that was only in a small way physical. A flurry of motion and the barriers burst. He moved back and forth quickly lighting a fire that burned like the sun. They both lost identity in the blaze of ecstasy. And gradually they cooled, sighing and relaxing, fingers stroking, learning all that their initial urgency had given them no leisure to discover.

The candle flickered near the end of its life when Moriana awoke. She lay on her stomach becoming slowly and deliciously aware of Darl's hand caressing her back. He kissed her when he saw her eyes open.

"I can muster support among the City States," Darl said musingly. "Folk may not care much who rules the Sky City, but there are those who will follow wherever I lead. Still, we'll need funds."

She raised herself on her elbows. Her breasts swung gently, brushing her nipples along the sheets, giving her an exquisite sensation. The amulet around her neck burned like a white star.

"You mean you're willing to help me? After I told you what happened to the last man who aided me?"

"You forget, Highness. I'm a man in search of a cause. In truth, it doesn't matter what cause. I thrive on action. I see justice in your cause; that's why I feel bound to help. A just cause requires sacrifice."

"It wasn't Fost's cause."

"I spoke of your sacrifice."

Moriana reached out and ran a finger down the firm line of his jaw. She couldn't forgive what she'd done. But to know that another understood was comforting. Darl turned his face to kiss her palm.

"So," he said, "what about money?—before I become too distracted by your beauty."

"I hate to disturb you," said Ziore. "I fear I can control only this one."

"What? What do you mean?" demanded Moriana. "What are you talking about, Ziore?"

Someone giggled.

Moriana realized with an icy shock that the giggle she heard came not from Ziore but from outside the room. Her eyes turned to the door.

A man stood there, short sword clutched loosely in his fingers.

"Hello," he said, tittering. "I was supposed to kill you. Isn't that absurd? You're friends!"

"Assassins" hissed Darl.

The door flew open all the way and a second assassin rushed in.

Moriana and Darl rolled off the bed, groping for swords in the gloom. Moriana reached hers first. The blade hissed free and swung in a moaning arc to strike away a thrust at Darl's unguarded side. The second assassin danced back as Darl got his sword out and cut at him backhanded.

The first assassin giggled insanely. His comrade shot him a furious look, drew a long, thin poniard with his left hand, and backed toward the wall waving both weapons menacingly.

Naked, the pair advanced. Without conscious thought, Moriana's hand moved.

The dagger blocked her thrust with a sliding clang. At the same instant, Darl's sword darted for the assassin's groin. The shortsword swept down—too far. Before the killer could react, the broadsword's point raised and sheathed itself in his guts.

His partner laughed himself into a fit of hiccuping.

Moriana teetered back to the bed and sat. Strength flowed from her. Her sword tip fell to the floorboards and stained them with dark, rich blood. She felt sick. She glanced down at the familiar cool hardness of the amulet between her breasts. The blackness that had predominated was giving way to equilibrium.

"You hurt?" asked Darl. His voice was rough. Danger and death so soon after love had jarred his composure. Moriana shook her head. "Well, then, let's see what Chuckles has to say about whoever hired the Brethren of Assassins to come for us."

"Ask me anything," the assassin said. "Dear friends, how can I refuse you?"

Imin Dun Bacir knew opportunity when he saw it.

For fifteen years he'd held the coveted post of Chief Trade Factor for the Sky City in Tolviroth Acerte. In that time he had absorbed the true Tolvirot's appreciation for *opportunity*. And today fortune had granted him the most delectable opportunity of his career.

He had seized it.

When Derora V had died and Synalon assumed the Beryl Throne, Bacir had considered dropping everything and leaving. Synalon was utterly mad. He had never taken much interest in politics, but he knew that anything less than active support for Synalon would be construed as opposition. He had accumulated enough money as chief factor to make any Tolvirot proud. He could have gathered his treasure, bought passage on a fast ship, and spent his retirement in a villa in Jorea.

To do so, however, would have been to pass up a fabulous opportunity.

It had called just as he was sitting down to dinner in his Medurim-style mansion in the suburbs of Tolviroth Acerte.

"Tulmen Omsgib to see you, Notable," Trune, his majordomo, announced. Bacir looked longingly at the steaming spread before him. He could not delay speaking with the banker. To defer business until after a meal would gain him a reputation for frivolity. To a Tolviroth the pursuit of gain was not like a sacrament, it *was* a sacrament. He arranged an expression of heartiness on his ample features and followed Trune to see what Omsgib had to say.

Imin Dun Bacir heard from Tulmen Omsgib how the Princess Moriana had come begging for money and how her request had been turned down on the grounds of not wishing to alienate his bank's best customer. Bacir solemnly thanked the banker for the interest in the Sky City, but his brain shifted into high gear as he figured ways of turning this tidbit to his own interest.

Omsgib gave him a clue by mentioning that he had assigned agents to watch the princess surreptitiously. Bacir quickly assured the banker that the Sky City's own men would assume these tedious duties.

Synalon would be lavish to whoever informed her that her sister still lived. And to the person who finally rid her of the threat Moriana posed, her generosity would know no bounds. Bacir considered capturing Moriana, then regretfully discarded the idea. Part of success in business was not to allow greed to overcome good sense. If Rann had been unable to eliminate Moriana, Bacir was not eager to risk capturing her alive.

The Brethren of Assassins was notified of a task as soon as Omsgib left. Bacir then turned back to his long-awaited meal. He scarcely noticed the food was cold. He wolfed it down, barely tasting it, then retired to his leisure rooms to inhale narcotic fumes and soothe his jangled nerves listening to a quartet of naked female musicans play archaic Medurimin chamber music.

Naked girls and archaic chamber music were his twin passions, after the accumulation of wealth. But not even they kept him diverted. After an hour, he dismissed them with an irritable wave of his hand. He turned to pacing grooves in his plush rug, waiting for word that the Brethren had fulfilled their commission.

The water clock had just dripped the eleventh hour when Trune appeared at the door of the leisure room.

"The assassins?" Bacir demanded harshly. Seeing his majordomo nod, he said, "Well, don't stand there. Send them in at once."

He quivered with tension and felt as if fat blue sparks would leap from his fingers like static electricity. He bounced up and down on the balls of his feet, chins jiggling, until he heard Trune's subtle footsteps padding down the corridor.

"G-good evening, Notable," the assassin said. He laughed a squealing laugh through his nose. Bacir wondered if he'd been sniffing vapors, too. It hardly seemed appropriate for an assassin to indulge in such vices while on business.

Another, much larger man came in behind the first. Bacir sensed a third presence in the corridor. He frowned. Three assassins? The Brethren evidently considered Moriana formidable.

"Did you kill the princess?" he demanded, using the word "kill" in spite of the Brethren's touchiness about its use. Bacir was in no mood to humor the hired help.

"Why, no, Notable. I've done much better than that." He interrupted himself with a giggle. "I've brought the princess to you."

The third member of the small party came into the room. Her hair was spun gold, her eyes green balefires.

"Princess!" gasped Bacir. Trune started to move for a bell rope hanging by the wall. Darl's sword materialized and touched its tip to Trune's neck. The majordomo grew very still.

"That's right, cur," said Moriana. "Grovel. Grovel for your worthless life. You've earned a traitor's death, Bacir. I may not be as cruel as my sister, but do not mistake my motives. Give me one reason why you shouldn't pay for the attempted murder of your rightful sovereign."

"Mercy," sobbed Bacir. Tears rolled down his round cheeks onto the rings on his fingers, now clutched beseechingly before his face.

"There is a way, foul one," she said, her voice low and menacing, "for you to redeem yourself. You can aid me, dropping of a carrion-eater. To do so is no more than your sworn duty, but if you perform your task well, I shall be magnanimous. I will allow you to continue your wretched existence."

"Mercy, bright one! Have mercy on me, O Mistress of the Clouds!" He rolled a tear-sheened eye at Moriana. She remained unmoved by his use of the title reserved for the Queen of the Sky City. "I dare not help! Synalon will have my life for it!"

"That may be, but Synalon is far away. *I* am here."

Bacir stopped snuffling and peered at her from beneath quivering brows. It might have been a trick of the light, but at that moment Moriana bore a startling resemblance to her cousin Rann.

Squalling seabirds rode on the morning wind. Captain Uin Ragalla lounged at ease on his poop. He puffed great clouds of blue smoke from his pipe and contemplated the day's sailing. The wind blew northerly and the sky was clear. He could ask for nothing more. The *Black Flame* could warp out of harbor, run south with the wind through the Karhon Channel till it cleared the southern tip of the island, and be well on the way to Jorea by the noon bell.

A hail from the dock roused him from his reverie.

"What's that?" he demanded, looking up at the annoyance.

"Hail the ship." The man calling to him was short and so fat as to be almost globular. The roundness of his face was accentuated by a black fringe of beard clinging to the uppermost of his myriad chins.

"What would ye?" Ragalla asked. His grasp of the

Imperial Tongue spoken throughout the Realm was good for a Jorean.

"I would take passage to Jorea," the man said, clutching a ragged cloak about him as the wind whipped up.

"And what'll ye pay with, then?"

"I have no money."

Ragalla spat.

"Some chance. Nothin' for nothin'—that's what you Tolvirot always say, innit? Well, then." He nodded and sucked aggressively at his pipe. Blue clouds rose from the bowl.

"But I'm not a Tolviroth," the fat man protested.

"Nooo," he said, studying the man. "I suppose ye ain't. Fact be, I suppose you're that Factor fellow from the Floating City, then? Hey?"

The fat man nodded.

"Well, fancy that. The high-and-mighty trade fellow from that Sky City a'beggin' passage 'cross the sea without two sipans to clink together."

"I've fallen on misfortune," the man said with a certain dignity.

"So? May happen I'll fall and get misfortune all over my face one day, then." He motioned to the man. "Come aboard. I can always use another cabin boy, hey?"

Imin Dun Bacir took ship for Jorea as he had long planned. He left without the fortune he had spent so long accumulating. But he went with his life, and where he went not even Synalon's wrath could reach.

Imin Dun Bacir knew an opportunity when he saw one.

The Sleeper sensed a Presence.

The demon's subconscious groped for that nearness, a response born of loneliness. It drew back just as quickly. The first outpouring of joy crusted over with bitter resentment.

Words formed in its mind: *Why turn away?*

Blank refusal met the query. Again the Presence probed, gently, insistently. *Why turn your face from those who love you?*

Asleep, the demon could shape no coherent thought. Yet the emotion wrenched from it was as unmistakable as it was inchoate.

Betrayed!

The Presence read the outpouring of agony, the loneliness and helpless cruel confinement.

Help me! silently shrieked the demon. You could have helped me!

The Presence recoiled from the plaintive violence of the last emotion. It poured forth its own thoughts like balm into the tortured Sleeper's mind.

I have not power to help you. Not even those I serve—whom you serve—can free you unaided. But I bring tidings of joy. Soon, your time may come. You must prepare yourself to again serve.

NO! The Sleeper's denial was an eruption of negation. The Presence rode the blast like a free-floating leaf making no attempt to oppose its strength with the Sleeper's. Even asleep, the Demon of the Dark Ones possessed power of cosmic scope.

But freedom, the Presence promised. *You may soon stretch your limbs to the skies again. Is that not worth much? All?*

The Sleeper felt anger. Betrayal had become ingrained in its view of the universe. It knew the Presence lied. The emotion dropped low and sullen. It knew it would receive no help. It was alone, doomed, betrayed!

The Presence stifled its own surge of annoyance lest it anger the Sleeper more. The sleeping demon's mind only functioned in the most basic fashion, considering only appetite and the simplest of feelings. In its hurt anger the demon would spurn any offer of help hoping to wreak infantile vengeance on those who had betrayed it.

The Presence bided its time. It felt Istu's hatred. Reason would never pierce the shell of truculence.

Yet time grew short. The Aspects neared a critical conjunction. And the Lords of Infinite Dark had to know that their sole begotten child would be obedient to their wishes were he released.

A child cannot be reasoned with, the Presence thought to itself. *Yet a child can be bribed.* It turned from the sleeping, imprisoned giant and fled through the corridors of night. A plan formed in its mind.

CHAPTER EIGHT

"I have been betrayed before," Synalon raged at Rann. "I have been spurned by my own family, I have been schemed against, lied to, used, abused, and made to suffer for the failings of others. But never have I been subjected to a more humiliating failure. *Never!*"

Rann's guts trembled before his cousin's fury. If he got away with only being skinned alive, his luck would be extraordinary.

It was impossible for anyone else to have survived the ice fall. It had only been the wildest chance that an edge of the block had struck the portico of the Palace of Esoteric Wisdom and thus failed to crush all life from Rann; for all his resilience and the sorceries of the palace mages he had still not healed. None of the others could possibly have gotten out alive. Not Moriana, not Fost. Even the demon Erimenes should have had his jar pulverized.

Yet not an hour ago a messenger had arrived from Tolviroth Acerte with the stunning message: *Princess Moriana lived.*

Bringing the word to his royal cousin had been the hardest task the warrior-prince had ever faced.

Synalon stalked paving stones that carried the scars of her last foray into demonomancy. Not even Rann knew what the queen had done that night, though he had a few shrewd guesses. The next morning five mages of the palace had been found dead in their beds with expressions of horror twisted into their features. Whatever Synalon had done was potent.

It had also left her in a state of nerves that had sent

125

eight of her lovers and three advisers into exile through the Well of Winds. Whatever else Synalon's ensorcellments had granted her, she had not been given peace of mind.

"You have my life, Your Majesty," the prince said, eyes locked on the floor. "You should have taken it before when I allowed your sister to escape."

She gazed at him narrowly. Today she wore a gown of rich purple, almost indigo, which clung to her like mist. The fanciful condiment of feathers adorning her head fell in wild disarray.

"You—" she began, but her lips trembled so badly she had to start over. "You *dare* accuse me of misjudgment in leaving you with your foul life? Oh, you wretch, you rogue, you *groundling!*" Along with the epithet Synalon hurled a bolt of lightning that shattered a five-thousand-year-old statue. Guards and attendants scattered in all directions.

" Dark Ones!" she shrieked. Her hair began to crackle. "Witness my mortification! I am served by dolts!"

She hauled a quivering Anacil from under the Beryl Throne by one skinny white ankle.

"Must I cast all my advisers down the Skywell? Come out of there, you miserable old fool!"

"Majesty," he quavered. "Y-your headdress, O Mistress of the Clouds. It's on fire!"

Synalon raised a hand to cinder her chamberlain. The hand stopped in the region of her right temple. With it frozen there, the queen cocked her head and sniffed. Then she snatched her bonnet, now billowing smoke, and hurled it into the arms of a guard.

"Throw that out the window, worm!"

The man trotted to obey.

"Very well," Synalon said at length, struggling to control her rage. "We are on the verge of taking the first step on our road to conquest. I know the penalty of failure as well as any. I cannot dispose of you, my cousin, if for no other reason than that your Sky Guardsmen will follow only you. But be warned. I will tolerate no further failure from you. The invasion will succeed or you will know my *full* wrath."

Rann's mouth went dry. He remained kneeling, unable to believe what he'd heard. His cousin allowed him to live.

"Do not fear, Majesty," he cried, springing to his feet. "I will lead our troops to victory!"

He bowed and turned to go.

"One moment." Synalon stopped him with that smoothly seductive, bitchy voice she used when she had something particularly vicious in mind. He swung slowly to face her. "Those captives we took, spies trying to get into the City. How many still live?"

"Twelve, Majesty."

"And they are in your safekeeping?"

"Certainly, Your Majesty. I plan to attend to their disposal personally."

"How thoughtful." She touched a finger to her chin and smiled wickedly. "You have so much to do with the preparations for the coming invasion. I cannot ask you to sacrifice your time on such pursuits. Captain Tro!" The commander of her personal guard stepped forward. "Send a party for my cousin's prisoners. Convey them to my dungeons. I shall see that they receive due punishment."

The queen favored all in the room with a special look, seductive and promising. Rann's groin was empty but the nerves remembered. Too well, they remembered.

"See what a gracious sovereign you're blessed with," she declared.

Rann tightened his face into an impassive mask. Twelve prisoners, twelve! And she robbed him of them. The torments he'd planned, the sweet expectation he had been nurturing, carefully allowing it to grow so that his ecstasy would be complete—all wasted.

"Your Majesty is too generous," he said. "I only hope to repay you in kind someday." He left quickly before his queen spoke again.

The rulers of Bilsinx officially scoffed at the notion that their town had anything to fear from the Sky City. The townsfolk were in an uproar and weren't calmed when a score of rumormongers were flogged in the Central Square. The rumors stopped totally when Mayor Irb had five housewives dismembered by dray hornbulls.

Despite his official posture, the good lord mayor was plagued by a private uneasiness as he revealed to a distinguished visitor on the eve of the City's arrival.

"We are honored by your presence in our fair city, Count Ultur," he said, slopping rakshak into his visitor's cup. "Quite honored."

"I thank you, my lord mayor," said the Count Ultur V'Duuyek as he sipped at his potent liquor.

The mayor plunked his mug down on the arm of his chair. The green velvet upholstery was a mass of circles matching the underside of his mug. Irb was a man who liked his rakshak.

"Well? You're bound for the Sjedd, is it? Help them put down those beastly Thail savages?" He looked closely at the count and framed his eyes with what he thought to be a look of perspicuity. Dissolute shrewdness was all he managed.

"My dog riders are versatile and up to the task, I'm sure," said the count. "Besides, the Thails are quite low at their southern end, and the Sjedd is mostly savannah. A shaman has identified some of the southern tribes as those who've seized Sjedd territory. I will retake the country, then proceed into the foothills to chastise the tribesmen."

The mayor nodded his understanding in the manner of those who don't really understand. He had heard of the disturbances in the Sjedd. Quite alarming. The

Sjedd lay across the end of the Thails along the side of the Quincunx running between Brev and Thailot. Upheavals there always had a deleterious effect on trade. The military ramifications were beyond him.

He knew little of military matters, but he did know that the count's twelve hundred, heavily armored dog riders from the Highgrass Broad constituted considerable force.

"The Sky City goes overhead tomorrow," he said slowly. "You've doubtless heard the rumors, milord, that they plan to attack us. I've squelched such talk, to be sure, but still the rumors persist."

When the count said nothing, Irb persisted.

"Do you think there's anything to it?"

"If they were to try it without substantial ground support, they would be foolish, indeed," V'Duuyek said, his manner scornful.

The mayor sat back, nodding with satisfaction. The Bilsinx militia wasn't large, but it was kept in reasonable practice battling brigands and occasional nomads drifting in from the steppes. The token Sky City garrison of two hundred dog riders and a score of flyers could be dealt with easily.

"If the Sky City were to attack us, ridiculous as that seems—but *if* they did—your people would not idly sit by?"

"My lord mayor," V'Duuyek said, smiling thinly and smoothing one horn of his meticulously waxed moustache, "should fighting break out, I quite honestly doubt I could keep my people out of it."

This satisfied the mayor, who bellowed out for more rakshak. With the problems of defense all solved, it was time for serious drinking.

For once, Erimenes found nothing to carp about in Fost's choice of a destination. Even the spirit's obsessive appetite for sensation was almost glutted by the brawling, splendid bazaar that was Kara-Est.

From its vantage point at the tip of the Gulf of Veluz, Kara-Est laid claim to being one of the great cities of the day. Younger and more vibrant than Medurim, earthier than the City in the Sky, possessed of an exuberance foreign to the staid merchants of Tolviroth Acerte, and vastly more cosmopolitan than her sister cities of the Quincunx, Kara-Est dinned her self-image into a visitor like an unceasing clangor of cymbals. Built on a cluster of hills that rose steadily as they marched inland, bounded to the northeast by swampland, and giving way to the steppes in the southwest, the seaport looked anything but prepossessing. Boxy homes clumped like hives on the hills. Each painted a different hue, they caught the morning sunlight and presented a chaotic impression. But after the initial shock wore off, the garish splashings of color assumed a curious harmony of their own.

Like giant balloons, the ludintip of the Mires swamps floated lazily above the city, propelling themselves by venting gas through sphincters in their air bladders. The beasts had long been domesticated by the Estil. The Estil alone of all the Realm's inhabitants shared the dominion of the sky with the Floating City. The occasional contrivances of hoops and rings and cross-braced frames on the higher rooftops were engines for defense against attack from the air.

Fost and Jennas rode in from the steppe side by side. With his usual lack of grace, Erimenes jounced along in his jug. A Northern stranger and a barbaric warrior woman from the south mounted on immense and fearsome bears would attract attention enough without a pale blue spirit hovering beside them like a friendly cloud.

The sentries on the New Wall gaped at the newcomers as the bears rolled through the city gates. The guardsmen fingered crossbows. The barbarians from the steppes seldom penetrated to Kara-Est, but when they did they seldom came for peaceful reasons. Nonetheless, this pair seemed well enough behaved.

To Erimenes' immense glee, Fost set a course for the waterfront district.

"At last!" crowed the spirit. "To visit the fabled fleshpots of Kara-Est! From anecdotes I've heard, the cultural demonstrations to be seen at Madam Tinng's, particularly those involving Highgrass Broad warrior-girls and their dogs, are most educational." He chortled. "I'm sure healthy, hot-blooded youngsters such as yourselves will require no schooling from me in the full appreciation of Kara-Est's fabled vices."

Fost sighed. The philosopher, after giving up his ascetic principles on death, had settled into a perpetual adolescence. Since he lacked the physical equipment to sate his newly acknowledged drives, they grew constantly sharper all the time. Jennas eyed the satchel with more pronounced distaste than usual. Erimenes' mention of the fanciful displays put on by the warrior-maidens had touched a raw nerve. From the morning they'd set out, Erimenes had been suggesting a novel manner for Jennas to improve rapport with her bear. While the Ust-alayakits lived on terms of intimacy with their beasts, the kind of intimacy espoused by Erimenes was regarded by the nomads with acute horror. Jennas in turn had taken to proposing new and colorful ways in which Fost might dispose of his all-too-familiar spirit.

"I thought you'd been to Kara-Est before, Erimenes," said Fost, as they jogged down a cobbled street accompanied by the stares of the townsfolk.

"Not so. I am always receptive to experience, even repeated experience. In my wisdom I've learned to eschew the young's insistence on novelty." He sighed. "Besides, when I came through here before I was in the charge of an acolyte mage from Duth. He'd taken some silly vow of celibacy and wouldn't sway from it. Were it not for your sterling example, Fost, I would sorely fear for the manhood of those from the north."

"I hate to damage your high opinion of me," Fost said sacrastically, "but we aren't going to be exploring the dives. We haven't time. And don't protest," he continued over Erimenes' outraged cry, "or I may reconsider Jennas's suggestion that we sell you to a merchant captain for a chamberpot."

The spirit shut up. Fost smiled. The verbal infighting helped take his mind off the three weeks he'd spent in the saddle—and Moriana.

They climbed a hill, the bears' strong claws giving purchase on the ice-slicked cobblestones. Jennas gasped as the harbor came into view. They paused to take in the impressive sight, then rode down into the city's heart.

For Jennas it was almost too much. She'd been briefly in small trading towns south along the Gulf of Veluz; Kara-Est was a hundred times larger than the greatest of those. Even Fost, raised in the Teemings, the stench-ridden and overcrowded slums of High Medurim, couldn't help being impressed.

Bars and brothels, houses of gambling and houses of worship, government offices, warehouses, theaters, dwellings rich and dwellings shabby, all jostled each other around the wide sweep of the bay. Hundreds of ships rode at anchor in the largest harbor of the Realm. And with the ships came sailors from around the world: surly, shaggy traders from the Northern Continent; blond savages from the Isles of the Sun who powdered themselves with gold dust and were followed by gaggles of mute, drugged slaves; wide-eyed scholars of the Far Archipelago, their wan otherworldliness reminding Fost of the Ethereals of the Great Crater Lake; black merchant captains from hot Jorea forced by the coming antarctic winter to supplement their usual garb of kilts and sandals with heavy fur cloaks.

They tethered the bears to a hitching post in front of an establishment whose sign proclaimed it the *Storm-Wrack Inn*. Riding dogs whined and cringed away from the gigantic newcomers. A stout townsman started to protest. Jennas glared at him and hitched at the strap of her greatsword. He gulped, unhitched his mount, and rode off looking nervously over his shoulder.

They went inside. Fost made his way to a hardwood bar with a gleaming rail of juggernaut fish ivory, ordered sack for himself, and with a shudder, *amasinj* for Jennas. The barkeep, a tall man with a glazed eye, took the order without comment. He didn't even comment when Erimenes demanded loudly to know when the indecent displays began. In a cosmopolitan town such as Kara-Est, not even disembodied voices emerging from jugs excited comment.

Fost elbowed his way back to Jennas in time to be nearly bowled over by a sudden commotion. Yelping bar patrons shoved by him. In the space they left vacant, he saw Jennas pitching a bearded docker out the door. She turned away, dusted off her hands with an air of satisfaction, and resumed her seat.

"What was that all about?" he asked, handing over her mug.

"The lout wished me to kiss him," she said, downing a slug of her drink that would have stretched Fost on the floor. "I refused. When he persisted, I put him out." Fost nodded. He'd never doubted the hetwoman was capable of taking care of herself.

He sipped his own drink more conservatively. They hadn't come to the tavern to indulge Erimenes, who was now suggesting that a redheaded serving girl at a table nearby give into the importunings of a Northlander with checkered trousers and one hand on her rump. Fost was looking for information. He was certain Moriana headed for the Sky City. What he didn't know was its exact location.

Jennas tensed at his side. He glanced at her, following her gaze. Across the table from them stood a tall, dark-skinned woman with the brassard of a Jorean sea captain encircling one arm. She was a handsome, robust woman with gray strands mingling with midnight curls. Her cloak dangled from her shoulders, revealing bare breasts, big and firm and gleaming like polished ebony. She stared with frankly sexual interest—at Jennas.

"Ho there, missy," she said, saluting the startled Jennas with a foaming jack of ale. "You're quite a sight, and that's for certain. What say you you ditch this jocko and come with me? I've never seen a lass the likes of you."

Jennas's eyes went round. Clearly, she was uncertain she'd heard the mariner clearly—which Fost thought for the best. If she had, her next move would have been for the wire-wound hilt of the greatsword leaning against the stuccoed wall. The Jorean was no more the sheltered type than Jennas. She was as tall as the tribeswoman and carried the cutlass familiarly at her hip. Except for the fact she was bare-breasted while Jennas wore her mail, they looked well matched.

She leaned forward, smiling widely.

"Well? What say you? I've a string of pearls on board my *Wavestrider* that'd ride right lovely around your throat."

"No, thank you," Jennas said a bit unsteadily. "Your offer is kind, but I'm happy where I am."

Fost looked at her in surprise. The mores of the Ustalayakits being what they were, he'd expected Jennas to carve up the other woman for suggesting such a liaison. Later, he learned that such relationships, between two males or two females, were not unknown among the southern tribes; like other sexual matters, they were regarded as the private concerns of the participants.

The captain shrugged and turned away, looking sad.

"Just a moment, captain," said Fost. "Have a seat and drink with us. We're new in town and would hear the latest news."

"You're a good sport, friend," said the Jorean, cocking her head to one side. "I'll say that for you." She sat on a stool across from the pair. "It would do me poor credit to spurn such generosity. Never let it be known that Captain Karlaya, mistress of the cog *Wavestrider,* ever turned down the invitation to drink."

"I'm Jennas, hetwoman of the People of Ust. My companion is Fost Longstrider. He's a Realm-road courier. We're pleased to make your acquaintance."

"A nomad chieftain and a road-rider, eh? I can pick 'em, that's for sure. Good for me neither of you took offense. Damn mainlanders squall so when a simple proposition is laid on 'em." She eyed Fost more carefully. "Aye, a good thing you took no offense. I know enough of this Realm of yours to know what a handful you can be."

"You might have introduced me," piped up Erimenes peevishly. "But then again, I can't expect reasonable behavior from you, Jennas. You proved that by turning down the captain's gracious offer. I'm sure she'd be much more stimulating company than this sluggard Fost."

"You wouldn't need a new slop jar, would you?" Fost asked the captain, who stared wide-eyed at the satchel.

Fost explained Erimenes' clay-prisoned existence, there no longer being reason to keep his existence secret. Karlaya was fascinated by Erimenes and offered to buy him on the spot. For reasons he didn't fully understand, Fost turned down the generous offer. Erimenes did not seem upset at remaining with Fost. He might have been afraid the captain would put his jar to the use Fost had proposed.

Fost bought another round of drinks. Eyeing the serving maid, Karlaya ordered *amasinj.* When it came, she tasted it, pronounced it unfit to drink, drained her mug, and ordered another. As she worked on the second mug, she related some rumors she'd heard.

Mostly it was standard gossip, incomprehensible to Jennas and useless to Fost. Port Zorn was raising its harbor fees; the Emperor in High Medurim had decreed a new pleasure dome, the fourth of his brief reign; sundry border skirmishes occurred. When the captain mentioned the Sky City's unusual activity the courier pricked up his ears.

"Is there any word of the Princess Moriana?" he demanded.

"Surely, there is." Karlaya mulled over a mouthful of drink as Fost fumed. She swallowed, studying the two. "You look to know how to swing those swords of yours, so maybe this will interest you. You looking for employment?"

"What do you mean?"

"The Princess What's-her-name, she's in league with Darl Rhadaman of Harmis. They're recruiting mercenaries up in Tolviroth Acerte."

Snow drifted from a low-hung sky. An appearance of business as usual prevailed in Bilsinx as the City in the Sky floated in from the north. Mayor Irb stood on a balcony of his palace at the exact center of the Great Quincunx, the point over which mystic forces steered the City to a new destination.

Despite his official insistence that nothing was to be feared, Irb had mobilized his city's militia. Afraid that an obvious show of force might provoke an unfortunate response, in the air or on the ground, he had ordered many of his troops to remain under cover in the government buildings around the center of the town. The rest mingled with the crowds—merchants, dockers, casual shoppers, and the curious who thronged the cruciform Quincunx Avenues that followed the possible lines of the City's flight.

Titanic fungus-shaped balloons sprouted from the City even before it passed the northernmost walls of Bilsinx. Irb nodded, reassured. He had dreaded the possible explosion of eagles' wings from the Sky City's battlements. The appearance of the familiar, harmless, cumbersome cargo craft was anticlimactic.

The wind streamer dropped from the City's forward piers, a weight dragging a long orange banner behind to tell the Sky Citizens how the wind lay so they could guide their balloons with the least difficulty.

Messengers materialized at Irb's elbow. The barracks of the Sky City garrison had been discreetly surrounded. If anything was tried, the birdsmen would have no support from the ground. And word came from the camp of the Highgrass Broad mercenaries east of town that they were saddling and arming. In case of real trouble, Irb could expect rapid reinforcement from a well-trained cavalry.

The wicker gondola of the lowest balloon bumped cobblestones. The waiting crowd surged forward, handlers reaching for line to dog the balloon to earth. The gondola's side fell away.

Someone screamed shrilly. An instant later, a barrage of arrows burst from the knot of men standing beneath the balloon. The crowd stood stunned. Another volley and frightened townspeople began to run.

Irb gestured frantically. A company of dog cavalry issued forth from the gate of the Palace of Just and Perfect Governance and headed for the outbreak. Elsewhere along the north-south axis of the city, balloons touched down, disgorging their lethal cargo.

And now the dreaded wings of the Sky Guardsmen gripped the sky. Like malevolent spores, the birds dropped from the City, streaking down to preselected Bilsinx targets. Irb shrieked orders to his personal bodyguard. A hundred eagles dived straight for the ramparts of the palace itself!

In the Sky City, commands were shouted to waiting work gangs. Muscle was applied to levers, and heavy stones that had been hauled up from the surface were jacked over the side. Trajectories calculated by City

mathematicians, the missiles fell in advance of the landing parties, smashing against pavement to send lethal
shrapnel whistling in all directions. Fleeing citizens were
shredded by the fragments. Another rock landed on the
lead elements of the column riding from the palace.
The commander was killed instantly and the remaining
dog troopers scattered.

Wounded dogs wailed. Women shrieked. Men fell
gurgling with arrows through their throats. The bird
riders swept low, shooting indiscriminately into the
panicked mass below. The soldiers Irb had ordered
interspersed with the mob died where they stood, unable to form any effective fighting force.

But resistance did gather in the Central Square. Footmen with shields and short spears poured from nearby
buildings. Dog riders loped to join them, their mounts
baying bloodlust. The Bilsinx cavalry were mainly un-
armed bowmen equipped to meet the threat of mounted
brigands. Their bows sang and arrows arced skyward.
Infantry bowmen guarded by their comrades' shields
added their missiles to the defensive barrage.

The leading Sky City men died screaming. Shots
from the ground did not need to reach riders. Transfixed, eagles plummeted like giant snowflakes, their
riders cast helplessly down to smear the cobbles with
their lifeblood. A wounded eagle fluttered near the
cube-shaped palace as though trying to land on the
roof. Two-score arrows feathered its rider as he cast a
javelin in pitiful defiance.

Southward floated the City, silent and still deadly.
The battle roared and howled and clashed below. Sky
City arrows and javelins slaughtered defenders in the
Central Square. But officers of initiative were counter-
ing the aerial threat. On their orders, troops dragged
tables and other furniture from surrounding buildings
to erect lean-to shelters to protect the archers while
they shot. Others barricaded the avenues leading to the
square.

Outside the square there was little organized resistance. But the problem the Sky City strategists had foreseen—and dreaded—had arisen. Their balloon-landed assault teams lacked strength to storm the square and were taking casualties from the archers sent scurrying from the central strongpoint. Given time, the bird riders would wear down the defenders, clear out the square, and then land soldiers to finish the battle. Wherever resistance cropped up, bird riders could harry from above and drop troops to take the defenders in the rear. Already, flight after flight of eagles dove down on the palace, raking its roof with storms of arrows. They would land on its roof very soon.

But only at a fearful cost in lives of men and birds, lives the City in the Sky could not afford.

This was of academic interest to Irb. He nodded in irritation when the Captain of the Palace Guard informed him of the fact; what did it matter that the might of the Sky City was broken when *his* city was captive? He was about to snarl a rebuke to his commander when the skirl of trumpets drew his attention to the east.

The Highgrass cavalry of Ultur V'Duuyek rode to action under bright swallowtail pennons.

"There," said Irb with satisfaction. "*Now* we shall see results."

The scale armor of the dog riders shone dully in the gray morning light. The leader, a compact rider with blue and green ribbons fluttering from the spired top of his helm, raised his sword above his head and dropped it with a chopping motion. Arrows rose from the ranks.

And fell among the startled defenders of the Central Square.

The mobs that had clogged the streets leading to the center of Bilsinx had evaporated, leaving behind only still, dark forms. Nothing hindered the dog riders as they charged down the broad avenue, loosing flights of arrows at the defenders. Militiamen fell among carts and tables and crates in unfinished barricades. Archers returned the mercenaries' barrage. Steel scales clanked like the wings of a billion locust-encased men and dogs alike. The Bilsinxt arrows had no more effect than the gently falling snow.

Bilsinxt dog riders charged to meet the new threat. Their arrows finally took a toll among the Highgrass Broad riders. The mercenaries slung bows across armored backs, unclamped lances from brackets set alongside their saddles, couched, and charged. Heavy riders met a light wall. The Bilsinxt countercharge melted like a sandcastle struck by a sea wave.

Irb had time to call down the curse of the Dark Ones on the treacherous Count Ultur. Then a five-ton rock from above smashed into the north face of the palace, obliterating Irb and the balcony on which he stood.

Weakened, the battlemented edge of the roof slumped, falling into the street in a stately, horrid silence. The City's savants had reckoned well. As planned, a picked commando unit of six-score Sky Guardsmen swooped in the wake of the giant stone. Their eagles' claws scraped to landings on the roof, even as the defenders tried to grasp the horrifying fact that fully a quarter of their number had been dashed to ruins by the huge rock.

First to touch down was a huge black eagle, head crowned by a crest the color of blood. The bird named Terror voiced its bulging war cry as its rider leaped lithely from its back, scimitar and hornbull-hide buckler in hand. Though not fully recovered from his wounds, Prince Rann Etuul led the attack. He had to be there when the stricken city received its deathstroke. With a deft blow, he laid open a spearman from clavicle to hip. Then he was running for a stairway, his Guardsmen shouting triumphantly at his back.

The Grasslanders drove like a lance into the Central Square. Raked bloody from above, ridden down by iron riders from behind, the defenders broke. The lucky ones made it into nearby buildings. The rest were shot down by flying archers. Other bird riders dropped their mounts onto the backs of fleeing militiamen. The defenders' cries rang hideous and defeated as the warbirds disemboweled them.

Prince Rann's men spread throughout the palace like a black and purple plague. Rann cut his way through a shouting rabble to the courtyard, swept the last defenders from the gates, and swung the portals open to clasp his leather glove in Count Ultur V'Duuyek's bloodstained steel gauntlet.

The City in the Sky had won the vital first battle in its campaign of conquest. It had taken forty-three minutes.

Snow fell softly, laying a white shroud over the dead.

CHAPTER NINE

Torchlight splashed orange and ominous down the snowy flanks of the hills to stain the listeners' faces.

"Free men of the North," Darl said loudly, "hear me!"

They heard. Standing in the snow with their breath coming in white plumes, the men of the Black March listened to Darl Rhadaman's words. Chores would be neglected that night, beds unoccupied until late. When Rhadaman spoke, men attended.

"Long has the City in the Sky held itself aloof from the affairs of the surface," he went on, voice deep and clear. "Even contemptuous, aye. But always apart, alone, trading its magic for the goods we produced. They are sharp traders; so are the Tolvirot. In all, we and they profited."

"Now they are discontented. They want to rule the surface as they command the air above. They have treacherously attacked the Five Cities. They came sowing death from the air and Bilsinx fell. So shall it be until every city in the Quincunx is theirs. But will they be content to stop then? No!"

He swept his gaze around the throng of onlookers. The night was as still as a cathedral.

"With the wealth of the Quincunx they will buy mercenaries as they bought the dogs of the Highgrass to bay after their foes and drag them down. They will spread their dominion like a creeping sickness—no!—like a fever, ragging, spreading, until all the Realm is infected with their evil."

"We must act. The time is now when their schemes are aborning, when their treacherous grip on the ground is tenuous. Now they are vulnerable. Soon they will build momentum and power. And then your steads and crops will be theirs, your wives and children sacrificed screaming to the Dark Ones whose worship the usurper has revived. Will you have that? *Will you?*"

"*NO!*"

The sound boomed forth like the roar of Omizantrim in full eruption. Darl stood erect in the full force of their rage and fury. His expression was transfixed, transported, ecstatic. He was in his element. He lived for moments of power like this.

The incoherent burst of hatred resolved into words.

"Lead us, Darl!" the mob howled. "Lead us! We'll claw the City down from the sky!"

Standing just beyond the full glare of the torches, Moriana shuddered. She felt the blood-hunger gripping the crowd. If they realized a Sky City noble was practically in their midst, they'd turn on her and rend her like enraged war dogs.

"You wish to destroy the City, then, brothers?" Darl called. He fixed a tall, vigorous onlooker with his gaze.

Singled out, the man waved his cap in the air and cried, "Yes!" The fever of destruction on him, he added, "Will you lead us, Darl?"

"No."

The word dropped like a stone among them. Exuberance left the throng. They stared at the speaker. Hostility began to replace adoration.

"You do not wish to destroy the City in the Sky. Who among you does not benefit from their magics? The metalworker whose captive elemental increases his production tenfold and more? The herdsman whose flocks are kept free of pestilence by Sky City wards and potions? No, my friends. To destroy the Sky City would be to destroy yourselves."

"But, Lord Darl," said the man he'd singled out as spokesman for the crowd, "what do you want of us?" He scratched behind prominent ears. "One minute you issue us the call to arms, and now you'd have us swear eternal friendship with the City. How can we do both?"

"Your quarrel is not with the City, brother," said Darl, "nor yet with its people. It is with those who rule the City: Synalon, the evil sorceress who calls on the Dark Ones. She and her minions would make you bend your necks to the yoke of slavery."

"You fear the Sky City, and rightfully so. Yet you cannot exist without it. So you ask, what are you to do?"

He looked around, eyes boring into the innermost recesses of each man's mind.

"You can serve yourselves and at the same time serve a higher justice as well. You can right the wrong Synalon did in seizing the Beryl Throne for herself. For you all know that Synalon is not the true and proper ruler of the City. Her sister, who would be friend to all the peoples of the Sundered Realm, desires only peace and prosperity. Her cause is just. Her cause is *yours*.

"You ask what you can do? I say to you, swear yourselves to Moriana's cause as I have done myself!" And he nodded to Moriana, who stepped forward into the circle of torchlight.

The acclamation washed over her like the ocean's tide.

They had gained over five million klenor from Imin Dun Bacir in Tolviroth Acerte, the sum total of his personal fortune. As Moriana told him, his life was a bargain at any price.

Moriana had thought they had all the money they needed. To her chagrin, Darl corrected her. They had nowhere near the requisite amount to mount a campaign—or a single battle—against the Sky City.

Moriana and Darl remained another week in Tolviroth Acerte winnowing the mercenaries who thronged to the island in search of employment. They looked for leaders of proven skill and experience to command, and a few especially battle-hardened warriors to act as cadre for the volunteer armies Darl promised to raise. With the majority of Bacir's money remaining, the pair *then* started putting together an army.

Even after the news of the fall of Bilsinx reached the North, Moriana got no support from the surviving Quincunx Cities. Each had plans of its own for meeting this new menace, plans in which the pretender to the Beryl Throne didn't fit.

They continued from Wirix northwest to the River Merchant, which bordered that conglomeration of feuding states still called the Empire. Here Darl enjoyed his greatest renown. Here it was that he hoped to garner the bulk of the army to press Moriana's claim to the throne.

The princess still couldn't believe her good fortune in meeting the count-duke. Who else in all the Realm would swear to aid her to victory or follow her to defeat on their first encounter? Mere infatuation was unlikely to motivate anyone of intellect and talent to be of service to her.

But Darl's attraction for her was not the reason he joined her. The reason was simply as he'd stated it: he needed a cause. Without some crusade, some quest, his life lacked meaning. Challenging the City promised the adventure of a lifetime.

Moriana only marveled at the coincidence that brought him and her to Tolviroth Acerte at the same time. It was part and parcel of the bewildering luck she'd been experiencing. One minute she was given great good fortune, the next it was snatched away. It was as if some mad god toyed with her destiny.

But it was no mad god. It was the Destiny Stone.

She still believed she possessed the Amulet of Living Flame. She had marked the fluctuations in color, dark to light, light to dark, in the amulet's great jewel. She had even connected the shifts in hue with her own fortunes. But it never occurred to her that the talisman caused the twists in destiny. She merely thought the amulet had a subsidiary property of measuring a person's good fortune at any given instant. She credited it to the wisdom of the Athalar and thought no more about it.

Again Moriana marveled at her luck in finding Darl. He possessed the means of effectively accomplishing her ends. And he was a magician whose skills rivaled Synalon's.

Sorcery had nothing to do with his talent. His magic was in his tongue and the skill with which he plied it.

His speech was like a torch. It set afire the souls of those who heard it. When she thought about the things Darl had said, it seemed to Moriana there was little remarkable about them. But something in his manner of speaking, his presence, lifted men up and out of themselves. This was the greatest gift he brought to Moriana.

The chorus of approval roared on and on. Moriana faced the crowd, her head held high, trying to look noble and resolute. They would get a hundred volunteers from this gathering, perhaps more, and this was only a small meeting. Success rode the air like a banner.

And yet she irrationally felt uneasiness dogging her at every turn.

Prince Rann stalked the vaulted corridor that led to the queen's throne chamber. His steel-rimmed bootheels rapped authoritatively, echoes diminishing behind him like the wake of a ship. He wore new boots in the fashion of the Highgrass Broad riders. Unlike the light, soft, knee-high moccasins worn by the Sky City flyers, these were of heavy grazer leather and came to mid-thigh when unrolled. Now the tops were folded rakishly below the prince's knees. He had been given them as a gift from Destirin Luhacs, V'Duuyek's second-in-command, in commemoration of Bilsinx. They were too heavy to wear astride a war bird, but it pleased Rann to wear them about the palace.

He contemplated the coming interview with his cousin with great satisfaction. In the flush of conquest, she had forgotten all about the Athalau affair.

From Bilsinx, the Sky City had proceeded southward passing over Brev and then veering toward Thailot. Of all the Quincunx Cities, Brev was the weakest, and the Hereditary Council governing her knew it. As the City approached, they held hurried consultation, then sent word that the Sky City was as welcome as always to trade there. The City did not answer. Yet when its vast oblong filled Brev's sky, the cargo balloons drifting down held only magic artifacts and other trade goods.

The Sky City had bigger game in mind.

The three remaining Quincunx Cities followed Rann's expectations. Thailot couched its submission in terms of caring little what befell those on the other side of the Thails, but submitted nonetheless. Not so with Wirix and Kara-Est. The Jewel of Wir interned all Sky Citizens on the island and sent its defiance to Synalon. Kara-Est contemptuously expelled the Sky-Born and sent no other message to their aerie.

After Bilsinx was secured and Sky City agents had informed Rann by means of communicator crystals that the news had reached the seaport city, he dispatched a squad of Sky Guardsmen to make an aerial reconnaissance of Kara-Est. Intelligence reports indicated that the Estil were devoting their whole attention to shoring up their defenses.

Observers riding baskets slung from ludintip spotted the patrols' wings far off. No other living gasbags rose to challenge the bird riders. The Sky City commander gloated until the ballistae mounted on revolving platforms on Kara-Est's rooftops engaged his patrol. A steel missile pierced a rider's leg, pinning it to his mount's chest. A frantic midair rescue attempt failed. He plunged to death with his mount on the steep streets below. Another eagle was grazed by a bolt before the patrol winged out of range.

Rann had been furious at the news. But the setback was only temporary. Fate—or perhaps the Dark Ones— had gained the City time to prepare for its duel with Kara-Est. Rann knew how to make use of time. When the Sky City passed over the seaport, the groundlings would be amply repaid for their presumption.

Far more serious had been the tidings that Moriana had formed a liaison with Darl Rhadaman. The possibility existed, as much as Rann hated to admit it, that the slippery bitch and her new consort would be able to scrape together enough second sons, criminals, and others in the degenerate North to harry the City's lines of communication. If that happened, he would have to divert precious manpower to avert the threat.

Amazingly, Synalon had taken even that news with equanimity. Rann had expected that more than antique statuary would fall victim to her lightning bolts. But his royal cousin had merely nodded distractedly when he gave her the word and had gone back to feeding gobbets of raw meat to one of her loathsome talking ravens.

Now he was on his way to report that the palace mages met with greater success than anticipated in generating new fire elementals. The salamanders had a special role in the upcoming battle.

"Highness?"

The familiar nasal voice stopped him in his tracks. He wheeled to face Maguerr the mage.

"What is it?" Rann asked. The network of scars covering his face whitened at the strain of keeping his tones polite.

Maguerr was a pissant; what affronted the prince most was that Maguerr was an indispensable pissant. No other sorcerer in the City had his skill with the magics of communications crystals. Though Maguerr's manner with Rann was as unctuous as ever, Rann had to be polite—and he hated it. The rumor had even started that Synalon toyed with the idea of inviting Maguerr to her chambers for nocturnal consultations.

"Word comes from our agents in Kara-Est, lord." Maguerr fingered sandy wisps of beard. The gray and maroon robes of his recently earned mastery had not lent him dignity. He looked like a scrawny waif who had pilfered a Master Mage's wardrobe.

"Well, what is it?" demanded Rann impatiently.

Maguerr's head bobbed up and down as though on a string.

"Two strangers of a most peculiar variety, lord. They came from the south out of the Southern Steppes, and they rode giant bears."

Rann stared at him, eyes suddenly without color.

"One of them," Maguerr continued through his nose, "was no less than the hetwoman of a clan of bear-riding savages. The other . . ." and he preened like a warbird, ". . . the other was a Medurimite courier, Fost Longstrider by name."

Rann felt fingernails digging into his palms. He was glad his sleeves hid his hands. He didn't want Maguerr to guess the intensity of his reaction.

"So the Long-strider lives," he mused, almost glad. In his bumbling way, the courier had been a formidable opponent. "And the chieftain of the bear riders accompanies him. What can this mean, I wonder?" His mouth stretched into a taut grimace. He had not forgotten the Ust-alayakits, how they came from the night to take his Sky Guardsmen in the rear and slaughter them like children when he had the Long-strider at swords' points and Moriana not much farther away. Not since that terrible day in the Thails had he suffered such humiliation.

"Glad tidings you bring me, Maguerr, glad tidings indeed." He patted the adolescent on the shoulder. "I must confer with Her Majesty now. But await me in my chambers. We must discuss how best to use this intelligence of yours."

Without knowing why, Synalon came instantly awake.
She lay for a moment in her bed, straining to hear that which made no sound. She slowly identified those she could hear. From without came the noises caused by the wind in its ceaseless dance past the high windows. The low creakings and settling sounds of the floating City seemed to rumble up through her mattress and naked body. Steam from salamander-heated boilers whispered through a coil of brass pipes across the chamber from her great bed. The radiated heat kept away the worst of the night chill, but it was cold outside and the heavy quilted comforters felt good.

Yet the silken sheets matted to her profusely sweating body. Her well-honed instincts sensed a deadly danger lurking. She summoned up the mental clarity needed to cast firebolts before she scanned the darkened, sparsely appointed bedchamber.

One advantage to the austerity was that it left few places for an intruder to hide. The queen lay motionless, flickering her gaze along the walls: nothing. Lids low and feigning sleep, she rolled onto her back to search the other half of the chamber. The delightful, skin-prickling caress of the Wirix silk sheets on her nipples went unnoticed.

Still, the subliminal message of danger gnawed at her brain. Menace was near. She knew it. Finally, reluctantly, she looked toward the last direction from which a person in a raven-guarded citadel a mile above the earth would expect attack.

As she turned her attention to it, the window exploded inward.

She lay stunned as the doubled arch of glass and metal bowed inward and burst in a blizzard of glittering fragments. The carnage occurred in absolute silence. And for all its violence, it happened with awful deliberation, as if time had grown tired of its endless race and had slowed to catch its breath.

A galaxy of shards cascaded to the floor. Her years of probing the dark corners of the mystic had inured her to both wonder and horror. Yet this was so strange, so unnatural, that all she could do was lie and watch as the glass became a diamond pool of granules on the floor.

She looked up. A figure stood on the sill.

"Guard!" she shouted, even as she reached for the sheathed dagger under her mattress.

The door slammed open. She winced at the abrupt loudness. Two Palace Guards stood with swords clutched in trembling hands.

Her coverlet had fallen away, baring breasts that shone blue-white in the light of the lesser moon. Making no move to cover herself, the queen gestured at the black dwarf crouching on the still. The guardsmen charged.

The figure shook its head. Synalon discerned no features in the darkness, nothing about the intruder save that its proportions were those of a human dwarf with head large, torso small, and arms and legs stumpy and short. It reared up, however, to the height of a tall man. She caught a glimpse of blunt projections from either side of the long skull, and then the thing turned to face the onrushing guards.

The being laughed. Its chuckle gusted forth like a desert wind. Synalon saw it emerge as a mist of darkness that blew toward her attacking soldiers.

The breath-cloud roiled about the leading guard. He stopped, dropped his sword, and clapped hands to his face. The chamber rang with the sound of his shrill scream. Behind him, his companion stopped. He raised his weapon. The cloud enveloped him. He began to quiver and a gibbering sound, half laughter and half sobbing, bubbled from his lips.

The first guard dropped to his knees. His fingers

turned mottled and dark. Synalon watched as the flesh dropped away, leaving the bones as naked as dead twigs. The flesh of his face blackened, too. His eyes met hers, immense orbs goggling from pits of bone, in a look of agony and supplication. Then he fell forward. Seconds later the other guard joined him in death. Through the rippling of mail on mail, the queen distinctly heard the soft squashing of putrid flesh.

She moved quickly from the bed, the chill of the flagstones against her soles. With a conscious effort, she forced down the nausea she felt. She raised a silvery arm and aimed her hand at the apparition, palm foremost, fingers wide.

Power raged within her, fueled by fear and hatred and hot anger. The coverlet, bunched and fallen against one smooth thigh, began to smolder. Her hair lifted in a crackling cloud.

White fire blasted from her palm. Her eyes glowed like beacons as heat waves shimmered up from her pale, naked body. Never had she called up such power. The lightning bolt should have spattered the black apparition all over the room. It should have fused the very frame of the window into a vitreous lump.

It should have, it didn't. The lance of stark, raw energy lashed fully into the being's chest, then disappeared.

Synalon reeled. The stink of charred feathers from her coverlet seared her nostrils. She squinted at the glowing suns orbiting in front of her eyes. Beyond them, solid and black and impervious, stood the dwarf.

The thing chuckled again. The harsh and lifeless sound seemed more familiar to her now. Synalon poised for rapid action, but no cloud of corruption accompanied the laugh.

"Poor child," the creature said. It stepped from the sill. The huge, ungainly figure seemed to float to the floor as if being lowered gently from a balloon.

Synalon let her head slump. Her hair hung in midnight swirls down the slope of her breastbone. Her arms hung limp at her sides. The intruder chuckled again in approval of her apparent submission.

But it was only feigned. As the black soles noiselessly touched stone, a wild cry ripped the night and a bird streaked in through the gaping window. The raven darted in for the kill.

With venom-gleaming claws inches from its broad black shoulders, the intruder raised a finger. The raven's wings shot from its sides. It veered in the air and hurtled toward its mistress, who had mentally summoned it to her defense.

So astonished with Synalon by the raven's perfidy, she could do no more than stand and stare. Talons reached to rip tender flesh. The intruder laughed again, gesturing.

The raven vanished. A black rose fell to the floor at Synalon's feet. She raised wide, stark eyes to meet the intruder's ebony gaze.

"Have you not guessed the truth, little sister?" the apparition asked. "Or is this the way you greet the answering of your most fervent prayers?"

Then she knew. She had heard this voice before when the messenger of the Dark Ones had assumed the place of the fire elemental. At the realization, the being's form became familiar. With the stubs of horns jutting from its head, it was like a dwarfed cousin of the Vicar of Istu that stood in the Circle of the Skywell.

She fell to her knees. Exultation filled her. But it was exultation tinged with dread.

"Pardon, O messenger of the Great Lords," she said. "I could not know. . ."

The being shook its head cutting off her protestations.

"No harm done, except to your unfortunate bodyguards. It is what they are paid for, however." It chuckled again. "Besides, your precipitate action provided a useful lesson in the futility of opposing your will to even the lowliest servitor of the Dark Ones."

The queen slowly stood. Her limbs had turned weak and fluttery. She knew something was amiss. The sense of danger heightened.

"How may I serve you, Lord?"

"No lord I," the creature said, shaking its head. "And it is not my will you serve but that of my masters."

"Convey their commands, I beg you." Such humility was as alien to her lips as the taste of spoiled food. Yet it wasn't hard to muster deference in the face of such power.

"No commands—now," the messenger said, placing blunt fingertips together. "I am merely to tell you that the Aspects are almost right. Soon will come the time."

"Soon?" Synalon cried, her heart lurching within her breast. "And will I be the instrument of the Dark Ones' will?"

"It is as I have said," the apparition said. "But you must reaffirm your obedience to my masters."

"How?" Synalon asked, breathless with eagerness.

The creature smiled. Its teeth sent back curved glints of moonlight like twin rows of dusky pearls. It dropped gnarled hands down past its belly. Something dark grew from the juncture at its squatty legs. Synalon watched in fascination as it stretched toward her like a snake. The blunt head glistened like a dome of obsidian.

The Queen of the City in the Sky dropped again to her knees before the dwarf. Her hands, as hesitant as a virgin's, reached up to enfold the black member. She felt the pulsing of the great veins, as hot and fervent as any man's. Yet the skin was dry and leathery, a perfect match with the being's voice.

She opened her mouth to receive the benediction of the Dark Ones.

In the womb of night a dream of hate turned to one of pleasure.

Istu moaned in eternal sleep. The sleeping portion tensed for new disappointment. The last time it had known this peculiar excitement, this tingling delight in stony loins, it had been cruelly jerked away by rending agony. The demon slept, but it remembered.

But this pleasure was no ephemeral delight. It lingered. It grew. It crept like a vine up the imprisoned demon's spine. Softness, moistness, supplication, filled the sleeping mind with lusty sensation.

Images swarmed before the sleeping demon: a white body spread-eagled on a stone altar, with golden hair strewn in wild disarray; a silvery pale body bathed in moonlight, kneeling, faced a whiteness glimpsed through jet hair. The images expanded. The Sleeper felt the brush of thighs on hips taut with fear and horror; willing lips caressed its stony pillar. Hot tightness and futile struggle for escape drew the Sleeper's soul into a knot of delectable tension. Wet pressure, slipping, sliding, moving faster and faster. No longer chained to the altar. But still helpless. The demon's excitement soared.

And the familiar black hair, the pallid skin, the musk scent of excitement reached the Dreamer's nostrils. The one who had summoned him before only to tantalize and torture moved before him with deliberate actions. Certainty pervaded the sleeping demon that it would not be denied again. The black-haired one would make good on the pain she'd caused him before.

Hands reached to grip her. Black hands, thick-fingered and familiar, yet alien felt and caused the Sleeper to feel. They gripped, twisted, pulled. Blue eyes flicked up, wide with anxiety. Istu felt himself sinking into a bottomless pit of ecstasy.

Vicarious ears heard the equal of pain and fear. The Sleeper felt acquiescence enfolding it and gave itself up to pleasure.

A rushing dragged the Sleeper onward filling it with tautness, and the pressure exploded outward in a blaze of dark light. Squeals mounting like steps came to its ears like a song of joy. Blind delight pounded in its loins.

In time the fury ebbed. The Sleeper's mind sank into a soothed and peaceful slumber. The bribe had been accepted.

Sleeping, the demon was little more than a child. It might not be reasoned with, but it could be bought with pleasure.

The Dark Ones would have Istu's obedience when released from bondage, even if his mind remained locked in the torpor imposed by Felarod. And far above the stone bubble still ringing with the bellows of a demon's ecstasy, the messenger of the Dark Ones reflected that a job well done brought more rewards than one.

"Aren't you worried that Gabric will find you, Fost?" asked Erimenes.

"That eunuch!" said Fost, making a face in his ale. "He'd be too busy counting his klenor to notice his own building burning down around his ears."

The tavern bustled around them. Locations might change, Fost mused as he sipped his brew, but taverns, never. The alehouses of Kara-Est differed little from those of Medurim; those here in Tolviroth Acerte weren't distinguishable from any others. Perhaps inland taverns had a different milieu, but seaport taverns were all the same.

In his current state, this insight represented profound thinking on Fost's part. He had drunk too much. At his side Jennas, who had been induced to try the local dark ale instead of her *amasinj,* matched him mug for mug and showed no effects. He displayed a tendency to rock gently from side to side as though he stood on the slickened deck of a sea-tossed ship.

It might have been newly acquired habit, though. The pair had just spent twenty-three days beating up the choppy Karhon Channel in Captain Karlaya's

Wavestrider en route to Tolviroth Acerte. It had been a trying voyage. Two days running they had to stand in along the coast while a gale blew down the channel. Winter weather wasn't too extreme due to the slight axial tilt, and the considerable extent of the polar caps owed mainly to the smallness and coolness of the sun. However, the world also orbited near the primary, giving moderately short seasons. Midwinter had come and gone while the *Wavestrider* worked her dogged way toward Tolviroth Acerte.

Karlaya's predominately female crew inspired Erimenes to new heights of inventiveness. Sailors the world over being what they are, the spirit's imaginative lechery was greeted with much amusement by the crew.

Fost had a vague suspicion that some of his companion's more outrageous proposals had been carried out. The equinox celebration had occasioned much merriment and consumption of potent Jorean rum among Karlaya's crew. The Jorean mariners kept on good terms with Somdag Squid-face, God and Protector of Realm seamen. But he was not their deity. Instead, the Joreans worshipped Gormanka of the Wind-Wheel, like Ust the Bear, a patron of the Realm couriers. But so they would slight no one, they saluted all the deities, singing and dancing, during which the revelers became progressively less clad. Naked bodies, black and white, goose-fleshed and sweat-polished, writhed passionately under the yellow light of the torches. And after that, in Karlaya's snug cabin in the sterncastle . . .

He didn't really remember more than the gaiety on deck. But the next day Jennas seemed more subdued than called for due to the aftereffects of the rum, and Fost had overheard her informing Erimenes in a low, lethally serious voice that if he ever so much as alluded to the activities of the night before, she'd heave him into the channel.

Now Fost did his level best to recapture the state

he was in for the equinoctial festivities aboard *Wavesrider*. He had arrived in Tolviroth Acerte to find that Moriana, Darl, and their carefully screened cadre had departed eight days before for the Continent. Jennas could hardly hide her satisfaction at the news.

Fost's reaction to his latest failure to catch the princess was to get stinking drunk.

"And whom are you calling a eunuch?" a voice bellowed from the tavern door.

Fost pulled his snout out of the earthenware flagon. The rude, grating voice hailing him sounded familiar, though in his befuddlement he couldn't quite place it. Nonetheless, his guts tensed in anticipation of trouble.

Broad shoulders blocked the tavern door. Below them the shape gave way to an equally broad chest and still broader belly, strong legs widely planted. Above, the outline rose to something of a point without the apparent intervention of a neck.

The image snapped Fost's brain into focus. He raised mug to lips, sipped insolently.

"Well met, Merchant Gabric," he said. "How's business?"

"As good as may be expected when my top courier takes unauthorized leave." Gabric stepped into the room, arms laid like hawsers across his chest.

"If I'm your top courier, you should pay me top money." He took a measured draft. "But that's academic now. I don't work for you any longer. You can consider my resignation retroactive to the beginning of my last assignment. That way, you needn't worry about severance pay."

"It's not that easy, you rogue," Gabric shouted, his jowls turning ruddy. "You have commitments to me! You've taken my coin. You can't just say, 'I quit,' and have done with it."

Fost shrugged. He turned away, feigning disinterest.

"Fost's right, you know," a voice commented at the courier's crooked elbow. "You *are* a eunuch, Gabric.

In fact, has anyone informed you that you bear the most striking resemblance to a gelded hornbull?"

Gabric's face slowly went from the hue of a cherry to a beet to a ripe eggplant. Worn-thick blood vessels throbbed at his bald temples as he leaned forward, blinking in the gloom at the thin, translucent figure wavering beside Fost.

"Aha!" the merchant roared in a voice that made his earlier outbursts sound like whispers. "You're not just a contract breaker, you low cur. You're a thief, as well!"

Some inches taller than Fost, he drew himself up to his full height and pointed accusingly at the black-haired courier.

"I hereby charge you with commercial malfeasance. To wit, that you did willfully and without authorization take leave of your duties in violation of your contract with Gabric Exports, Inc., and did furthermore misappropriate to your own use property paid for and duly consigned to one Kest-i-Mond, mage, county of Samadum." He lumbered forward with heavy menace, looking like some shaved cousin of Grutz or Chubchuk. "I take you into custody, as called for by the Tolvirot Commercial Code, Section Forty-six, Sub-paragraph A."

Fost leaned back against the bar. He had no contract with Gabric, and there was no wrongdoing in his having possession of Erimenes. Kest-i-Mond had been dead before the courier delivered the wayward spirit to him. The courier started to explain this to Gabric. He had forgotten, however, the full extent of Erimenes' waywardness.

"You and what army, blubber-belly?" taunted Erimenes cheerfully.

"Great Ultimate," Fost moaned. Gabric had no claim against him. But if a scuffle broke out thanks to Erimenes' vicarious bloodlust, Fost could wind up in serious trouble. The Toviroh authorities would not look kindly on anyone damaging a merchant as prosperous as Gabric.

Jennas hissed beside him. He looked toward the door and tensed.

"Fortunate you asked us along, good Gabric," said a whip-thin voice. "This ruffian seems of a mind to give you trouble."

The owner sauntered through the door, gauntleted thumbs thrust through his sword belt. He was a small man, his wiry frame clad in an impeccable livery of black and purple. The sword at his waist was curved as were the sidearms of the five men following him into the tavern.

"Aye, that he is," smirked Gabric.

"When did you expand into the novelty pet line, Gabric?" asked Fost, eyeing the sextet of Sky City bird riders.

Gabric's pig eyes rolled from the soldiers to Fost. Beads of perspiration gleamed on his brow.

"I knew you might prove difficult since you've always been inclined toward fiscal instability and might prove unwilling to retire your debts. I asked these gentlemen to accompany me. They're the new Sky City trade delegation."

"Trade delegation," snorted Fost. If any of these bird riders had even been involved in any exchange other than sword thrusts, he'd eat Grutz, hair and all.

A sinking sickness settled into Fost's belly. The soldiers' presence meant Rann had found out he still lived. At this stage in their conquest, the City in the Sky did not want to risk murdering a man in Tolviroth Acerte who was nominally a citizen of the City of Bankers. But if its agents accompanied someone with a commercial grievance against the courier in the expectation he might prove obstinate . . .

"Do what you want to the courier," said the leader of the bird riders. "But we get the barbarian girl. *Re-*

member." His voice snapped at Gabric like a lash. The merchant bobbed his head.

The crowd pressed back. Gabric closed in and a sliver of steel sprouted from one hand, incongruously slim in the vast paw gripping its hilt. Behind Gabric the bird riders drew swords.

"You've an insolent tongue, Longstrider," growled Gabric. "I think I'll cut it out."

Fost swept his arm around in a blur, his half-filled mug slamming into Gabric's face. The merchant dropped like a bag of wheat. Seeing this, the bird riders lunged in. A whining arc of steel sent them leaping back as Jennas whirled her greatsword. The leader spat a command. They spread out. Inn patrons vanished like quicksilver. Gabric moaned and tried to rise, fingers groping for his gilded dagger. Fost kicked him hard in the belly.

"Bravo!" cheered Erimenes.

Fost feinted at a bird rider, spun, and hacked at another who'd closed in quickly believing the courier's back exposed. A frantic move interposed the smaller man's scimitar between broadsword and his flesh. The bird rider fell, stunned by the force of the blow. As he tumbled backward, he carried the others with him.

Fost couldn't fight well in the cramped interior. He motioned Jennas outside. She lunged for the door, then paused to look back at him. The courier waved her forward again. She ran out into the street with Fost close behind while the Sky City men tried to reorganize.

A staggering patron stumbled into Fost's way. The courier considered the cries from behind him, the drunkard and the impossibility of escaping quickly through the door. So he tucked Erimenes' satchel safely behind him and hurled himself through the large leaded-glass window fronting the tavern.

Glass exploded into the street. Riding dogs barked in surprise. Jennas had already mounted Chubchuk, waving her sword in the faces of a fresh trio of the men in Sky City colors.

Fost threw himself over Grutz's broad back and clung. Pursuers boiled from the door of the tavern, trampling the drunk. As Fost hauled himself to a sitting position, Jennas kicked Chubchuk into a shambling lope up the brick street.

Finally astride, Fost set off after Jennas. Grutz rumbled smugly to himself as he ran with surprising speed. From the other end of the block came a new commotion. The watchmen from Peacekeepers, Inc., had arrived on the scene.

Tarinvar the Steersman sat by the rail of the lugger *Gallinule* scrimshawing a piece of juggernaut fish ivory none too skillfully when he heard a frightful thrashing in the water.

He raised his head. The carving fell from numbed fingers. Clambering up the far railing was a demon twice the size of a man and dripping with water and weeds. Tarvinar's eyes tried to pop from their sockets. The demon returned his stare with a red-rimmed scowl.

"Grrr," said the demon.

Tarinvar leaped over the side, not waiting to hear more.

The bosun emerged from the midship's cabin and came running aft. The first thing he saw was the inexpert idol of Somdag Squid-face which Tarinvar had left behind. The second thing he saw was the monster. Dark and malignant, it hunched near the stern, swiveling its misshapen head. Its gaze came to rest on the bosun.

Heart threatening to explode from fear, the bosun leaped to the railing, then pressed the back of one of his hands to his lips, wagged his fingers in imitation of Papa Squid's squiggly visage to invoke the deity's protection, and dived overboard.

"Monsters!" the cry came from the rigging above. A seaman dived past. He fell in the greasy water of Tolviroth Harbor with a prodigious splash, just as a second intruder clambered over the gunwales.

Blinking saltwater from his eyes, Fost cleared his vision in time to see another dozen men in seamen's garb erupt from a hatch, dash to the railing, and jump overboard in a formation that would have done credit to a squad of Sky Guardsmen. Every one piously wiggled fingers in front of his face before diving. The cry, "Demons" came floating up from the water like a seabird's call.

Fost looked around in surprise. He had thought the skirmish in the tavern had sobered him up. A few feet away, Grutz pawed irritably at the seaweed wound around his head. Water had soaked his fur, matting the hair into flat, scaly wedges.

Chubchuk hoisted himself up through a gap in the rail, a thoroughly sodden Jennas still clinging to his back. She shook limp auburn hair from her eyes.

"Where is everybody?" she demanded.

"I may be insane," Fost said, the eerie silence making him shiver, "but I swear the crew jumped over the rail as I came aboard."

A spashing by the hull drew their attention. They leaned over the rail in time to see a flotilla of bobbing heads round the *Gallinule*'s stern and strike, out for the wharf a hundred yards away.

"Demons," they heard one call. "Blessed Samdag deliver us from the dreadlings of the deep!"

Fost and Jennas stood for a moment, looked at Grutz, then broke out laughing. A damp, seaweed-festooned bear emerging from the sea had to qualify as startling.

"When you collect your feeble wits," said Erimenes acidly, "you might find out if there's someone aboard who knows how to steer this contraption. And you'd

best be prompt about it. Your oaf of a former employer
has just arrived at the wharf with his associates."

Fost glanced shoreward. A crowd gathered on the
dock. A number were plainly onlookers, but among
the mob Fost spotted a knot of Sky City soldiers.

"You're right, Erimenes," said Fost. "Time to de-
part."

"Before you rush off," said Erimenes, "Would you
please empty this damned water from my jug? I shipped
a gallon of the foul stuff. It sloshes unmercifully. I
just know I'll become seasick if you don't do something quickly."

Laughing, Fost emptied a brown stream from the
jar. Then he turned away in search of anyone who remained of the *Gallinule*'s crew.

A breeze quested through tufts of dry, dead grass.
Tiny hints of green could be glimpsed at the bases of
the tufts where new shoots pushed up through the earth.
Snow lay in clumps; more would fall before the season
ended. But the hardy growth of the Sundered Realm
began its annual struggle for supremacy quite soon after
the days began to lengthen and grew imperceptibly
warmer.

Moriana walked along a bluff with the stiff grasses
brushing her legs. The grass clutched at the skirt of her
pale beige gown. She nodded absently to herself, mark-
ing the feel of the cloth swaying against her skin. After
so long in tunic, boots, and breeches, it was strange to
be clad in this fashion.

A strap crossed one shoulder. From it hung the
Athalar spirit jar, its lid open. Ziore hovered at Moriana's side like a benevolent pink cloud.

The princess sat, gathering her cloak about her.
From her vantage point, she saw the camp marching
before her: orderly rows of tents, columns marching
and countermarching in a fallow field, soldiers at practice with sword and spear, shooting arrows at targets,

the cordoned kennels for the cavalry mounts, the bawling herd of one-horned ruminants penned beyond to serve as provender for men and mounts alike. Banners sprouted from flagpoles of tents like exotic blossoms. Paramount flew Moriana's own device, an eagle's claw clutching a scarlet flower against a field of pale blue.

"I should be happy, Ziore, shouldn't I?" she asked, watching the banners dance in the wind.

"You make it sound like a duty," the spirit said.

Moriana shrugged. She had picked a bare spot of earth to sit on. Her forefinger drew random shapes in the dirt.

"Look, Ziore," she said, sweeping her hand in a gesture encompassing the camp. "Almost eight thousand men gathered at my feet. If Darl is right, we'll have ten thousand by the time we march south. Ten thousand men, Ziore—the whole population of the City is less than three times that. It's power, more than I ever thought I could muster against my sister."

Ziore poised, waiting. The wind sighed through the bottomland of the tributaries of the great River Marchant. The main flow ran northeast a quarter mile away; on the far bank lay the Empire. Eastward, Omizantrim squatted like a stone effigy. A thin spire of vapor rose from its maw and was lost in the high haze drifting overhead. Ominous as the mountain was, it had laid a blessing on this land. The vomitus cast up over eons from the entrails of the earth was rich in minerals. Crops grew lush to the very brink of the badlands kept desolate by lava and poison vapors from the volcano.

Somewhere to the south floated the City in the Sky. In the weeks since Moriana and Darl had left Tolviroth Acerte, it had passed over Thailot where trade proceeded as if nothing untoward had come to pass. Wirix met the City's passage with sullen defiance—it was almost certainly the last the Sky City would assault. Brev and Thailot were easier targets, Kara-Est immeasurably more valuable. A few days before, the chance that guided the Floating City had turned it southward to pass over its new dominion of Bilsinx.

Ziore's patience had a relentless quality to it that Moriana could never outmatch. She inhaled, held it, then let it out slowly.

"I'm grateful to Darl," she said. "No one would— no one could—do for me what he's doing. And yet . . . yet it begins to feel wrong somehow. Events move past my control. And how can I complain? He's doing me a favor."

A many-throated shout caught her attention. She turned to see Darl riding in from the wooded hills on his tall war mount. He raised a hand. Instantly, a mob surrounded him. Idlers, officers, soldiers at their soldierly tasks, all gathered around crying out their devotion and their love. He raised a salute now, turning his head this way and that. Moriana knew he grinned that grin of his, a look she had come to know well in the last few weeks, a look she thought turned to love.

Ziore laid a hand on her shoulder. She reached up to stroke it though she knew the warmth was no more than a comforting illusion produced by the spirit.

"Such devotion," the nun's ghost said. "It borders on adoration. These men had never before laid eyes on Darl Rhadaman six weeks ago, and now they would lay their lives at the feet of his war dog." Moriana looked up at her. She looked deep into the living woman's eyes.

"I know little of this world, child, but it seems to me such loyalty is a potent force, as potent in its way as force of arms or numbers."

"Loyalty, aye," she all but spat, her face hardening involuntarily into bitter planes. "Loyalty to *him*."

"And this troubles you? You resent that their loyalty is given to him but not to you?"

"No." But she turned her eyes away.

"It can be no other way." Ziore smiled sadly. "You admitted that your resources were inadequate to muster support among the northerners. Not even among the people of the Quincunx could you raise an army. Thanks to Darl's persuasion the emissaries of Kara-Est and Wirix have promised to help provision your armies en route." She touched Moriana's cheek. "I know it is hard on you. But you cannot evade the knowledge that without him you'd be unable to challenge Synalon."

Moriana tried to hold in the tears that stung her eyes, tears of anger, of frustration, of the self-disgust that had grown to be an inextricable part of her soul in the weeks since that terrible day in the glacier when she'd had to murder the man she loved for the sake of her City. Her fingers groped blindly for the amulet hanging about her neck. She clung to it as if she could find strength in it.

"There's more to it than that," she said.

"That, too, cannot be changed," Ziore said. "This is the North. Customs differ here."

There was another reason Darl had become the focal point of the crusade against the City, and Moriana drew ever farther from it. In the southern lands of the Sundered Realm, women and men existed in general parity. Armies frequently consisted of both sexes in the same proportion of the population. The second-in-command of the mercenary band Rann had hired as ground troops was a woman. Women had equal say in governments as well, from the chief deputy of Kara-Est to warrior-chieftainnesses of the steppes like Jennas. In the Sky City women ruled by law and custom; though the rank and file of its military was male, Moriana had first been blooded while commanding troops in the war five years before with the Golden Barbarians who had invaded the savannah west of the Thails and terrorized the country between Deepwater and the Sjedd.

In the northern half of the Realm it was different.

Darl's triumphant procession reached the pavilion he shared with Moriana. He dismounted, handing the reins to a soldier eager to do his least bidding. Then, as was his custom, he turned and knelt, abasing himself before Moriana's banner.

Moriana didn't need to turn back to Ziore to know what the spirit felt. The words ran through her mind: *his loyalty is to you.* She shook her head.

Darl's loyalty was unquestioned. And he reaffirmed over and over that he followed Moriana's flag, turning the suspicion of the earthbound toward her into a kind of reverence. Yet that very reverence passed *through* Darl, just as (according to pagan priests of the Far Archipelago) divine essence passed through them to the faithful.

"I'm a figurehead," Moriana said quietly. "A symbol, a living emblem. Not a shaper, not a leader of all the forces gathered in my name."

That's unworthy of you, Ziore mentally rebuked her.

Moriana's hands clenched the amulet as if to crush it. Yes, the thought was unworthy. She knew it and despised it. She loathed herself for the ingratitude that made her resent her greatest benefactor.

But deep inside her mind festered a suspicion that more lay behind her concern than childish petulance, that the channel along which she felt her crusade being diverted might dash everything to ruin. The thought tingled and stung like a pulled muscle. She suppressed it. It was rationalization, nothing more.

Within her hands, darkness slipped across the face of the Destiny Stone.

CHAPTER TEN

Tapers burned low, flickering in figured sconces. Gargoyle faces graven into the stone of the chamber by some long-dead, inhuman hand winked at Prince Rann from shadowed walls. He pored over his plans to meet the threat of Moriana's ragtag army.

A knock on the chamber door broke his concentration.

"Her Majesty would speak with you, Highness," a voice came tentatively. "She awaits your pleasure in her chambers."

"I come," said Rann, draining his goblet. He rose, paused to take a fur-trimmed cloak from the outstretched talon of a fiend on which it hung, and draped it around his shoulders. Synalon's latest fancy was to keep the windows of her throne room wide, day and night. Spring was still weeks distant.

He followed the servant down the corridor to a steeply pitched flight of stairs. Two palace guards stood erect in their sculptured breastplates and greaves. They thumped their weapons' butts ceremoniously on the floor as Rann walked between them without acknowledging their presence.

Clad in a filmy gown the color of her hair, Synalon lounged by an open window. The landscape spread before her, yellow and white, patched over with shadows of drifting clouds. Off in the east, past where the land fell away from the central massif and rolled gently to the sea, Kara-Est readied itself for war.

"Greetings, cousin," said Synalon without turning. The way she draped herself against the window's frame made her seem part of the design, a sinuous and erotic embellishment. The gossamer material of her gown clung to her limbs like lover's fingers.

"What is your pleasure, Majesty?" asked Rann, bowing deeply.

"Are you ready to crush the upstarts challenging me in the name of that slut Moriana?" she demanded.

"Quite, dear cousin. V'Duuyek will ride north with nine hundred of his men leaving the other three hundred to garrison Bilsinx in case the Estil try to be clever. We've five hundred of our own dog riders accompanying him and eleven hundred infantry. Additionally, we have a thousand Bilsinxt light-dog bowmen for scouting and skirmishing." Synalon raised an eyebrow at this. Rann smiled with a touch of impudence. The thousand Bilsinxt mounted archers represented a victory for him.

Rann did not possess the preternatural gift of oratory that animated Darl Rhadaman. Yet he was a skillful enough speaker and he knew well the ways and weaknesses of humankind. He had called the citizenry of Bilsinx before him in the Central Square the day after the assault. It wasn't subjugation the Sky City offered, he'd told them. Partnership, rather, in a glorious enterprise that would make the City the foremost power in the Sundered Realm. Mere aggrandizement at the expense of the Quincunx had not been the City's goal. Instead, the City's ruler, the bold and brilliant Queen Synalon, wished to streamline the inefficient process of trade among the Cities and the City and meld the Quincunx and the Sky into one powerful, smoothly functioning entity to stand against an envious world.

He reminded Bilsinx of the "merciful" character of the conquest. There had been no fires, no looting, no widespread slaughter or property destruction. The only ones who had been harmed were those offering resistance. He had told the populace he regretted even those deaths. The shedding of Bilsinxt blood, the martyrdom of so many brave soldiers fighting nobly—if misguidedly—in defense of their homes, would not have been necessary but for the obstinate unreason of Irb and his sycophants. The wicked mayor had been punished; Bilsinx and the Sky City were now one. It remained only to put hard feelings behind and forge a bond of eternal friendship between two great peoples.

A wave of restrained approval met his words. Irb had not been popular among his subjects. But the Bilsinxt had heard tales of dark and bloody retribution meted out by Synalon and Rann. This avowal of friendship and the chance to share in the Sky City's greatness were unexpected. The cheers had been sporadic at first, then turned into a wave of acclamation.

The Sky City need have no fear of rebellion in Bilsinx.

"We can't spare many flyers," Rann went on. "I believe that a squadron of two hundred fifty common bird riders will suffice. Moriana notwithstanding, the Northerners have no experience fighting bird riders."

Synalon turned. One leg was cocked, the foot resting insouciantly on the windowsill. The other dangled downward to the floor. She nodded slowly.

"And who commands? Not Count Ultur, surely?"

"I will, Majesty." Rann frowned.

"Really?" said Synalon, feigning surprise. "You intend to desert the City at the crucial moment of our preparations to conquer Kara-Est? You disappoint me, cousin."

He could scarcely believe what Synalon was saying. He had to lead the expedition against Moriana. Their best intelligence—and it was good—indicated that her army outnumbered the City's forces two to one. In spite of this, Rann felt confident of success. Had he not led the combined armies of the City, Thailot, Deepwater, and the other cities of the West, outnumbered and disorganized as they were, to victory over the nerveless slave-warriors of the Golden Barbarians?

"Majesty," he said, voice rasping with sudden dryness. "Surely you don't expect me to stay!"

"Oh, but I do." Her voice was like the caress of a silken whip, soft and yet deeply cutting. "You are needed here, cousin mine. At such a juncture I cannot chance the loss of your cogent brain." She allowed her lips a subtle curl.

"But I have to lead the expedition! However much you value my . . . cogency, we cannot have Moriana's rabble rampaging through our supply lines. With all due modesty, Majesty, only *I* can guarantee that they will be stopped before they endanger our hold on the ground."

"Your post is here!" rapped Synalon. Then the harshness flowed from her features and she smiled with mocking gentleness. "Besides, good cousin, you don't think any Northblood savages can defeat our armies, do you?"

He stood without responding, feeling his limbs turn leaden, feeling the tightening in his bowels, the stinging at the backs of his eyes. For some reason, he was reminded of the frustration of his youth when his best efforts had failed in learning even the simplest magical lore.

Synalon watched him. Her head tipped forward, slim brows sweeping up like wings, her mouth curved into a coquettish smile. Yet her eyes were mad lamps. She inflicted her insane whim on him, punishing him for his failure to make an end to Moriana Athalau. That her petulance could make her dreams crumble like a dead, dried leaf did not stay her. Perhaps she didn't realize the danger of holding Rann back now. Perhaps she did.

With bile burning his throat, he bowed, turned, and was gone.

Synalon's laughter followed him like the chime of a tarnished silver bell.

* * *

An arrow thumped sod an arm's length from Grutz's churning haunch. Fost turned in his saddle and flung back a defiant curse at his pursuers. It was all he had to hurl at them.

"Curs! Cowards!" shrilled Erimenes, his vaporous being shaking with rage. "Stand. Turn and fight the rogues. Oh, the dishonor of it all!"

"Is he always like that?" called Jennas from Chubchuk's broad back.

"He's worse at times," Fost said.

The two bears loped across the undulating hills of the Highgrass Broad. The tall grasses that gave the land its name whipped their flanks, urging them to greater speed. Erimenes hovered at Fost's elbow, occasionally blurring and dissipating in the breeze but always reforming to heap further curses on the fleeing pair. Looking back in exasperation, Fost saw that the score of dog-mounted archers was gradually falling behind. Relief flowed through him like liquor. Not even Jennas, ferocious as she was, favored giving battle when they'd been ambushed. All the courage in the world wouldn't prevent the lethal steel broadheads from finding their marks.

As if to reaffirm the fact, an arrow sped past Fost's ear.

"On!" he shouted at Grutz, drumming his heels into the bear's ribs. Armored in fat and fur, the beast never felt him. But he heard the nasty whine of arrows and the baying of twenty hounds. Even a war bear of the steppes knew when not to buck the odds.

"You call yourselves heroes!" cried Erimenes disdainfully. "Yet you turn your backs and flee like rabbits at the first sign of danger. Oh, that my poor eyes must witness such craven, fainthearted cowardice!"

"When did we ever call ourselves heroes, you blue flatulence?" shouted Fost. "If you want to fight the dog riders, go back and do it yourself!" Jerking savagely at

Grutz's reins, he wheeled the bear around to face the onrushing riders. Howling like their dogs, the men rushed forward.

Fost snatched at the satchel strap and began whirling it around his head like a sling.

"What are you doing?" Erimenes wailed.

"Giving you a chance to taste the joys of battle first-hand."

"My jug!" moaned the spirit. "You'll break my jug! Oh, how can you be so heartless?"

"If I don't throw you at them, will you, by the Great Ultimate, *shut up?*"

"Y-yes!"

Jennas was a hundred yards away and moving fast. "Come on, you Ust-forgotten fool!" she shouted.

Fost turned Grutz around and booted him. A flight of arrows moaned by and were lost in the weeds.

"For this I gave up being a courier," muttered Fost. Then he was galloping full tilt down a hill to catch up with Jennas.

The Red Bear rolled the sun down the sky. The pursuers gradually fell back as the land became more uneven. Finally, they became lost in the settling evening gloom.

Fost and Jennas camped on a bank above a stream. The crisp, cold water made a sound like sipans clinging in a beggar's cup as it tumbled its endless way toward the Wirin River. The bears drank greedily, splashing and snorting, their muzzles black with water. Most of the year, water was scarce on the Southern Steppe. It had turned warm early in the north this year; all but a fringe of ice at the edge of the stream had melted. Grutz and Chubchuk fished. Their long talons swept a half-dozen fish wriggling onto the shore where Fost dispatched them by slamming their heads against a rock.

Jennas squatted on the bank, face bronzed by the

maiden glow of the fire she was building. Snow had already given way to rain here at the northwestern edge of the Highgrass country, but many peasants had stored more firewood than they needed last autumn and were willing to sell the fuel. Grutz and Chubchuk sat haunch to furry haunch attacking shrubs growing above the water. Fost grimaced. Snowberries had a powerful purgative effect on humans, as he'd discovered to his acute embarrassment early in his career as courier. Apparently the tiny blue-green berries didn't have the same effect on bears. They had been eating them all the way across the broad without showing any ill effects.

"Ah," said Erimenes, swaying slightly in the breeze. "Nothing like a fine fire on a cold winter's evening." Fost scowled at him but said nothing. Whether in affectation or simply by habit (what with surviving fourteen hundred years of afterlife), he held his spectral blue hands over the fire as if to warm them.

Fost dropped the fish on the grass at Jennas's side. The bears continued noisily consuming their berries. They would catch their own fish later on. Their talent for fishing had been an unexpected benefit of their presence. Since neither Fost nor Jennas had the slightest skill with missile weapons, hunting meat posed a problem, and not even Fost's dwindling supply of gemstones looted from Athalau would survive the prices the peasants charged for livestock, a precious commodity in this war-torn land.

Fost cut a branch from a bush stripped by the bears and whittled it to a point. The fire blazed up eagerly, as if anticipating the roasting fish.

Fost impaled a fish on a sharpened twig and handed it to Jennas. He stuck another on the branch he'd sharpened for himself. The nomad woman stuck her fish into the upper reaches of the flame where it soon began to crack lustily. A succulent odor drifted from the fire.

As his own fish browned, Fost eyed his companion. Her face was as impassive as ever, even in the orange firelight. But he could tell she was troubled.

"We'll reach Moriana's army tomorrow," he said. He watched the woman closely. A muscle tightened at the corner of her jaw. "Why did you come, Jennas? I know you . . . you care for me. This has to be painful for you."

She said something he didn't catch. He asked her to repeat it.

"I didn't come for your sake," she said softly.

"I'm glad of that," he said in a neutral tone.

She looked at him sharply.

"You don't believe me?" He didn't reply. "I could say you flatter yourself, but that's not so. I like the nearness of you. I'd make you my mate if I could, and it's a sorrow to me that you stay set on this Sky City wench who stabbed you once already. But it is not for your sake that I left the steppe. It is for my people."

He said nothing. One of the bears licked noisily at a paw smeared with sweet juices and ambled down to the stream. A moment later the other joined him. There soon came a splat-splash! of their broad paws slapping fish from the water.

"I have dreamed again," she said. "Ust warns me that time is short. He has not told me so, but I feel this coming battle will be crucial. That somehow its outcome may lead to a release of powers once thought chained forever."

Fost felt a prickling at the back of his neck. The only powers he knew that were "chained forever" were those of the demon Istu, offspring of the Dark Ones, who slumbered beneath the streets of the City in the Sky. Having encountered a fragment of the demon's subconscious, Fost found it disconcerting to face the prospect of the demon actually being loosed.

"Maybe you read too much into these dreams, Jennas. I've never had a god appear to me, but I've read accounts of those who have. The gods seem fond of generalities. I'm sure if you looked at whatever it was that Ust told you, you'd find it to be no more than the customary calls for charity, pious thoughts, and good hygiene."

"Do not mock me."

"I don't. I'm serious, even if I'm too flippant in the way I put things. But I can't credit all this talk of a War of Powers. The old one, yes, I'm willing to admit it happened as legends say. But that was ten thousand years ago, Jennas, a hundred centuries. Most of the magic's gone out of the world. The gods have grown tired with it. They've gone on to other playthings."

Jennas stared at him, her expression one of wonder.

"But you are the Chosen of Ust. You owe your life to his intercession. Don't you believe in him? Can't you feel his nearness, here, now, in this place at this moment?"

A bear snorted behind Fost. He jumped, turned around. Grutz grunted to him and continued shoving a fish into his mouth.

"You're ready enough to acknowledge the existence of evil beings," Jennas said, reproach in her voice. "You can't deny the reality that is the Demon of the Dark Ones, can you? Why do you turn from the Wise Ones, then?"

Gingerly, he plucked his fish from the spit and broke it apart. The meat inside was still steaming. He took a mouthful, chewed it thoughtfully, and swallowed before answering.

"I can't deny the truth of what you say," he conceded. "I do find it easier to admit the existence of personified evil than of good. It fits in better with the way the world seems to be." He broke off another chunk of flesh and tucked it into his mouth. "And my experience," he added wryly, "shows more evil than good all around."

"I think," said Erimenes, "that the real question is what motivates you on this fool's errand, Fost."

"What?"

"You may not have the Amulet of Living Flame but you have its gift. Or have you forgotten? You lay dead, stabbed by the Princess Moriana about whose welfare you wax so solicitous. And the amulet returned your worthless life to you." He spoke bitterly. He had desired the amulet to restore his own life, to permit him the worldly pleasures he had denied himself so long ago.

"You have your life. You are young, strong, presentable. You have a pocketful of gold. And what do you do with these precious gifts, these things for which I would give even my immortality? You spurn them. Instead of enjoying them to the fullest, you go rampaging off across the countryside in pursuit of the very golden-haired witch who killed you, not to wring from her your just revenge but to warn her of the peril of the Destiny Stone!" He shook his head. His long, ascetic nose was pinched in distaste. "You are indeed a fool, O Fost."

"So I'm a fool," said Fost angrily. "What of it?"

"It is time to consider your motivations, as I said. I think you know what drives you to this foolishness."

"Pray enlighten me," Fost said sarcastically. He felt his anger smoldering. What right did this treacherous, lecherous old wraith have to speak like this?

"When you were a child," said Erimenes, "did not your parents die? Were you not left an orphan?"

"Yes," Fost said, puzzled. "They were killed in a riot. It was the day young Teom assumed the Imperial yellow. Word had reached the Teemings that the food dole was being cut back. Rumor had it that the reason was the high cost of his coronation. The populace rose." He rubbed his chin. "I never found out who killed them, civil guard or rioters. Makes no difference, I suppose. They were dead."

"And they left you, the parents you loved, alone on the streets in a slum. Is that not so?" Hesitantly, Fost nodded. "And in all your life, you've never known lasting affection."

When Fost only scowled at Erimenes, the spirit went on. "Old Fimster, the thief who took you in, died of fever, did he not? And Ceratith the pedant, who opened to you the doors of human knowledge, he was murdered by alley bashers." He shook his head. "It is indeed small wonder."

"What is small wonder?" snapped Fost. His fists were tightly clenched.

"That you cling to any slight scrap of affection offered you. You became enamored of Moriana and thought she felt the same way about you. So now you pursue her the length of the continent to protect her from her own greedy folly. You are as loyal—and pathetic—as a foundling pup. You follow anyone showing attention, even someone kicking you in the ribs."

"That's ridiculous," said Fost. His cheeks felt as if he'd held them too near the flames. "It doesn't make sense, dammit!"

"Then why are you shouting?"

Fost became acutely aware of Jennas's eyes fixed on him across the dance of fire.

"Because it's untrue! It's absurd. It's not a matter of some fixation on my part but of saving Moriana's life."

"Why?" the spirit asked with malicious inflection. "She took yours."

Fost jumped to his feet. He raised his fists menacingly at Erimenes, who stood calmly by with arms folded across his insubstantial breast. Slowly, Fost lowered his arms.

"I don't know why," he whispered. "But I must."

He sat by the fire, his face averted. Desolation seeped like a blight into his soul.

He felt Jennas beside him. He tensed, unwilling to

face her. She didn't speak. She simply put her strong, smooth arms around him and held him close.

After a time, he turned to her.

Uncertainty about the coming battle formed a lump of lead in Moriana's stomach. She felt the age-old worries of a commander. Would she win? Would Synalon triumph and be free to loose the evil of the Dark Ones on the Realm once again? Either way, win or lose, many would die.

"At times such as this, I don't resent my cloistering," Ziore said somberly.

"What do you mean?" asked Moriana, distracted momentarily from her worries.

"The dilemma you face, child. If you act, you condemn thousands of men and women to death or disfigurement. Yet if you don't act. . . ." She made a helpless gesture with her hands. "Your sister will return the Dark Ones to the world and there is no Felarod this time." She shook her head. The folds at the outer corners of her eyes deepened with sorrow as though her face was still flesh. "We knew no such brutal questions in my convent."

"Perhaps that's reason enough to forgive poor Erimenes," said Moriana. Ziore's mouth hardened, and she turned away.

Moriana looked out across the valley. To the north stood a conical hill crowned with a gay pavilion, the one she shared with Darl Rhadaman. Her banner snapped from its staff in the crisp evening breeze. She pulled her gaze from it, unable to bear the thoughts welling up inside again.

Her gaze swept back across the shallow, broad valley. A small stream, tributary of Chanobit Creek flowing on the far side of her army's camp, crossed it and nourished the still-brown grasses. To her right, a long bluff hid the enemy camp from view. Riders shuttled ceaselessly along it, keeping watch. The day's overcast had broken and light from Omizantrim turned the day to splendor.

"My lady," came a voice from behind her. "Is it safe for you so close to the enemy?"

She turned to see Darl standing ten yards away. Something in the way he held his head told her he'd been there unnoticed for some time, simply watching her. She felt strangely touched.

"I'm not alone," she said. "Ziore is with me."

"She won't be much help if the Highgrass riders come upon you."

"I can take care of myself." The words came out more sharply than she intended.

"You shouldn't wander off," Darl said, a half stubborn and half indulgent look on his face. She was almost disappointed now that her words hadn't cut deeper.

"The morrow weighs heavily on me," said Ziore, swirling about her jug. "I need to meditate. Will you please reseal my jug, Moriana?" The princess looked at her spirit companion in surprise. Ziore had never expressed an urge to meditate before.

Then Moriana realized the spirit's motives. With a grateful smile she replaced the carved stone lid of the pot. The nun's figure wavered and became a formless pink cloud dissipating in the afternoon light. Moriana put the jug in her knapsack on the ground beside her.

Darl stood close by. She felt his eyes on her. His gaze had become a burden she couldn't explain.

"How are you this evening?" he asked quietly. Moriana almost laughed at the seriousness and formality of his words. A look at his face kept her from it. He was very solemn. And very vulnerable.

She had an urge to reach up and stroke his cheek, but something caused her to hold back. After a moment, he stretched out his hands and she took them in hers. His skin was cool and dry.

They simply stood there. The early evening sounds came slowly to fill the silence. The buzz of voices peaking sporadically into shouts, the bleating of livestock, hammers ringing off breastplates and blades at a dozen forges all provided reason enough not to speak.

Darl released her hands. He turned away, walked to the lip of the hill, and drew a deep lungful of the brisk air.

"When I was young," he said, "I saw my mother and father killed. It was on a day similar to this one, seemingly peaceful but actually seething with death and forces beyond human control. The Earl of Jav Nihen coveted Harmis—don't ask why. There's nothing there but mountains. At any rate, he invited my family to his summer palace for a revel. So we went, my mother and father, my uncle and I. I was only five then. We ate and I drank watered wine sweetened with honey. It was a great outdoor festival with pavilions by the score and huge bonfires roaring. We watched the players, mimes, acrobats. In many ways it was the finest night of my life.

"The Earl's men circulated through the crowds. Finally, when I stood yawning and ready for bed, Earl Maunrish rose from his chair of state and bade my parents rise. He lifted a great, golden goblet—how it gleamed in the firelight!—and drank to their health. They raised their goblets to return the honor.

"It was a signal. As they drank, they were seized from behind and cut down."

He turned to Moriana. She stared at him, speechless. She knew the story. Like the rest of his life, it had passed into legend, but she didn't know the details—or his reason for recounting them now.

"I was seized, too. I was too horrified to cry out or even to struggle. Seeing my mother and father hacked apart made me feel as if I'd died with them.

"My uncle Luu saved me. He used a stool to break the man's skull holding me. Seeing me free, he drew his sword and rallied our people. Then he cast a firebrand into the nearest pavilion."

Darl paced now, hands locked behind his back. She saw the veins standing out on the forearms below the sleeve of his green and silver tunic.

"We escaped, my uncle and I, with me slung across the saddle of his wardog. Harmis-town fell shortly, betrayed. My uncle had to flee to the mountains with those remaining loyal. I was deemed too young for such a life. I suppose I was. I must have been in their way constantly. But how I protested when I was bundled off to Duth!"

The sky turned to bands of slate and indigo while he spoke. A few rumpled clouds remained, dark above and dull red below. Darl clasped his big hands in front of him, each massaging the other as he stared up into the evening sky.

"The treachery of that summer's night I never forgot. Nor was I blind to the evil in Duth. The lords of that city are harsh and proud and suffer no insolence, real or imagined, from their peasants. I saw wrongs done—fathers cut down for failing to doff their caps when some petty lordling rode by, daughters taken for failing to hide their loveliness from some baron. I came to feel each injustice as my own.

"The end came quickly for Earl Maunrish. His mistress refused to be cast aside for a serving lad and poisoned the earl. The people of Harmis rose in revolt, and my uncle drove the invaders back across the border when I was thirteen. Within a fortnight of his triumph, Uncle Luu died of a cancer. Before I could lay claim to the throne, Harmis fell into a civil war. Kubil and Thrishnor invaded Jav Nihen and Duth pledged itself to Harmis' security against invasion from outside. Yet none would intervene to restore order or grant me my birthright. I was too young to muster men to my cause. I ran away and went a'wandering."

He stopped and stood, head down, unspeaking. Moriana came and touched his shoulder. The watch on the enemy-held ridge was changing, riders in leather jerkins and the black and purple tunics of the Sky City replacing the mercenaries amid blaring trumpets and clanging of weapons. Moriana watched as she laid her head on Darl's shoulder.

"That's how I came to be as I am, bright lady," he said. "I eventually returned to Harmis, put down the bandits who festered like pus pockets in the mountains and reunited my land. But I found myself different, my attachment no longer to my country but to an ideal. I couldn't bear the knowledge that ill is done, that evil prospers. Battle pulls me like a magnet draws iron; it is my excuse to war on the side of the oppressed. It will kill me one day. I'll fall in a ditch by the wayside and be forgotten before my corpse grows cold. Evil will march on like a procession of skeletons as if I'd never been."

"Poor Darl," she said lamely, unable to find the words to comfort him.

"It's what I've chosen. Don't pity me."

"I . . . I hate to think that the cause you fall in may be mine."

His hand gripped hers painfully hard. She made no attempt to draw away.

"My lady," he said hoarsely, "this time I've something to fight for beyond an abstraction. You are a cause for me, my lady. Were you a bloody-handed murderess, a lover of the Dark Ones, were you more vile than even Synalon, still I'd follow your banner."

"I do not ask this of you," she said in a small voice.

"You need not ask. I give it freely."

Premonition made her step forward, grasp his face in her hands, and kiss him hard. He kissed her back eagerly. Moriana felt nothing now, nothing but sorrow and self-hatred for using this man.

Still, when they broke apart, he said the words she had tried to dam up. "I love you, Moriana."

It was so easy to say and yet those were not the words she wanted to hear from him. Her eyes turned bleak and bright with tears.

"Thank you for your loyalty, Lord Harmis," she said, turning away. She walked away forcing her spine to stay straight, her shoulders braced and her sobs unvoiced. She hadn't felt this way since her dagger drove through the mail on Fost Longstrider's back on its way to his heart.

She picked up her knapsack and ran down the hill heedless of falling in the dark. She felt Darl's despair following her like a shout and knew that even a brief look back would ease his torment. But she couldn't make herself look back.

It was a long time before he followed her down the hill.

Count Ultur V'Duuyek rode along the ridgeline overlooking his camp. At his side rode Destirin Luhacs, her heavy face grim, her hair swirled into a pale yellow helmet atop her head. Sentries hailed them. The count acknowledged the challenge with a nod and rode on. The sentries were only Bilsinxt rabble.

The count was troubled. He had agreed to this expedition because he thought Moriana would be leading only a mob of criminals, misfits and fools who thought war a glorious adventure. With the admitted genius of Rann to guide it, the smaller army should have had little trouble routing the larger.

But Rann wasn't leading the army. And command hadn't gone to V'Duuyek. Rann had sent his second-in-command, a thin neurotic man named Chalowin. Perhaps, as Rann believed, the colonel was the best possible replacement. Nonetheless, he had not been a happy choice.

V'Duuyek saw his army fracturing, turning to dust. Rann would have been acceptable as commander to

V'Duuyek's nine hundred heavy riders simply because of his renown. Chalowin was unknown, an alien speaking in abrupt, disjointed bursts. V'Duuyek had accepted this commission and taken the City's coin. He wouldn't criticize his employers. But his second-in-command felt no constraints. Twice he'd cautioned Luhacs that her tirades against both Chalowin and the Sky City had a poor effect on morale. That in itself bothered him. Luhacs lacked his reserve, but she seldom required such chastisement.

A small animal broke from the bush under the forefeet of V'Duuyek's mount. The dog gave an excited bark and sat on its haunches. Luhacs's red set off in pursuit. The hare fled with all the strength in its powerful hind legs. Cursing and shouting, Luhacs finally controlled her mount. Without a word, she turned its head to camp and rode down the face of the ridge. Even in the evening dimness, V'Duuyek saw that her neck burned with anger.

Another man would have sighed. Perhaps this was an omen. A Grassland soldier's mount was supposed to be better trained. Not even the lowliest trooper's dog should have bolted in pursuit of a rabbit.

Count Ultur felt more apprehensive than he had before his first battle as a boy of thirteen. The enemy was camped only two miles away on the south side of Chanobit Creek. Tomorrow would see battle. And Count Ultur feared the result.

He did not fear for his own life. The stories telling of his ice-hard courage did not lie. He was afraid for the one thing that mattered to him, the thing he had created twenty years ago and nursed as lovingly as a gardener.

He feared that the regiment to which he had dedicated his existence might not survive.

A cold wind blew, carrying the thick smell of rain. The count allowed himself a grimace of irritation. It had rained the last seven days out of ten, and on such days the Sky City eagles could not fly. They rode in cages wrapped in oiled cloth, swaying in the beds of wagons, their yellow eyes glaring from the darkness in accusation. That was an inconvenience. If it rained again tomorrow, it would be disaster.

Damn Rann! Chalowin went with the army because political considerations demanded that a Sky Citizen lead it. But his function was to see that the plan of battle conceived by Rann back in the City was faithfully executed.

V'Duuyek had little enough faith in running a battle from a hundred miles away. But what would Chalowin do if rain made the plan unworkable?

There was nothing to be done now. The morrow would bring what it would bring. Pausing to smooth his moustache back into symmetrical spikes, be nudged his own mount's ribs and cantered down to camp.

"It won't work!" Moriana insisted, slamming her fists down onto the map spread across the table commandeered from a peasant's cottage. "I'm telling you, it's what Chalowin wants you to do. His bird riders will tear you apart."

She stared at the faces ranged around her, reading expressions by the light of the lanterns and candles set about Darl Rhadaman's pavilion. Iatic Stormcloud, his face that of a dissolute angel, regarded her with the same smile he'd shown her since he had been recruited as Darl's co-commander in Tolviroth Acerte. The countduke's other assistants looked at her with a mixture of impatience and something she thought with increasing anger looked like condescension. Darl was looking off at the wall of the tent, a light, pained expression on his face.

"Come now, Your Majesty," quavered an ancient voice. "These are battle-seasoned knights. Surely . . . surely they can withstand the assault of—uh—of birdmen."

Moriana stared at the oldster, schooling herself to

patience. Darl had been elated when the Three Notable Knights of the March had volunteered to follow Moriana's claw-and-flower flag. And they were notable knights whose deeds resounded as loudly as Darl's. Unfortunately, the days of their great deeds belonged to an earlier generation. The youngest of the three was a fussy and precise gray-haired man of seventy-six. The eldest was a remarkable one hundred and twenty-three. He spoke slowly, looking at her with his great, sad hound's eyes.

"No one doubts the mettle of your knights, Sir Rinalvus. But mettle is small protection against arrows falling as thick as hail from above," she said quietly.

"Arrows." Sir Tharvus spoke the word distastefully as though he had said "offal." He sniffed. "We are not the sort to be afraid of such child's toys, Your Majesty."

In exasperation, Moriana looked to Darl.

"Can't you explain to them? Bunching together like this is asking to be slaughtered by the bird riders. It's exactly the formation our—the Sky City's—war college regards as ideal for attack."

Before Darl could speak, the third brother put in smoothly, "But my dear, our knights fight best when used as a solid mass. If they lose cohesion they lose much of their effectiveness."

The speaker favored Moriana with a kindly smile. The middle of the brothers in age, he was still a handsome man and powerful of frame despite his ninety years. Moriana heard a voice within her begin to yammer in panic, but she answered him as reasonably as she could.

"Sir Ottovus, your men will be perfect targets. How much effectiveness will they have when they're dead?"

Ottovus only smiled. Lip twitching, Tharvus turned to Darl.

"Is all this discussion necessary? This is speech for men, my lord."

Moriana colored.

"Now, sir," Iatic said in his golden voice, "we are pledged to serve the princess's cause. She has a right to join our councils."

"As I—um—understand it," said Rinalvus, "the good princess—or queen, I suppose I should say since we're trying to restore you to your throne, and begging Your Majesty's pardon—I thought she was going to explain to us how her magic will aid us tomorrow."

"Yes," said Tharvus, "I'm certain *that* is a subject Her Majesty is amply qualified to discuss at length."

"I have told you before, lord, my magic is not of a sort to be used in battle," said Moriana.

"But what is this?" Rinalvus asked. "I . . . I thought magicians threw fireballs and lightning bolts, that sort of thing. Should be quite useful. Yes, indeed."

"My sister would be able to oblige you with ease," snapped Moriana. She tried to keep the edge from her words because she admired the aged knight. It was merely that he, and all of them, failed to understand that her participation in the battle was vital for success. They seemed slave to so many misconceptions about the nature of war waged by the Sky City that she had to try to correct them. "It requires far more involvement with powers best left unnamed to become that facile in destruction."

"What can your talents accomplish then?"

"Healing the injured. Scrying—you've seen me look into the enemy's camp often enough. Manipulating the weather."

"That'll be fine," nodded Ottovus. "You can stay atop the hill out of harm's way and tend to the wounded. And if you can whistle up a few clouds to keep the bird riders out of the fight, so much the better!"

He beamed at her. It dawned on the princess that he thought he was doing her a favor, that he offered a way to stay out of the fight where no woman would wish to be. But Moriana wanted to be in the thick of it, dealing blows in what was her cause.

She sagged, the table's edge pressing against her thighs. She felt more frustration and sick fear than anger. It was as if she exchanged words with a charlatan's puppets. They spoke to her and she to them, but she no more communicated with them than she could with effigies of wood or ivory. She wished for Ziore. She desperately needed the spirit's calm strength. But Darl had said it would make the others uncomfortable. And Moriana, always aware of the immeasurable service he did her, had given in. As she had done so frequently of late.

"Hear me, lords," she said, leaning forward on anger-stiffened arms. "You have agreed to help shoulder my burden, and my gratitude to you is profound. But the burden is mine, and I mean to bear as much as I can."

"Well, to be sure . . ." began Ottovus.

"I do not mean to languish on a hilltop while my fate and that of my City is decided by others. I have led troops in battle and have been victorious. I have led Sky City troops; I trained throughout my early years as a bird rider. I know my folk. And I fight as well as any of them."

She glared at them defiantly. Slowly, her defiance softened and melted away like the wax in the burning candles scattered around the pavilion. The others' eyes showed condescension quite openly now. It came to her that they thought her martial experience to be like that of the Emperors of Medurim and other idle aristocrats of the North, that like them she "trained" by dressing in gilded armor and reviewing the troops once a month.

"Come, this is absurd," said Tharvus. "A woman going into battle. Indeed!"

Moriana snapped her lips shut on the challenge that rose to them. Her furious impulse had been to offer a challenge to single combat. That would have only reinforced the others' notion of her as an impetuous creature, ruled by emotion and not to be trusted with the serious business of war. She turned a despairing look to Darl.

The Count-Duke of Harmis stood blinking rapidly. For some reason, Moriana was reminded of a small boy whose fellows will not play nice and who is on the verge of tears because the game goes other than his way.

She knew she was being unfair. He'd done much for her and was only trying to do what he thought right.

"I think Your Majesty misunderstands," spoke Ottovus in round, comforting tones. "It is only that the idea of exposing yourself to harm is unacceptable to us. We would be remiss in our duty if we failed to protect you."

Darl moved to her side. He took her hand and fell to his knees.

"Trust us, Your Majesty. We have proved ourselves in war. We know how best to serve your cause."

And I don't? she thought savagely, without voicing the words.

He kissed her hand fervently. The others nodded benign approval. Even Tharvus was smiling at her now.

"Trouble yourself no more, my queen!" Darl cried, leaping to his feet. "Leave this to us and we shall give you victory tomorrow!"

The others joined in.

"Victory! Moriana and victory!"

The tension was swamped in the sudden wave of loyalty and passion. The waves of exuberance broke over Moriana. She felt herself eroding bit by bit like a castle built of sand.

CHAPTER ELEVEN

The new day appeared much like the gemstone set in the talisman Moriana wore around her neck: mostly white.

"See?" said Ziore to her as the guards Darl had assigned escorted them to the crest of a hill overlooking the battlefield. "I knew things wouldn't turn out as badly as you feared."

Moriana surveyed the scene. Normally, the hill provided a vantage above the broad valley where her army and Synalon's would clash today. But a thick fog cloaked it, making the landscape appear as if it were layers of wool. She couldn't see farther than a few feet. Ripples in the mist now and then exposed shapes, shadowy and indistinct, of men preparing for the day.

Under the blanket of damp, clinging mist, Chalowin's eagles would be grounded. Unless the weather changed, the Sky City's chief weapon would be rendered impotent.

Moriana clutched her amulet. Pale light glowed between her fingers.

"Your amulet has not been wrong yet," said Ziore. "See how its color foretells good fortune?"

Moriana looked at it ruefully. She wondered if it was worth the sacrifice.

From below came a shout. It was followed by a strange clanging sound like a cook banging with an iron spoon. Moriana's breath caught in her throat.

The Battle of Chanobit Creek had begun.

* * *

"My birds cannot fly," Colonel Chalowin stated flatly. "There will be no battle today."

V'Duuyek's gaze was steady from beneath the rim of his helmet. He had foreseen such an objection.

"We fight, with or without your eagles. Our army is in place."

Tension turned Chalowin's usual facial tic into myriad twitching, writhing components. Now the Sky City colonel looked like some insect in his nervousness.

"The prince's plan requires the eagles," he said. "They cannot fly. We wait for better weather."

V'Duuyek smoothed his moustache. He boiled inside. Knowing that Chalowin might try to forestall action, he had taken steps to prevent it. If those steps were discovered . . .

"We must prevent Moriana's army from bypassing us. If they succeed, they can cut the City's lifeline at Bilsinx. Is this what Prince Rann commanded?"

"We have the greater mobility," said Chalowin doggedly. "We can catch them."

"As long as this foul weather holds," said V'Duuyek, speaking with his usual precision, "we have little mobility at all. Our army moves at the pace of the wagons carrying your war eagles. If Moriana's army gets past us, we may never catch them."

They stood on a bluff across the valley from the invisible hilltop where the enemy had erected their command post. V'Duuyek gazed into the formless fog, his blue eyes bright, as if by straining he could pierce the dirty fleece clouds and see their foe. In fact, he strained his ears to catch a certain sound that would tell him his mercenary force stood a fighting chance of survival.

Chalowin glared at him. His left eye pulsed closed with an arhythmic beat so disconcerting to V'Duuyek that he turned away. He felt no concern that this would make the colonel suspect. Chalowin, unlike Rann, was not overly perceptive.

"Our enemy has the initiative," he said. "If we hold back, they will attack us with every advantage of momentum. It isn't an advantage I'd advise we give the knights of the City States."

"We will withdraw then." Chalowin slapped himself on the chest without being aware that he did so.

"In that case, any offensive move on their part will catch us unprepared and in disorder. We can expect to be overwhelmed. They have a considerable advantage in numbers, colonel."

Chalowin's pallor grew more marked as the mercenary spoke. When V'Duuyek finished, it took the Sky City officer half a minute to control his angry twitching sufficiently to speak.

"The prince has given us the plan," he said, raising his voice. Wraithlike figures stopped to turn and stare at the men. "We must not deviate from it! Order the withdrawal now, my lord. When we make our attack, it will be as Prince Rann decreed."

V'Duuyek stared at him. He felt sick to his stomach. He knew why Rann had placed a man of such unswerving devotion in command: another might decide on his own to alter Rann's plan. With the Sky Citizen's disdain for groundlings, he might even neglect to inform a subordinate V'Duuyek of any change. Such lack of coordination brought only disaster. And in V'Duuyek's learned opinion, Rann's plan was an excellent one. Chalowin could be relied on to follow it exactly, as if its every detail were graved on his brain. But, as the count had feared all along, events precluded its use. And Chalowin could not conceive of an attack that differed from the original.

V'Duuyek made a production of removing his gauntlets, his left one heavy and backed in steel, his right of dog's hide, thin and pliant so his fingers could grip the string of his bow. He listened for the sounds he counted on so heavily. But he heard nothing. Tucking his gloves into his baldric, he turned to face Chalowin.

From below came a cry, the deep, fierce barking of a dog yelping in pain. The count paused, smiled and took his gauntlets from his baldric, and began putting them on again.

"We are already engaged, colonel," he said. Even in his triumph, he kept his tones even, his words trimmed neatly to fit. "We've no choice now but to give battle. Unless the men of the Sky City are inclined to flee from a battle already joined . . ."

Chalowin's jaw worked open and shut. V'Duuyek saw the anguish on his face. Rann wouldn't hesitate to back away from battle if his keen mind told him that was the shrewdest move. But Chalowin was no more capable of briging down what he saw as dishonor on the City's forces than he was of defying Rann.

Almost choking, he said, "Give the order to attack."

"The curs have left their kennel!" cried Darl from the back of his great white war dog. "To me, O men of the North. Let's whip them back to whence they came!" He brandished his broadsword above his head. Even in the mirk, it flashed with a deadly light.

A roar of approval rose from the hilltop and the valley below. Though most of the troop couldn't see their commander, they heard the ringing clamor of his voice. That was all they needed. The men drawn up in ranks felt their blood take fire with excitement and the nearness of battle.

Moriana heard her voice joining the rest. Though she was condemned to wait out the day on this hillside, she couldn't help sharing the exhilaration of these men who would struggle and die for her.

Darl rode over and jerked back on his reins. The huge dog reared back with a snarl, pawing at the air.

Darl caught at a lance thrust into the soil. From its tip fluttered the arms of the princess. He waved it high over his head.

"Moriana!" he cried. "Moriana and victory!" Then he wheeled his mount and loped into the fog.

Moriana heard his laugh, high and full of boyish excitement. Then a thousand throats took up the battle cry. The men of the Northland who had come by the thousands to offer service to an alien princess swept forward to attack.

Against all Moriana's warnings, the army had been drawn up in a conventional formation. In the center stood a mass of infantry, almost six thousand strong. They were farmers, mercenaries, vassals of lordlings who had offered their swords to Moriana, armed with the short spears and shields of Realm footmen. Flanking them were thirteen hundred archers split roughly in half between the left wing and the right. They were men of proven temper, mostly foresters from the Great Nevrym Forest or deserters from the Imperial Border Watch risking Imperial displeasure for a chance to strike a blow at the forces of the Dark Ones. Moriana was glad of such men, but she feared they would prove inadequate. Although the army they faced was small, it boasted more than twice as many missile troops. There were ominous numbers of Bilsinxt riders, V'Duuyek dog riders, and seven hundred infantry skirmishers with bows and javelins.

But the knights of the City States scorned arrows, as Sir Tharvus had been at such pains to make clear the night before. It was on those knights that Darl depended most. Seven hundred of them poised on the left flank, their dogs snarling at each other, keyed to a frenzy by the excitement charging the air. At their head rode two of the Notable Knights, Tharvus and Ottovus, the first in his armor of gold and the second in crimson. On the right were the seven hundred under Darl's personal command. Almost half of the knights and men-at-arms came from his home county of Harmis. Backing them were twenty-five-hundred light lancers, their armor mail instead of the glittering enameled plate of the knights.

A heavy guard ringed Moriana's hilltop. She was not alone, at least. Two other figures impatiently paced the perimeter, casting covetous glances into the fog, eager to take part in the battle even now beyond their eyes' reach. Young Iatic Stormcloud, his hair a golden wreath and the fine lines of his face slightly blurred by dissipation, paced with the scabbard of his longsword clacking at his thigh. And ancient Sir Rinalvus, visor raised to allow his rheumy old eyes to peer into the mist, stood leaning on the haft of a massive ax backed with a hook. The angelic young mercenary commanded a reserve of a hundred knights and two hundred lesser cavalry. Sir Rinalvus was supposed to oversee the battle and keep his fellow commanders apprised of any new developments—if the fog thinned enough for him to see them. Moriana suspected that the oldster, wearing the same suit of polished blue plate in which he had accompanied so many exploits over the course of more than a century's adventuring, had also been set to watch over her and make sure she neither meddled nor came to harm. He didn't pace and glare like a caged falcon as did Iatic. But looking at him, pitifully shrunken within armor built to encase one more robust, Moriana felt her heart go out to him. Though he didn't accept her as an equal on the field of war, it pained him not to be able to strike a blow on her behalf.

"This is . . . most impressive," said Ziore, her voice intruding on the princess's thoughts. "In my days as a nun, we were taught war was a horrible thing, brutish and distasteful. Yet the air is filled with hot vibrations, energies. I find this . . . stimulating."

Could the spirit, cloistered throughout her life, be turning into another Erimenes?

"No, child," Ziore laughed. "I am unlike the evil

man whose false teachings blighted my life. I can take no joy in the pain of others. But I can feel the eagerness pulsing through a million veins. It flows like lightning along my nerves."

Moriana started to reply to the pale pink figure. A sudden blaring cry of triumph made her turn and look out across the valley. She saw figures surging and striving together. The knights of Harmis, with Darl at their head, rushed down. Her blue, red, and gold banner snaked behind. Among them were others in long linen surcoats. Their armor overlapped like a lizard's scales; their helms were high, worked into curious knobbed spires. From them flew streamers of a dozen bright colors. Dogs snapped at one another, tearing at exposed throats. The foreigners' dogs were bulkier than Darl's. Unlike the knights, who armored only the chests and heads of their war dogs, these riders covered their beasts' bodies with scale armor like their own.

Moriana had no difficulty recognizing the famed dog riders of the Highgrass Broad. Yet she was puzzled. Some of them, trying to avoid Darl's knights, loosed arrows tipped with broad steel heads. Even as Moriana watched, one struck the breastplate of Darl's armor. It hit at an angle and bounced off amid fat blue sparks. The princess was uncomfortably aware that she had screamed aloud in horror.

But although the dog riders were risking the tension of their strings and the glue that held their bows together to the treacherous damp, none seemed to carry the long lances traditionally used. A number of men lay still on the ground, their blood a red cloth spread on the wet grass. For all their steel, they had suffered terribly at the first shock. They turned and fled before the knights of the North.

The bulk of Darl's army advanced at a slow walk. They cheered frantically at the apparent rout of their vaunted enemy. Darl's knights started to follow up their advantage and spur their mounts into the mist. Darl's voice halted them. He had charged with only a few score of his knights. He was not reckless enough to take his whole force when attacking an unseen enemy.

He saw what Moriana had seen as soon as the melee separated itself into sides, one fleeing, one victorious. He had just beaten a mere handful of cavalry. Darl held his followers back to wait for the other knights to catch up with them. They sat impatiently, tugging at their reins to prevent their mounts from licking up the spilled blood.

Moriana let out her pent-up breath. She admitted she had underestimated Darl. She had known with ugly certainty that he would follow the fleeing troops with his small band right into the concentrated arrow flights of two thousand archers. But Darl had reacted as coolly and precisely as might Rann, under whose command Moriana had fought the Golden Barbarians half a decade before. She reached to the bodice of her gown to feel the hardness of the amulet. Perhaps its augury was true. Perhaps success would be theirs this day.

Then she gasped. The fog, the vital fog that kept the lethal bird riders helpless, was beginning to lift.

She turned to the brazier that sent a wistful spiral of smoke to blend with the fog. A stand with herbs and other substances had been placed next to the iron tripod holding the brazier. A pair of boys in the crimson, blue, and gold livery of the Brother Knights stood a few paces away, alternately punching each other and giggling, staring at the battle and eyeing the princess at whose beck and call they'd been placed. Ignoring the adolescent lust glowing in their eyes, she walked to the brazier and gestured for them to attend.

"Look lively," she snapped. "I must keep these damned clouds in place!"

Ultur V'Duuyek steeled himself. Torn, broken bodies flowed by. He had sent two scores of his men to probe the enemy position. Only fifteen dogs returned with riders still aboard.

They had known the nature of their mission, every man and woman of them. They were to be risked— sacrificed—so that Chalowin would be forced into battle. V'Duuyek and his officers knew full well that Darl and Moriana, who cared little enough for what Rann decreed, would not merely permit their foes to decline combat until better weather arrived. And for the Sky City army to be caught at any sort of disadvantage by their horde of foes would be catastrophic. To save his regiment, V'Duuyek had no choice but to send the forty on their suicide mission. He had been like a loving father forced to choose which of his children are to be sacrificed so that the others may survive.

And his favorite of all had been one of the volunteers. Though his face remained impassive, his eyes searched for the familiar red war dog with the heavy jaw.

A moment later he saw the dog. His lips pressed into a thin line. No rider occupied the saddle of Destirin Luhacs's mount.

Wounded men rode double with their comrades— risky business because one rider and its own armor brought even a Highgrass charger near the limits of the burden it could carry. Others had improvised stretchers from cloaks and the coils of rope they carried by their saddle bows.

Two dogs trotted straight for the commander. V'Duuyek scarcely dared glance at the figure slung between them. Its spired helmet had fallen off. The hair coiled about the head was matted pink with drying blood.

"Destirin . . ."

The figure stirred. The head lifted. The face was a horrid mask of blood, a black slash across the forehead. Yet the apparition grinned, teeth shockingly white against the fog-dulled red.

"I live, Count Ultur," said Destirin Luhacs, "but I fear I'll have to go easy on the rum for a while. My head spins even without it."

Count Ultur V'Duuyek did not smile, but between him and his second-in-command passed a look of perfect understanding. With a nod, he gestured Luhacs's rescuers to bear her to the ridgetop where Sky City mages might attend to her wounds.

Calmly, surely, he drew the oiled case of his bow from over his shoulder. Clamped firmly in place, his lance jutted from its stirrup. He undrapped the bow, felt the string for tautness and nodded. Chalowin was at the rear, behind the long ridge on which the command post had been erected. Foiled of his chance to carry out Rann's strategy, Chalowin had given over conduct of the battle to the mercenary.

V'Duuyek looked right and left. Messengers sat on quivering, long-legged dispatch dogs waiting to carry his commands.

"We go," he said quietly.

Following Rann's concepts, the Sky City army had been deployed in a way to maximize its strengths. Its fifteen hundred spear-and-shield infantry, in black iron helmets and tunics and breeches of purple and black, were ranged in three blocks of four hundred, with a reserve of three hundred backing up the army. In the left gap waited a thousand Sky City dog riders, heavily armed with bow, lance, and black-painted shield. In the right gap stood the Highgrass Broad riders. Before them, the seven hundred foot skirmishers provided a living screen. These were the half-breeds born of groundling women and of Sky Citizens on garrison duty. Their morale was not as high as that of their pureblooded comrades, but it wasn't their function to stand and fight. They harassed and delayed the foe, keeping them from seeing exactly how the army behind was set forth.

The thousand Bilsinxt auxiliaries swarmed in nervous clouds at either side. At V'Duuyek's order to advance, they galloped forward, drawing bowstrings to ears. Like the half-caste foot skirmishers, they had no armor save for the green tabards they wore over yellow tunics. The mercenary expected no great performances from them, but they were meant only to annoy the enemy and then fall back.

Like a curtain being raised, the mist ascended to a height of twenty feet. The top of Moriana's hill was in the clear. The ridge around which the City's men were arrayed remained cloaked in fog. Behind it, the eagles uttered dispirited cries. The unbroken blanket of fog screened the enemy from arrows fired from above; the lancers could not strike without flying along the ground itself, a role more suited to V'Duuyek's dog riders in their shiny, surcoated carapaces. A bird rider wore no armor but a conical cap of thin steel and a hornbull-leather buckler face with metal.

Darl rode at the head of the other army, lance held upright, Moriana's banner streaming behind him. Men and dogs growled at his back as the Bilsinxt poured around the infantry in twin streams and rode toward them. They felt their skins crawling with the need to be at their foe. But Darl did not intend to waste the momentum of his knights on mere light cavalry. The Northern army, the army of the Bright Princess as Darl had dubbed it in a poetic mood, moved forward at a stately pace, its gay colors muted by the fog.

If the Bilsinxt swarmed like bees, they had their stingers as well. Arrows buzzed up to fall among the Northerners. Shelled in steel, the knights and their dogs were almost impervious to the missiles. A few dogs yelped as hindquarters were grazed, but none fell and no riders were injured.

Among the lightly armored footmen, it was a different story. Men of Harmis, men of Thrishnor and Duth and Samazant in the Empire, men who had come from Port

Zorn to fight for the beautiful Princess Moriana, from Wirix to fight Synalon, from Kolnith and Deepwater and the Sjedd to champion the cause of the Wiser Ones—men who had come from all over the Sundered Realm to find adventure, booty, or fulfillment of some pious vow, found death instead.

Moriana's archers loosed before a second volley came from the Bilsinxt. Riders screamed and fell from saddles to be dragged across the ground by dogs maddened by pain and the bright stench of blood. The Northern infantry had only light armor and shields. The riders of Bilsinx had no protection but the speed of their swift dogs. For many, it was not enough.

For once, Count Ultur had misjudged. Far from breaking at the first taste of death, the Bilsinxt wheeled their dogs and swept across the front of the hostile ranks for a second pass. Closer they came. Their bows were less powerful than those of a bird rider, but now the lesser range told.

An arrow socketed itself in the gap between the brassard and breast of Sir Ottovus's armor. He smiled and pulled it free. Yet those nearby noted that its tip came out bloody. The man riding at Darl's right uttered a sharp cry and fell with a shaft jutting through the slit in his visor. Darl looked back once, face white beneath the raised visor of his own helm. Then he turned resolutely to the foe.

With a courage as fanatical as it was unexpected, the Bilsinxt circled again and again and again inside the narrowing gap between the armies. More and more of the steel-plated war dogs fell out of the ranks to stand snarling over fallen masters.

Glancing up from her brazier, Moriana groaned as she saw the left-hand array of knights break from the ranks and charge their antagonists. Like men freed from a geas, the Bilsinxt broke off their death ride and raced for the rear.

The Sky City dog riders lunged to meet the knights.

They hurtled forward and then broke to their right, spitting arrows into the faces of the onrushing knights. Driven by stouter bows, these arrows punched through the plate armor. Dogs began to fall, spilling their riders in the path of those behind. Confusion blunted the force of the charge.

· Darl's hand was forced. A quick sally or a blizzard of arrows might shatter Tharvus's men completely. The Count-Duke of Harmis slammed down his visor, dropped the tip of his lance, and charged.

Sound boiled from the valley floor as the armies collided. Steel glanced from steel with sonorous bell notes. Arrows moaned like spirits of the dead. The soft thump-thump of dogs' feet gave way to barks and snarls. The screams of the wounded floated over all like carrion birds.

"I don't like it," said Moriana, glancing from brazier to battlefield, then at Sir Rinalvus and back to the brazier again. The knight watched Ziore in fascination. He held one hand above his eyes as if shading them from the sun.

"What do you mislike, princess?" he asked.

Moriana frowned at her brazier. With senses not those of the flesh, she felt the sun pour its heat down from the sky, trying to melt away the snowy bank of cloud overhead. Since nature had provided the clouds, she would work them, keep them in a soft ceiling, a lid to trap the eagles against the earth. But it took constant effort.

"The dog riders. It doesn't look as if there are nine hundred."

"I know little of these things," said Ziore, "but wouldn't they leave some back to take the place of wounded or plug gaps in their line?"

"Yes, but fully half their number? I'd swear there are only four hundred there, five at the most." She squinted into the rising smoke. She felt control slipping.

She took a pinch of maroon powder, scattered it on the tiny flames, and recoiled when gray smoke rolled up into her face.

"They probably have some hidden beyond the ridge." Ziore sounded doubtful. Moriana realized the spirit was trying to bolster her courage and ease her fears. She felt the touch of Ziore's mind on hers, as light as down and twice as soothing.

No! she thought so violently that Ziore winced. *Stay out!*

She glanced up and saw the hurt look on Ziore's face.

"I'm sorry," she said aloud. "But I don't dare let you soothe me. I can't let you into my mind at all. It blunts my powers." The spirit lowered her head.

BOOM!

With a rolling crash like thunder, V'Duuyek's dog riders met Darl's knights. Lance broke against shield or armored beast. Men and women were hurled down, mortally wounded. Dogs lunged at each other, toppled riders, and tore at them until fierce lance thrusts dropped them where they stood.

Like waves, the armored riders smashed into each other and then fell back. For all Darl's prowess, the knights of the City States couldn't break through the wall of iron they faced. Time and again both groups withdrew, only to reform and surge in again. The tide slowly turned. More dogs from the Empire bayed lament over fallen masters than those reared in the tall grass country of the east. But numbers told.

Blood streamed down Count Ultur's face. His helmet had been torn just above his right eye by a lance. The wound wasn't serious but it bled profusely. He nocked an arrow, drew, sighted across the few yards of corpse-strewn grass separating the riders. He cursed. He was denied a clear shot at Darl.

The count loosed his arrow. A man stiffened, struck dead as his head was turned. The man dropped. Darl saw how close he had come to hearing the Hell Call, waved the hand that still held Moriana's banner, and urged his forces on.

The armies splashed against each other again.

Moriana scarcely dared to look. Her army was winning; somehow that was harder to watch than when the outcome was in doubt. Old Rinalvus thumped on the butt of his ax and yelled himself hoarse. Iatic Stormcloud paced and scowled, angry at missing a fight that came closer to victory every minute.

"Lord Iatic!" a voice cried. Moriana's head whipped up. "Sir Rinalvus! Your Highness!" A man rode up the hill from the woods along the right flank. Moriana recognized him as a squire with the reserves. Iatic stared at him, holding one hand upraised and cupping the elbow with the other like a messenger of a Wise One about to deliver Law.

"What is it, boy?" Rinalvus demanded.

The youth looked from face to face as if unsure whom to address. Finally, he blurted out to everyone in general, "We were riding through the woods, lords—uh, and lady—and we saw riders coming this way. They had streamers on their helmets."

"A flank attack!" Moriana cried. Without a word, Iatic spun and ran to his own mount. Shouting for his reserves to follow, he pelted down the hill. He was too canny to rush into the woods where his knights would be at a disadvantage. Instead, he readied his men at the foot of the hill where they'd be in position to strike the mercenaries as they emerged from the woods.

"Stay clear of the fire, boy," Moriana told the squire. "And keep your dog away. The magic may scare him."

Something popped in the heart of the fire. The dog jumped, slipped on wet grass, and fell onto its side. The squire left the saddle and fell on top of Moriana. She yelped as hot metal seared the back of her hand.

The squire bounded up as though Moriana were a mattress.

"Oh, Your Highness, forgive me! I didn't mean! O Gods, I wouldn't dare to . . ."

Moriana didn't hear him. She was on hands and knees trying to steady herself against the waves of horror breaking over her. In her tumble she'd upset the brazier. The magic holding the cloud cover intact had broken.

And her amulet had slipped from her gown. Moriana stared at it numbly.

It gleamed dully on its silver chain, as black as a lump of coal.

V'Duuyek's men were pushed back for what the count knew to be the final time. His gamble had failed; the troops he sent through the twisting valleys to come upon both flanks of the enemy had not arrived. His beloved regiment was being chopped to shreds before his eyes.

Then a trumpet call drew his eyes outward. An involuntary shout escaped his lips. From first one side of the valley and then the other broke his men, streaming from the woods and a gully. The shouts of consternation among his enemies were sweet music to him.

Darl's knights turned to meet the Grasslanders. On the far side of the field, the knights under the command of Sir Tharvus and Sir Ottovus readied for their charge. V'Duuyek sat, his short, heavy sword in hand, prepared for the final charge.

Something made him glance up.

"Great Ultimate!" he cried. His soldiers tipped back their heads. In a moment, the knights did so, too, pausing and milling as they did.

Breaks appeared in the cover above, revealing patches of blue. The battlefield lapsed into silence as the clouds dissipated with eldritch swiftness. Those below felt a chill, but there was no wind.

Behind the ridge, Chalowin shrieked, "The Dark Ones have delivered victory to us!" Like bolts shot from twelve-score catapults, the eagles surged into the naked sky.

They fell into the roles assigned them in the master plan. Like a new fog, a hundred eagles spilled over the ridgetop and passed with a drumming of wings. Their riders raked the ranks below with arrows. The riders' aim was good. Most of their arrows found homes in Northern flesh.

Moriana caught sight of Sir Ottovus sitting tall in his saddle, sword raised in defiance. Slowly, like a collapsing tower, he toppled to one side. Moriana saw the ugly black butt of a lance protruding from his neck.

Beside her, Rinalvus sobbed and covered his face with his hands.

A flight of bird riders made straight for the hill. Moriana felt her arms gripped. Two spearmen had stepped up and hustled her toward the pavilion she shared with Darl. They had been ordered to keep her from joining the fight.

She recognized the emaciated figure astride the lead war bird. He shouted a command. Arrows sliced down, striking half a dozen spearmen.

Moriana's guards let her go at the tent flap and ran to join the handful of their number who still survived. Eagles landed, their riders leaping off with javelins and short curved swords in hand.

"Here, old one," one said to Rinalvus, "give over that chopper and we'll not hurt you. Don't do anything rash and you'll be in your dotard's bed by nightfall."

Rinalvus's answer was a deft ax-blow. The man gurgled, teeth spilling from his head like pale seeds. He died.

Shouting their anger, his fellows closed in. Rinalvus moved with fantastic speed. He knocked a sword from a gloved hand, spun his ax to split a javelin, and lopped the arm off another who leaned in to thrust.

"Come down, damn you!" he yelled at the sky. He

looked neither frail nor wasted now. "Come down from the sky and meet the avenger of Ottovus the Golden!"

Chalowin screeched fury. He drew his bow and shot. The arrow glanced off Rinalvus's breastplate. The old man staggered back a step, then straightened, strong gnarled hands resolutely gripping his ax haft.

The bird riders circled him. They shot again and again at the lonely figure on the hilltop. Rinalvus's armor, redoubtable though it was, could not withstand them.

Moriana screamed as one sank into his chest. Another punctured his thigh. Still he stood his ground. His throat was pierced, his upper arm, his cheek. The indomitable old man stood as though the arrows were no more than insect bites.

Moriana rushed inside the tent, picked up a bow and quiver, and stepped back outside. The bird riders still circled Rinalvus like cultures waiting for a wounded beast to drop. But Rinalvus did not stop. He stood watching them defiantly, a dozen arrows in his body.

He turned and looked at Moriana with his sad eyes.

"My lady," he said, though the words were scarcely recognizable. "Forgive my failing . . ."

He fell.

Cold as the water that now ran red in the stream below, Moriana nocked an arrow, pulled, aimed. Chalowin caught sight of her.

"There!" he shrieked, face twisted in ecstasy. "The slut who plots the fall of Queen Synalon! Take her alive, my . . ."

He never finished.

The arrow struck him in the left eye. He gave a maniacal shriek as he backflipped out of his saddle and fell to the ground, as limp as a bundle of rags. He fell beside the body of the ancient hero he had shot down so ruthlessly. Their blood ran together.

Before he landed, another arrow arched upward. A

bird rider screamed more fearfully than Chalowin as the missile split his groin and drove deep into his bird's neck. A third rider turned his eagle toward the princess and dived. She stepped forward and calmly loosed again. The arrow went through the eagle's neck and plunged into the rider's belly. They swooshed overhead to collide with the top of the tent.

The remaining rider lost his nerve. Seeing the Sky Guard officer who commanded the army brought down, he fled.

But instead of a straightaway climb, trying to gain as much altitude and distance as possible, he turned his bird in a wing-pumping spiral. Moriana watched him climb almost vertically, a cruel smile wracking her mouth. Had he been a Sky Guardsman, he wouldn't have made such an error. He might even have survived.

Moriana let him get two hundred feet in the air. She raised her arm, slid back the string, aimed, and released.

The eagle jerked, squawked, began to tumble. Its rider came free, arms and legs wheeling wildly. The princess savored his scream until the ground cut it short. Then she walked over to Ziore.

Ziore's face was desolate.

"How can such things be?" she whispered. "How can the Wise Ones permit such horror?"

Moriana felt deathly tired.

"Perhaps they have no choice." She threw her bow away. "Or perhaps it's a game to them and we're merely pawns to be moved at random."

"You are wrong, child. Oh, Great Ultimate, you *must* be!"

"I fear," said Moriana slowly, "that all too soon we shall find out whether or not I'm right."

The battle reversed itself with stunning swiftness. Darl's army melted like snow beneath a warm rain as the arrows streaked down from above. Within five minutes, the army that had been within sword's reach of victory was a fleeing, fear-drunken mob.

The man who had done as much as any to bring this turnabout victory was not content to let the bird riders win it themselves. Count Ultur V'Duuyek led a charge head-on into Darl's knights. This time it was the wiry count who cut through foes like a scythe through weeds.

Finally, he and Darl faced each other above upraised swords. Darl's shield was gone, smashed to ruin by a hundred blows. It was blade against blade, man against man.

Sparks shot in all directions as the blades caressed each other. Snake swift, V'Duuyek laid open the armor coating Darl's thigh and drew a bright line of blood along the leg. Darl winced, grinned, and made a quick cut at his opponent's head.

The count's blade flashed up. Darl pivoted and thrust. With a crunching sound like shellfish dropped on a rock by a hungry seagull, Darl's point broke.

Through armor.

Through ribs.

Through heart.

Count Ultur V'Duuyek sat bolt upright in the sadde. His foe's blade slid free with a grating sound. Feeling nothing, the count swung around and came to rest with his head in a clump of grass.

"The Count is fallen!" A woman's voice rose to heights of despair. "Avenge him!" And crying *vengeance,* his men burst forward and swept the surviving knights away in a torrent of madness.

Count Ultur V'Duuyek's last sight was that of his regiment charging to its last and greatest victory.

He died content.

CHAPTER TWELVE

When V'Duuyek fell, Darl wanted to stand his
ground and die beside the body of his foe. His surviving men wouldn't allow it. They gathered around him,
fending off the howling dog riders. A young knight
caught the reins of the commander's mount. Darl was
led off the field weeping like a small child.

If Moriana had not been allowed to participate in
winning victory, there was none to stop her from saving
what she could from defeat. She had no hope of ever
gathering another army such as this. It was not hope of
using the survivors of this field to form the core of yet
another attempt on the Sky City that motivated her.
But these men had left their homes and their loved
ones hundreds of miles away to fight for her, though
her cause was not theirs. She felt it her duty to save
as many as possible.

It was difficult to recognize the refined and beautiful
princess in whose cause the battle had been fought.
She had become a green-eyed fury, straightsword in
hand, elegant dress hacked off above the knee to keep
it from tangling her legs. Yet the battered remnants of
defeat who drifted her way did as they were bid. She
ordered them away through the woods where the eagles
could not get them and in parties large enough to make
it hard for the enemy to pick them off piecemeal. With
her training in command and assistance from Ziore,
Moriana put together a successful defense when a band
of dog riders swooped down on her little group.

Ziore was still appalled at what had occurred and
wanted no further part of fighting. Moriana had pointed

212

out that this was a fight to save lives—the enraged Grasslanders were killing all Northerners they could find. Ziore acquiesced with the sad observation that it was such compromise that led decent people to butchering each other in the first place.

Chanobit Creek ran behind the hilltop holding the Northern command post. And when time permitted, Moriana felt a certain bittterness that the battle had, in fact, been waged by a Northern army and not *her* army. In the trees on its north bank, Moriana worked at organizing the survivors and sending them on their way. She was careful not to let too many group at one time for fear of attracting attention that would be fatal. Fortunately, the death of the two supreme commanders had left the enemy disorganized.

Shortly before night lowered the curtain on this bloody day, a party of knights rode up, leading Darl. The Count-Duke of Harmis seemed stunned, unable to conceive of the disaster that had come to pass. Moriana came out of the thicket to meet them. Her face was grave with more than the concerns of the moment.

"Your Highness, Your Highness," one said, tears streaming down cheeks barely touched with downy beard. "We've brought you failure and disgrace. How can we restore to you what our worthlessness has lost?"

She shook her head sadly.

"You cannot." The boy looked stricken. She wondered how old he was. "The way you can best serve me now is to live."

He brightened.

"Will you permit us to fight for you again?"

"If you wish, perhaps you shall. Some day." She held back tears of her own. "But that's not what I mean. I mean survive. Live out this day and many more so that I'll not have your death on my conscience, too."

He blinked in bewilderment. Moriana turned to Darl. He looked at her through strange, old eyes.

"I'm . . . sorry," he whispered.

Something blocked her throat. She reached up to take his hand. She pressed it against her cheek.

"You tried."

"What will you do now?" Darl voiced the question listlessly, as though he was reading lines in a boring play.

"I can do two things," she said. "I can quit—which I shall never do as long as I draw breath. Or I can go elsewhere for assistance."

He shook his head, a distant expression on his face.

"Where will you go? I have used up my stock with the folk of the North. Where will you find the men?"

"I will not use *men*," she said. "Or at least, not humans."

"I don't understand."

"The builders of the City, the Hissers—*Zr'gsz*, as they call themselves. They live at Thendrun in the Mystic Mountains."

A gasp burst from the listeners. They milled about, shuffling their feet and not looking her in the eye.

"It is a matter of personal interest to the rulers of the City in the Sky to know how things are with them."

"What can you offer them?" Darl asked. "You can't offer them the City."

"By the Five Holy Ones, no! But there are things, artifacts, sacred relics, which they would be overjoyed to recover. Without human aid, they have no chance of regaining them. And I think those trinkets are a small price to pay for my City."

"But what of your soul?" asked another youthful knight. "They are evil—they are the soul of evil. How can you bargain with them?"

"They are not the *soul* of evil, friend. You know little of the Dark Ones if you think any earthly evil can surpass theirs." The intensity of her feeling sent a shudder through her. "I hate the Dark Ones and fear them more than you know. More than you can know. But I would sell myself to them . . ." Her listeners gasped and drew back. "Yes, I would do that if it would free my City from Synalon. She seeks to return the City to the Dark Ones, then give them the entire world. Do you think my soul's too great a price to save your wives and friends and children from that?"

The young knight looked away. She swayed, suddenly weary to the point of collapse. She put one hand to the blood-flecked flank of Darl's dog. The other went, almost by instinct, to clutch the amulet within her bodice.

She felt a sudden impulse to tear it off and throw it into the clear, cold waters of the creek. It had brought nothing but doom and death. Then she recalled the high price she'd paid for the talisman and took her hand away.

"We must go," she said.

A knight gave her a spare dog he'd caught fleeing the field. She mounted, casting a look at the sky. Its hue deepened inexorably to azure night.

They skirted the fringe of the wood when the bird rider squad swept over them like a glowing cloud from the guts of Omizantrim. The young knight who had led Darl to safety fell with an arrow through his back. Only Darl and Moriana made the shelter of the trees alive.

Moriana looked back. The Sky City troopers hadn't recognized them in the gloom. They passed once more over the bodies of their victims looking for signs of life. One figure stirred, trying to raise himself from the mud of the streambank. A sheaf of arrows drove him down face first.

Moriana clutched a fist and ground it against her forehead. Darl looked on, shaking his head numbly.

Turning their backs on the slaughter, they rode into the north. North to the Mystic Mountains and the last stronghold of the ancient enemies of humankind.

The Sleeper dreamed of battle. Armored figures on dogs fought across a valley bisected by a stream, shoot-

ing arrows, jabbing with lances, falling bloody and
torn and dead. The battle surged, then great winged
shapes appeared in the sky. One army broke and fled.

Istu felt pleased. It made his sleeping mind happy
to think of the hated pale ones butchering each other.
And in some dim corner of his subconscious he sensed
that what he saw had meaning for him. It boded well.

The image changed. The blue and green banners
fluttering from lances faded and were gone. In their
place the demon dreamed of a gem, a huge, brilliant
diamond. And black. Though it hung suspended in
darkness as complete as that which enveloped him, it
glowed with blackness more intense. The Sleeper
sensed that this gem, too, was imprisoned not within
walls of cold, solid stone but in a stone that flowed
like liquid from heat.

He sensed the stone's pulsations. Even under intense
heat and pressure it remained solid, its facets sharp
and smooth. But he felt the rhythmic emanations of
power and was soothed. The emanations pulsed in
tempo with his own heart.

And a voice came to the demon in dream, a voice
unheard for a hundred centuries, a voice that wakened
in the sleeping mind whatever a demon can feel of . . .
love.

Soon, child it crooned. *Soon, beloved, soon.*

Content, the demon slept.

"We're too late," said Fost, slumping in Grutz's
saddle. The bear grunted in sympathy with his master's
despair. "The battle is already lost."

Jennas made a bitter sound.

"No, 'tis won," she said, pointing. "For them." Her
outstretched finger indicated the carrion crows gathered
like mourners around the bodies. Fost smiled in grim
appreciation. One side, the other side, human, dog,
eagle—it was all the same to the vultures. Whatever
misfortune befell others, they fed.

They rested their tired bears in a copse of trees beyond what had been the right flank of the Sky City army. The field lay deserted now, save for the dead— and the vultures.

They finally rode through the eerie stillness of dusk. Fost couldn't rid himself of the sensation that the limp bodies strewn so recklessly about would rise up at any instant with a friendly greeting or outstretched hand of friendship. He was no stranger to death; he'd dealt it himself on occasion. But he had little experience with—and no stomach for—such wholesale slaughter.

He had been horrified at the carnage at the battles of the cliffs when he'd helped the Ust-alayakits defeat the Badger Clan and slay their evil shaman. That had been nothing compared to this. Together in a heap lay more men and women than lived in either Bear or Badger tribe. Fost shuddered. He wanted to throw up.

Though they kept careful watch, they saw no eagles. The bird riders were off chivvying the defeated, butchering the stragglers and the wounded. The wind babbled to itself of the sights it had witnessed that day, stirring fallen banners and mocking the dead.

Fost hoisted Erimenes' satchel high.

"See, old smoke," he said. "This is what your passion for bloodshed leads to. Shed blood, what else? Don't your nonexistent nerves pulse with excitement at the sight?"

Erimenes sniffed.

"What could I possibly find to excite me here? This is rubbish."

Furious at the spirit's callousness, Fost swung the satchel up to dash the jug to pieces on the ground.

"No," said Jennas. "Let him be."

Humbly, a little ashamed, Fost put the strap back over his shoulder and let the satchel fall back into its riding place.

Following the path the routed army and its pursuers

had taken, they passed the hill with its crumpled pavilion and heard the sound of running water.

"I'm thirsty," said Fost, "and there were too many corpses in that stream back there for even the bears to touch the water. Let's see if this one is less clogged with dead."

Jennas agreed. They rode toward the sound, at the same time angling toward a stand of trees well beyond the hill. Though none of the bird riders had shown themselves so far, neither felt like taking chances.

They were almost to the water when they heard the moan.

Without thinking, Fost booted Grutz's sides. The big bear rolled over the bank and into the water without breaking stride. The icy water numbed Fost's legs. He barely noticed in his urgency.

Another sad knot of bodies lay in front of the trees. Dogs and men in the distinctive armor of the City States had been struck down by the equally distinctive arrows of the Sky City. The missiles protruded at angles that told they had come from above.

Fost pulled Grutz to a stop beside a young man who stirred feebly. His fingers raked furrows in the dirt. An arrow had penetrated his backplate and jutted with a horrible jauntiness from the center of his back, as if that was where in all the broad earth it belonged.

The knight had been trying to reach the stream. His first words to Fost confirmed this.

"Water. Need . . . need water."

Fost sat on his haunches, considering. A stream of bloody spittle ran from the corner of the young man's mouth. Of the boy's mouth. He doubted if the youth was twenty.

"You're in a bad way," said Fost, trying to remember his healing lore. "I don't know if you should have water."

"You don't honestly think it matters, do you, you dolt?" Erimenes said acerbicly from his jug.

Fost shrugged. The shade was right, though it surprised Fost that Erimenes had spoken. Compassion was not a trait he normally associated with the philosopher.

The young man drank greedily from Fost's water bottle. The courier held the man's head cradled in his lap as he drank. Jennas had arrived by this time and stood over them.

The young man coughed. The fit came on so violently that he jerked himself free of Fost's arms. Then to Fost's horror he fell backward onto the arrow still in him. His weight drove it deep and snapped off. He stiffened, coughed up bloody spittle, then sank back with a sigh, as though sliding into a warm and soothing bath.

Fost bit his lip. The young man's chest rose and fell raggedly.

"The princess," he asked, hating himself for troubling the dying man. "Do you know who I mean? The Princess Moriana."

"Princess," the boy nodded. He frowned then. "Failed her. Failed her . . ."

Fost felt a cold black hand clamp shut this throat.

"She didn't . . . she's alive, isn't she?" he demanded. To his relief, the boy nodded. Then the youth grimaced as if the movement caused him pain. "Where did she go?" The boy did not respond. By dint of effort, Fost kept himself from shaking the boy. "Where did she go?" he asked again.

"The . . . three of them," he said.

Fost frowned up at Jennas. "Three?"

"Ah—aye. Princess, Lord Darl and . . . Great Ultimate, is it getting dark so soon? And the spirit . . . the woman in the jug. . . ."

"Woman in a jug?" asked Jennas, as confused as Fost.

"It must be the spirit Guardian told us about," said Fost, trying to remember more of what the glacier had said. Seeing Jennas' baffled look, he added, "The glacier's name is Guardian. When we left Athalau, the glacier told us Moriana had a spirit jar with her. He said something about the spirit inside, but other matters pressed me then. Guardian had mistaken the other spirit for Erimenes. It put him into a fine rage." Fost glanced at the blue form wavering by his elbow. Erimenes' face acquired a faraway look.

"A woman," the spirit said musingly. "As I live and breathe, a woman! This has interesting aspects I had not considered. Imagine, another such as I!"

"By Ust's snout," muttered Jennas, "one of you is more than enough. And you do *not* live and breathe."

"A *woman!*" cried the philosopher. "I can at last vindicate my teachings! What the two of us can do together. . . ." The shade's substance glittered with dancing notes similar to those Fost had observed in Athalau. But the substance of his body didn't thicken. He took it for extreme agitation on Erimenes' part.

"Be quiet, you," snapped Fost. "This man is dying, and you rant on about another ghost."

"Not just any other ghost, friend Fost," crowed Erimenes. "A female! I wonder if it might be possible that we. . . ." His face glowed with a lechery so luminous it astonished even Fost.

Jennas scowled openly.

"The boy, Fost, the boy is dying."

Fost swallowed and turned back to the dying knight. He felt shame that Erimenes could carry on so. And he was no closer to finding what had happened to Moriana. He leaned close to the youth.

"Where did she go?" The boy did not respond. Fost dribbled water across the parched lips and asked again, "Where-did-she-go?"

The young knight tried. In his fading mind he was glad that with his dying breath he could help his princess, the bright princess whom he and his friends had let down so badly.

"She went to . . ." His mind struggled to focus. "Went to . . ."

Another coughing spell shook him. He sprayed bloody foam all over the front of Fost's tunic. Fost held his shoulders, trying to steady him.

The boy tried to say, "To see the ones who built the City in the Sky," but the coughing hit him again.

"To . . . City . . . Sky," was all Fost Longstrider heard in the instant before the boy's head lolled back on lifeless muscles.

Gently he lowered the boy. He rose and looked at Jennas.

"The fool," he moaned. "She went back to the damned City."

"And you will follow her."

"And I'll follow," said Fost. "I'll follow."

PLAYBOY'S BEST SCIENCE FICTION AND FANTASY

JACQUELINE LICHTENBERG
___16598 **UNTO ZEOR, FOREVER** $2.25

WILLIAM JON WATKINS
___16608 **WHAT ROUGH BEAST** $1.95

WILLIAM ROTSLER
___16633 **THE FAR FRONTIER** $1.95

GRAHAM DIAMOND
___16398 **THE HAVEN** $1.95
___16477 **LADY OF THE HAVEN** $1.95
___16524 **DUNGEONS OF KUBA** $1.95
___16631 **SAMARKAND** $2.25
___16717 **THE FALCON OF EDEN** $2.25